S.S. Mausoof grew up in Karachi and currently lives in San Francisco. He has written several screenplays and has multiple IMDB credits, including an award-winning thriller *Kala Pul – The Black Bridge*. His short stories have been published in several periodicals including the *South Asian Review Creative Writing Issue*. *The Warehouse* has been longlisted for the Karachi Literary Festival fiction prize.

D1215379

The map in this work is pictorial representation only, not to scale and is not meant to represent exact political boundaries. It is for general illustration only and is not intended to be used for reference purposes or reproduction elsewhere.

THE WAREHOUSE

S.S. Mausoof

hope**road** : London

HopeRoad Publishing Ltd
PO Box 55544
Exhibition Road
SW7 2DB

First published in Great Britain by HopeRoad 2017

A CIP catalogue record for this book is available from the British Library

Supported using public funding by
**ARTS COUNCIL
ENGLAND**

ISBN 978-1-908446-59-6

eISBN 978-1-908446-65-7

www.hoperoadpublishing.com

Typeset in Chaparral Pro 10.5 pt

Printed and bound by TJ International Ltd, Padstow, Cornwall, UK

For S. M. Sharief who did not get published.

LIST OF ABBREVIATIONS

ADC Assistant Deputy Commissioner
CIA Central Intelligence Agency
CO Commanding Officer
DFIP Detention Facility in Parwan
DRB Detainee Review Board
FATA Federally Administered Tribal Areas
FC Frontier Constabulary
IED Improvised Explosive Device
ISAF International Security Assistance Force
JTAC Joint Terminal Attack Controller
NAC No Objection Certificate
NATO North Atlantic Treaty Organization
NCC National Cadet Corps
NWFP North-West Frontier Province
SSG Special Services Group (Pakistan Army Commando Unit)
UNHCR United Nations High Commissioner for Refugees

1
Appetite Lost

Karachi, 15 September 2011

I don't drink before sunset. Breaking this rule is what got me into this mess.

It was a stifling Thursday afternoon in an endless summer. The clock hands stuck at 3 p.m reflected the lazy hours between *Zuhur* prayers and teatime. Looking out of the office window, I counted the drab NATO tractor-trailers that were caught in a major traffic jam from the seaport to the Native Jetty Bridge. At truck forty-two, I looked away from the sunlight and turned back towards the dim-lit office. A pedestal fan fluttered the pages of the *Jang* newspaper for Thursday, 15 September 2011. The news was sensational, befitting a newspaper named after man's favourite pastime – war.

'*Pakistan is an international migraine,*' *Madeline Albright*; *Suicide Bombing Kills 28*; *Karachi Stock Exchange Suffers Fifth Day of Losses* read the headlines. A commemoration plaque from the Pakistan Squash Federation for first place in the Under-18 Youth championship covered the less perilous headlines.

'Aziz, let's do squats.' I stood up. Even after twenty-five years, the plaque still inspired me.

But Aziz remained seated in front of his desktop computer. His face was very still, unlike his hands – one was under his desk and the other clicking furiously on the mouse.

'Stop watching anime porn,' I said. He scowled and then slowly raised himself off the chair. I had hired Aziz as an office assistant back when my business – Continental Surveyors (Insurance Claims) – was good. I had stopped paying him after the first year but he still came in, six days a week.

'One.' I crouched into a low squat. 'And up.'

On my fourth squat, the office phone rang. I exchanged a quick, curious glance with Aziz and picked it up.

'Cash,' said a female voice.

My name is Syed Qais Ali Qureshi. Only two people in my life have ever called me Cash, and one of them is dead.

'Yes?' I sat down.

'It's Sonia,' she said briskly. 'I'm calling from work. I have a job for you.'

'I thought Continental Surveyors was blacklisted by your boss.'

'Never on my list,' she said with a laugh.

'I'm glad, but I don't work for free,' I warned her.

'Relax, babe. It's an official survey. I'm offering you a job. Can I come by?' she asked. 'Are you still at the Karachi Port Trust building?'

'Fourth floor. Room 403.'

'Okay, I can be there within an hour. Wait for me.'

I put the phone back in its cradle before Aziz put down his extension.

'I have a client coming. Go home. I'll lock up,' I said and lit a cigarette.

'It's not peak time for commuter buses. Where can I go?'

'Why is that my problem?' I shrugged, taking another lazy puff of my cigarette. He had asthma, so I took a little more pleasure in dragging out my smoke.

2

Aziz took his time as he powered off the PC and collected his things in a cloth satchel. I waited. I was good at that. As he was walking out, I handed him the greasy bag of Hanifia Hunter's beef sandwiches.

'Take this.'

'You want me to take your lunch?' Aziz asked, surprised.

I closed the door on his face without a word and walked back to my desk. Sonia was the only woman in the world who made me lose my appetite.

*

She was an hour late and looked exactly as I remembered her. About five feet six inches, she had an oval face, a high forehead and fine eyebrows. Her long straight hair gleamed against her almond-coloured skin and her eyes were like those of a hunted gazelle.

'Cash, how are you?' Sonia offered me her right hand. Her left carried a Jafferjees leather briefcase. She wore a long patterned shirt, fashionably cut to accentuate her slender waist.

'I'm superb, thanks,' I replied with a smile but ignored the hand.

'How is business?'

'Not good under the civilians.'

'You preferred the General?' She settled into the hard wicker chair.

'I preferred the Governor General.' I pointed to the staunch portrait of the founding father.

'Who doesn't? But nothing fixes things in Pakistan like a man in a uniform. May I get a glass of water? It's quite a workout climbing up the stairs. Must keep you in shape.' Sonia spoke rapidly but her gaze remained steady.

I walked to the water cooler and poured her a glass of water. The air bristled with an awkward tension.

'How is that daughter of yours - what's her name again?'

'Shereen. She's waiting to gain admission into university. How's Omar?' I handed her the glass.

3

'He's doing better.' Sonia took a sip. 'I'm sorry about Jameela. It must have been hard to deal with her illness and sudden death.'

This was the first time that Sonia had said my wife's name out loud.

'It was not sudden and it's been two years,' I replied and averted her gaze.

'I should have come for condolences, but you know how Karachites gossip about affairs, *yaar*.' Sonia left a smeared lip-print on the glass rim.

'I am not your *yaar*,' I said, giving her a steely look.

'I forgot. Only male friends qualify as *yaars*. How come you never bother to call on your friend Omar?'

'Omar can't tell night from day. The last time I saw him, he was trying to seduce a green fairy,' I said.

'And whose fault is that? You took him to that homeopathic doctor who prescribed opium for back pain.'

'*I* never got addicted,' I said.

'Yes, Cash, you never got addicted, because you are a Syed, descendant of the Prophet. Your kind can walk out of shit smelling like a rose.'

I shrugged and, at the same time, all the electric power in the building went out, probably due to some unscheduled load-shedding. The world fell eerily quiet.

In the dim light of the room, she smiled, and the faintest smell of jasmine and feminine sweat brought back sticky memories. I reached for a pack of Gold Leaf.

'May I have one?' Sonia perched on the edge of the desk and I offered her a cigarette, took one myself and lit both. I blew a smoke ring in the stillness.

'Same old Cash, always Mr Cool.' She hissed a smoke stream through the ring. Back in the day, she would take in a lungful and kiss me, fill my insides with secondhand smoke that I would exhale.

'I have a claim that requires consultation. It's a case where the client doesn't want to file a claim even though the insurance company has booked the loss,' Sonia said.

4

'Who is this client?'

'A Pathan transporter named Malik Awan. His godown burned down.'

'Was it covered or an open-air structure?' I asked.

'It was a covered concrete structure and housed a consignment of duty free cigarettes – part of the Afghan Transit Trade.'

'Where was this go-down?'

'Jandola, just outside Tank.'

'Tank – as in Waziristan?'

She nodded and reached for her briefcase. I walked to the barricaded window and rolled up the bamboo shades. Sunlight streamed into the room and caught flecks of dust in the middle of their whirling ecstasy. Sonia covered her eyes. She looked older under the harsh light. I recalled that she was my age.

'I would have never come to you if I wasn't a hundred per cent sure about the legitimacy of this claim.' Sonia sorted through files until she found a green folder.

'Does Anthony know?' I asked. Anthony was her boss, who also sat on the board of the Pakistan Loss Adjusters and Surveyors Association.

'Yes. But it's my case. I hire the surveyor,' she said.

'So you decide to send the biggest chum you know to a fucking war zone?'

'That's why we will pay you upfront.'

She placed the green folder on the table and pushed it across the desk. I opened it. Clipped on top of the sheaf of papers was a cheque made out to Continental Surveyors from Anthony Lobo, Loss Adjusters. It amounted to two and a half million rupees. There were other notes, receipts for payments, and a contract on official stamped paper.

'The consignment of cigarettes was intended for a dry port in Kabul. They were reinsured by Lloyds for half a million dollars. Street value is one and a half million. You get a generous twenty per cent. The cheque you have is postdated a week from today. You get the rest when you come back.'

5

'A hundred thousand dollars is a generous commission. Who is on the policy paper?' My mind was already spending the money.

'The main underwriter is Western Federal. They cover sixty-five per cent. The rest was split between Capital and Bridge Insurance.'

'So what do you need?' I said.

'Do a survey, take photographs, write a report, and get the claim accepted.'

'The last surveyor sent to Waziristan was beheaded by the Taliban. His body was left on the roadside. The head was never found.'

'This is the deal, Cash. Take it or leave it. The Frontier Constabulary controls Tank and the Jandola Fort. It has to be safe enough for a certified surveyor, which means you,' Sonia said with conviction.

'Why this change of heart? He'll be the first Pakistani to reject half a million dollars.'

'He has gone *fundoo*. Under the strict interpretations of Sharia law, insurance is illegal.'

'Why did he have insurance in the first place?'

'Don't know.' Sonia shrugged.

'Why can't Western Federal fake a payment? It's been done before.'

'Half a million dollars is neither pocket change, nor is Malik Awan a corner shopkeeper. He owns dozens of warehouses along the N-55 highway. If he denies the claim while the insurance company has collected payment from the reinsurance, it could be problematic.'

'You mean Anthony might lose his licence?'

'Let's not go there. The regulators have been pretty tough since the Shikarpur incident,' Sonia said, zipping closed her briefcase.

'But will Malik Awan accept the letter if he is convinced of his newfound beliefs?'

'That is why we are sending you, Syed Qais Ali Qureshi, to put his fears to rest. Offer him salvation by setting up a charitable trust or an eye hospital in Karachi. I don't care. Just play the part of a Syed Muslim. You are one, aren't you?' She leaned over and winked. It was a dare and she knew that I would fall for it.

I nodded.

'Then be one. Our agent, Riaz Khan, will be your contact in Mianwali. He will help you with the locals.'

'Half a million dollars, Marlboro cigarettes and a fire bombing in Waziristan. Sounds like a conspiracy theory,' I said.

Sonia stood up and rearranged her hair into a chignon. Her breasts rose under the silk blouse as she set the knot with a butterfly clip, leaving a lonely wisp on her forehead.

'Come on, Cash. You know conspiracy theories come true in Pakistan. *Ciao.*'

2

Three Cups of Gin

As soon as Sonia left, multiple muezzins began the call for Asr prayers. Before the first verse of *Haya Ala Salat* (Make haste towards prayer) had died away, *Haya Ala Falah* (Make haste towards success) arose from another muezzin. If only the mullahs in Pakistan could agree to coordinate their melodious singing. But Pakistanis couldn't agree on anything, unless it involved cricket, Kashmir or the Bomb.

I twisted the cap off the pint bottle of Quetta Distillery's London Dry Gin and poured out half a cup. As I added cold water and stirred it with my index finger, my cellphone rang, playing a high-pitched Bollywood medley. It was Shereen. I can always make it up to Allah, but not to my daughter. I answered her call.

'*Abu*,' she said.

'Yes, Shereen?'

'When will you be home? You are supposed to take me to Naila's.'

I took a large sip. Thursday was the only night I stayed out.

'I'm waiting for a courier.'

'Good excuse, *Abu*, but today is your lucky day. There was a protest going on and the rioters burned a public bus. The police have cordoned off Stadium Road and traffic is blocked all the way to the White cemetery.'

'What are they protesting about? Drone attacks?'

'What world do you live in, *Abu*? Nobody cares about the drone attacks. An Italian newspaper published a cartoon about the Prophet and the *fundoos* have gone crazy. Anyway, the good news is that we got our own Mindstorm kit for the competition.'

'That's great news!' I was genuinely thrilled. I loved doing homework with my daughter. Being a father was one of the few happy surprises of my life.

'Professor Rameez told the class that he would endorse our project for the UNHCR camp. I need your help on the project brief and timeline.'

'Who else is on your team?'

'Tima, Zaheer and Kami, but they are useless. Tima is always chatting, Zaheer is slow and Kami plays Halo all day. Why should they worry about university scholarships and extra credit? They are rich.'

'You will get into the engineering programme, *inshallah*,' I said firmly.

'But only ten students are selected on merit. The rest get in because they are rich or associated with the rich. And you – I mean, *we* – are neither.' Shereen's voice reflected her frustration.

'Trust in Allah. I will find a way.'

'Or I will. What time will you be home?'

'I have work to do tonight, it might be a while.'

'Oh well, chew gum before you come home.'

My landline rang in the background.

'Okay, I have to go now. *Khuda hafiz*. Goodbye, God protect you.' I hung up and picked up the desk phone.

'Mr Qais?' The female voice on the other end sounded hurried.

'Yes.'

'Hold, please.'

I took another long sip of my gin while I waited.

'Qais,' said a new, raspy voice. One that had trampled my pride before.

9

'Anthony,' I replied curtly, the back of my neck prickling.

'Was Sonia at your office earlier?'

The sharpness of the gin caught a rut on my tongue. I mumbled a yes.

'Did she talk to you about the Tank fire claim?'

'Yes, I'm on it.'

'You are not my first choice, but Sonia insisted that you are the best man for the job,' Anthony said briskly.

'Don't worry, I'll give it –'

'She said you needed the money,' he continued as though I hadn't spoken at all.

'That's fine, but I'm not running a charity here. If you fuck this up or try to cheat me, I'll personally make sure that your licence gets cancelled.'

There was a pause. I imagined him wiping his fat face with a monogrammed handkerchief.

'I'll do my best, Anthony,' I managed to say, clenching my hand into a fist to stay calm. 'By the way, Sonia mentioned that the doctors have recommended a heart bypass for you?'

'She said *what*?'

'Poor Nadeem Khan died from a heart attack, and he was barely fifty-two. You must be near seventy! I'll pray for you. Allah knows best. Goodbye.'

Slamming down the phone, I poured my second drink as I fumed. Fuck Anthony. If there was one guy who could push my buttons, it was Anthony Lobo, head of the top insurance adjusters in Pakistan and a thoroughly pretentious bastard. He claimed Portuguese ancestry, but he was darker than my dick. I hated many people while drinking and, lately, the list had only grown longer. The in-bred in their Land Cruisers, the feudal elitist aunties with fake accents, the effeminate youths in skinny jeans, the black-bearded religious goons and the petty criminals with Mauser pistols. I hated them all for their hypocrisy, piety, wealth, and modernity.

And then there was Sonia Gonzalez, the only woman who challenged all my notions of Punjabi self-entitlement.

I met Sonia in '89 when I worked at the Shalimar mall. Sonia worked in the women's department and flirted with all the boys there – and, mind you, they were many. Saleem, fair, lanky and dopey-eyed; Rumi, a robust, boastful and married owner of an electronics store; and Vicky, tall, dark, with a Karachi grammar-school accent and proud to drive a Toyota Corolla with tinted windows.

And me, the one she called Cash.

I was young and had potential. I could run a mile in under six minutes, was a ranked squash player and could recite William Blake and Mirza Ghalib. At Bishop Carrera's sixty-fifth birthday party, we had finished a prized bottle of 'feni' spirits from Goa while dancing to Kajagoogoo's 'Too Shy'. That night I cupped Sonia's nineteen-year-old face between my hands and kissed her. As the summer went on, we met every other day, finding nooks and crannies to share our desires, our love – in friends' cars, on neighbours' phones, on abandoned avenues. She had me fitted for a midnight-blue silk suit for a New Year's Eve party. 'You look good in a suit; you have the shoulders for it,' she had said. That compliment had made me half the man I am today.

The office door flung open, breaking my reverie, and a big man with a handlebar moustache entered. Around his torso was a leather holster, and his silk shirt covered a paunch that was beginning to respond to gravity. Zahid Fareed could easily play the role of a villain in a film, but in Karachi he was Superintendent of Police in the CID.

'Never trust a man with two first names. How did you get into the office?' I asked.

'I have my ways,' Zahid replied nonchalantly.

'Did you bring ice?'

'It's coming. You started early today.' He settled his bulk on the wicker chair and placed his Dunhill Lights, a chubby wallet, and a Samsung S3 phone on the table. He then unbuckled his pistol holster and put that on the table, along with a spare magazine for the H/K 9mm pistol, his Saudi bracelet and Swiss

11

watch. Finally, he took off his police-issue sunglasses and tucked them carefully inside their leather case.

'What made you break your rule of not drinking before sunset?'

Before I could reply, I was interrupted by the entry of another policeman – a sub-inspector, no less – who brought ice and nuts. I waited for him to leave and close the door behind him before I told Zahid the story, ending on the prospect of visiting Waziristan.

'So ... the question is, should I go?'

'Nah, Shah-ji. The question is, do you still love Sonia?'

'Men my age don't fall in love,' I retorted as I poured two more drinks.

'Do you still get it up thinking about her?' Zahid snickered.

'Yes, often. She has the eyes of a hunted gazelle, the skin of a ...'

'What in God's name are the eyes of a hunted gazelle? Have you ever hunted a gazelle?' Zahid said with a laugh.

'It's a poetic metaphor, but don't worry, you wouldn't understand it,' I said as I pushed the drink towards Zahid.

'Isn't she the one you got pregnant?'

'No, it was Vicky's child.'

'But you helped her with the abortion, right?'

'Omar worked at U Lab. He fixed it. I was there. The lady doctor scolded me for being careless because she thought it was mine.' I crushed the ice between my teeth, savouring the chill spreading in my mouth.

'And then your gazelle married Omar.'

'He took care of her. She was in pieces, Zahid.' After a moment, I shrugged dismissively.

'Forget it, you won't understand.' I lit a cigarette and walked to the window. The twinkling lights added a veneer of serenity to the daily chaos. Even the drab convoy, trickling out of the seaport, looked purposeful.

'Did you ever fuck her?' Zahid asked after a brief pause. 'Probably not, *hain*? She plays you, Shah-ji. She got you by the balls. A Syed made a fool by a Catholic gazelle.'

12

'Better to get my heart broken by a gazelle than a Billy goat,' I retorted.

Zahid winced. He did not like being reminded of his sordid past of sex and sodomy. He was a killer and his tantrums were legendary. But I had known him for too many years to take his insults seriously or for him to take mine.

'Everything to you is a fucking joke, Zahid Fareed, just because you are a made man. The rest of us can rot in hell as long as you have your Rado watch and Samsung phone,' I said.

We sat in silence for a few minutes. We had known each other since we were schoolboys and the drinks were too crisp for petty resentment.

'So you are in love with her, Shah-ji. No problem. So when do you leave?'

'I have not decided yet. It is a very dangerous area.'

'I will come with you. I know the area and Tank is a daytrip. We can stay in Mianwali and I will take you to the best *karhai* shop in the country.'

'Bullshit,' I said. 'You always think everything is best in Mianwali.'

'I took you there, once. Remember our last trip for my sister's wedding?'

We reflected on our youth. Through the night, we said cheers a few more times, got drunk and made a plan.

It was all drunken talk. I did not expect him to follow through.

3

Loss Triangles

Pakistan has an unofficial three-day weekend. It starts on Friday, a half-hearted workday pivoted around the afternoon prayers, and ends on Monday morning. On this particular Friday, the Karachi Port Trust building was deserted; its sepia-coloured stones simmered under the blue sky like an over-exposed photograph. The air smelled of sea, prawns and camel dung. I took the elevator to the fourth floor, unlocked my office, turned on the AC, ordered coffee and got to work.

On paper, the Jandola claim in question appeared legitimate. Malik Awan had been insuring his bonded warehouses for twenty years. He hauled tobacco, a lucrative cash crop for Pakistan, to various production facilities and moved millions of cigarettes. I wrote down the facts of the case and added up the numbers. The policy was within the term limits and I calculated the earned premium and applied the deductibles. It added up nicely. I should know. Before Microsoft Excel and computers, I used to manually calculate loss triangles, a much sought-after actuarial technique, but that was a lifetime ago.

According to the claim file, the warehouse burned down on 29 May 2011. The imported cigarettes were destined for

14

Afghanistan, as part of the NATO non-military supplies. The shipment had been stuck in Jandola because of routine tit-for-tat games between the Americans and the Pakistanis. Militants provided ample excuse for rerouting the convoys on the N-55 highway. Not only are the Taliban active in the badlands west of Indus, there are frequent drone attacks, occasional sectarian violence, and a persistent refugee crisis. So an insurance claim like this warranted wariness on top of the usual suspicion that the policyholder might have purposely destroyed the insured goods to get the claim money. In rural Pakistan, the rule of law might be superficial but commerce still reigns supreme and a surveyor is seen by the 'insured' as a blank cashier's cheque. This means he must withstand threats and physical intimidation. It takes guts, but it helps to be likeable.

'The key for a surveyor is how he presents himself to the client,' Irfan Moeen Khan used to say when I had joined Continental Surveyors as an intern. 'Having an understanding of actuarial science also helps.'

I had worked with Khan Sahab for eleven years. He was a principled man, always immaculately dressed in a light worsted wool suit accompanied by a striped necktie and silk pocket-handkerchief. Above his desk hung an official portrait of the first Governor General of Pakistan, the founding father, Muhammad Ali Jinnah. A few years ago he had retired and now he lived in Houston, Texas. I had inherited his office, but not his principles.

The landline rang.

'Hello, this is Syed Qais.' I kept my voice low.

'Hello, Cash, did I wake you?' said Sonia.

'No. I'm looking over the Jandola claim.'

'You are going, right?'

'Not sure, I have a few questions.'

'Wait, not over the phone. Better to be discreet. I can come over and we can discuss it in person,' she said.

'No, I'll come over. Tell Anthony I want to see him.'

*

15

Anthony Lobo's office was on McLeod Road, the financial hub of Pakistan. Banks, insurance companies, the cotton bureau, stock exchange, and the media conglomerate – all have offices there. Parking and traffic are a nightmare, so I took a rickshaw. I had long figured out that the best means of transportation in the city were these motorised tricycles. All you needed was a strong back and earplugs and I had both.

It took twenty minutes to cover the few miles; the smog and the noise rekindled the hangover I had got from drinking with Zahid. I took a deep breath and galloped up the two flights of stairs, past the bleary-eyed guard with the pistol safety set to 'fire', and into the office. The peon eyed me with disdain, but the receptionist offered a warm smile.

'Salaam, Mrs Shameem,' I said.

'Mr Qais, how are you? It has been a long time since you graced us with your presence.'

'You haven't changed a bit,' I said with my best smile.

'Neither have you, only a little white in your beard,' she said. 'Meeting Sonia-ji?'

'Yes. Is she in?'

'Of course. She is waiting for you in Mr Lobo's office.'

I walked up a dim corridor lined with filing cabinets. The woody smell of inkpads, file folders, and dusty, crinkled papers filled the air. Framed photographs showed slim, clean-shaven men in twill suits, posing in front of jazz bands and Boeing airliners. The corridor opened to a large cool room with charts of loss triangles pasted on the walls; at the end of the room was a rosewood desk. Anthony Lobo was sunk into a well-worn leather chair behind his desk; his tweed jacket hung on a coat stand.

'Qais,' he said. A smile appeared on his lips but failed to reach his eyes.

'Anthony, It's been a long time. We should meet more often,' I said in English.

'I would prefer not to,' he said.

'Where is Sonia?' I said.

The side door opened and Sonia entered. She wore a lime-green kurta over black capri pants, and carried a cup of tea balanced on her laptop.

'Hello, Cash.' She kissed the air near my cheek. I wished I had shaved.

'You wanted to see me?' Anthony interjected.

I pulled a chair up to his desk and sat down.

'Should I be upfront or admire your cunning nature?' I said.

Anthony and I had never gotten along. I had slapped him once, a long time ago. It happened at a reception in the Taj Mahal Hotel, because he was mimicking my mispronunciation of the word 'competitive'. Since then, I had learned the right pronunciation but he never forgave me for the slap.

'We are all busy here. I sent over the folders and –' Anthony began complaining.

'The setup stinks.' I raised my voice but slowed the pace. 'The policy is valid, but the incident happened three months ago and after the initial inquiry, nothing happened. Now, all of a sudden, you want to send a surveyor?'

'That is the truth, I am not hiding anything,' Anthony said.

'You need to give me more details, because I am not buying this stale claim business.'

Sonia exchanged a look with Anthony. He remained silent, but picked up a fountain pen and started scribbling on a notepad.

'The claim was filed in June but the policyholder Saif Awan died. He is the son of Malik Awan and the claim remained open. At that time, we approached Malik Awan to follow up as he is co-signer on the policy, but he refused to talk to our agent. At the end of our quarter, the claim showed up in our books and we closed it as a paid claim,' Sonia said.

'You mean you claimed half a million dollars from the re-insurers?'

'Yes,' said Sonia.

I let out a low whistle.

'Who's it from?' I said.

17

'Lloyds of London,' Anthony said. 'They have transferred the money to our accounts, and we as the executing agents have to pay it out.'

'Except the beneficiary of the policyholder Malik Awan is now refusing to deal with the insurance company,' Sonia added.

'And I need to convince him to accept the claim, when I don't even know him!'

'You have to, Cash. You are resourceful. And we have a back-up plan.'

'What's that?'

'Saif Awan's widow – Mrs Ruqiya Saif – is an enterprising lady.'

'What does she have to do with it?'

'As Saif's widow she is the beneficiary and can accept the claim on his behalf.'

'How do you know she'll do it?'

'She reached out to Riaz,' Sonia answered. 'She expects to hear from an insurance executive from the city. This is where you come in.'

I looked around for an ashtray but found none. The room smelled clean but I lit a cigarette anyway.

'What if I fail? Do I get to keep the advance?' I said.

'Yes, but you will never be able to find work in the industry again,' Anthony said.

'And *you* will be investigated for filing a fraudulent claim with Lloyds. Either way, I win.' I walked out. Sonia followed. In the corridor, she touched my elbow lightly.

'You will not fail. You are the smartest guy I know,' she said softly. 'Just don't die on me.'

*

There was a large cake box from the Shahnama bakery sitting on the dining table in my apartment when I got home. Shereen was pacing around the table; a pair of white earphones peeped out from under her straight black hair. She was at the age where she still skipped.

'Hello? Is anyone home?' I called out to her.

'You are home early,' she said in an unexpectedly loud voice.

I pointed to her earpiece and she broke out in a grin. She looked so sweet that I had to smile, my first genuine one for the day. Someone had said it right – you need children to make a workday bearable.

'Sorry, *Abu*, got lost in music,' she said, lowering her voice to normal volume.

'Is that an iPod?' I asked.

'Yes. Shahrukh bought an iPod touch, so he gave me his old one.'

'He was here?'

'Yes, he came with Uncle Jamshed. They waited for you to join them for Friday prayers. So, you want to try it?'

'No. I am going upcountry – tonight.' I waited for a reaction. 'You take care of *Dadi* while I am gone, okay?'

'Of course I will,' Shereen said evenly. 'Keep your phone switched on, okay? In case we need to contact you in an emergency.'

'There might be reception issues, but I will keep in touch,' I promised. But she had already plugged the earphones back in by the time I spoke.

*

I smoked on the balcony while I waited for the dye in my beard to dry. I had shifted to the Seventh Heaven apartment six years ago, as a temporary move before I would buy a proper house. The dream of owning a house had remained impossible until yesterday, when Sonia offered me a chance to make real money. Fate had finally smiled upon me and I could leave this house of pain.

After a cold shower, I put the claim documents in a leather briefcase and lay out two shalwar kameez suits – one cotton

19

and one woollen – a windcheater, a brown woollen shawl, undershirts, socks, slippers and a prayer rug. I packed the toiletry kit with laxatives for constipation, Panadol for a cold, Amoxicillin for infections, Restoril for anxiety and Ritalin for alertness. I opened the side cupboard to get the duffel bag to pack all my things. Even two years after her death, the cupboard still smelled of Jameela. Her lawn-cotton kameezes were piled on the shelves, the dyed dupattas were hung on the sides and in the drawers were felt-lined boxes, containing the jewelry that she wore on our wedding day. I had wanted to sell off the jewelry several times to pay for her extended chemotherapy but she always reprimanded me for suggesting such drastic measures.

'It is my grandmother's heirloom; you must save it for Shereen's dowry. Promise never to sell it, Qais. No matter how bad it gets.'

It got bad. I had forgotten most of the anguish two years later, except for the sharpest memory – the first operation that removed her left breast, the months of suffering that followed and the final days that blended into a single painful chapter.

*

Begum Qureshi sat in the dining room with a yellow dupatta covering her hair. She was reading a *pansura,* an abridged version of the Quran, and watching her soap operas at the same time. She was my mother and I didn't intend to leave for a war zone without her blessing.

'*Salaam, Ammi,*' I said.

'*Beta*, you came home late yesterday. I was up all night, worrying,' she said.

'I am leaving tonight. I'll be back in a week.'

'To go where?'Ammi sat upright with her hands folded across her lap.

'Mianwali.'

'Why do you have to travel? I thought all business was done on the Internet these days.'

'You only waste time on the Internet. Real business still happens in the real world,' I said with another genuine smile. I was on a roll.

'Isn't that near Waziristan?' she asked as a frown formed on her face.

'It's a well-paid survey. I am lucky to have this opportunity.'

'If it is for work, you should go with faith. *Inshallah* it will be for the best. Before you leave, there is one thing I want to ask. Your Uncle Jamshed was here ...'

Captain Jamshed Ali Jamali was *Ammi*'s cousin and a recent retiree from the Merchant Navy. He lived in a mansion with his troop of servants and sycophants.

'You know, Rabia has moved back from Dubai after her divorce,' Ammi continued.

'Good for her,' I said.

'And Jamshed *bhai* wanted to discuss a specific business opportunity.'

'I am not a businessman.'

'Neither is he, but he trusts you like a son, and Rabia has always liked you. It is, after all, the way of the Prophet to support widows and divorcees.'

'Ammi, don't bring religion into this. The Prophet did not marry for money or business.'

'*Beta*, I was only thinking of Shereen. How can we marry her off while we live in this apartment? Our neighbours are all shopkeepers and electricians. If I had my way, I would move to Bahawalpur. But I sacrifice for you.'

'I have sacrificed enough for the family,' I said. I was getting angrier by the minute.

'Be ashamed! Meher-un-Nissa is happy and thankful to you, her brother. It is our tradition to exchange a daughter for a daughter-in-law. You have a beautiful daughter and Jameela was good to you. And you shouldn't speak ill of the dead.'

'I am not speaking ill of Jameela. You are the one who spoke badly of her when she was alive.' I stood up and yelled, 'Shereen, are you there?'

21

'Why are you always so angry? I open my mouth and you start yelling. She went downstairs to Fiza's flat.'

'You have the cheque book?' I glanced at the door, expecting Shereen to appear.

Ammi pointed to the drawer in the side table next to her bed. I still paid the bills.

'I will call Shereen. Are you leaving now?' She got up and put her hands on my shoulders.

'Yes, otherwise I will miss the train.'

I wanted to break away, but Ammi would not let go until she had finished her ritual. She continued leaning on my shoulder, reciting verses under her breath. Once done, she exhaled on my face and chest to ward off evil spirits. Her breath smelled of toothpaste and spices.

'Don't eat the food from the train station vendors. Say your prayers, and travel in the company of the Prophet. And don't let your anger get ahead of you.'

I nodded my agreement and left hurriedly, running down the stairs of the building. At each floor, I expected my daughter to appear and say goodbye. *Ammi* called out to her from the top of the staircase. Shereen was probably listening to music on her hand-me-down iPod or chatting with Fiza. I walked out of Seventh Heaven.

*

'Cantonment station,' I told the lean rickshaw driver. He threw his cigarette butt on the litter-strewn side street and pulled the lever on the meter. The rickshaw lurched through gaps in the congested service lane. Pedestrians swarmed between vehicles while passengers seethed in their static impotence. As he crossed the road, a lanky boy in pleated trousers giggled at a flirtatious *hijra*. 'Come on, smarty, give rupees, we will pray so that you find a sexy bride,' the eunuch hailed. A traffic policeman in a spotless white uniform argued with pedestrians, a raggedy street kid hawking trinkets competed

22

with a one-armed beggar for consideration from a madam in a Honda. The traffic billowed on the Teen Talwar roundabout. These upright columns, made of white marble, were built to represent the founding father's principles of unity, faith and discipline. Today the columns are plastered with posters promoting political hagiography and advertisements for soaps and tuition centers. Horns blared, tires screeched, curses were exchanged, but the rickshaw driver – used to the mindless chaos of traffic – cut across side streets, sped under flyovers and over train tracks with ease.

'Are you taking the scenic route?' I asked, amused.

'It's Friday evening. Everyone is going somewhere. Where are you going?' he asked, guiding the tri-wheel contraption past a roundabout.

'Mianwali.'

'Brave of you to go there. I give rides to refugees coming from Waziristan. It's a bad time, every day we hear of war. We are lucky in Karachi, even with all the bloodshed and targeted killings ... ' He continued on about his financial problems and difficult life. I drifted off. In Karachi, the working class has no time for other people's misery – we are all equally miserable.

At the station, I found that the train had been delayed. It was hardly unexpected so I walked along the station to pass time. It was a balmy night and squadrons of flustered robins flew from tree to tree. Seedy hotels lined the service lane, and the footpaths were packed with vendors selling provocative magazines, masculinity enhancement drugs and personal services – shaves, haircuts and massages. I smoked a cigarette under the peepal tree, which was known to have been planted back when Karachi was, as legend goes, crowned Asia's cleanest city. Today the trees were marked with stains of green *naswar* tobacco, splats of red betel juice and splashes of urine from pie-dogs and coolies. The station had been built by the British Raj and now, post Independence, was inhabited by shifty-eyed hustlers and touts. A bustling restaurant with a sign in Urdu warned customers not to linger, and from within it the singer

23

Musarrat Nazeer sang *'Chalien tu kat hi jayega, safar ahista ahista ...'*: if we start, the journey will end steadily, steadily.

I bought a copy of *Balochistan, the British and the Great Game* in Urdu and boarded bogey number eleven of the Khushal Khan Khattak Express shortly before it was to leave. The train was dark except for the bright LCD screens of my co-passengers' cellphones. I made it to my berth as the train inched through slums silhouetted by the halo of paraffin lamps. Half constructed multi-storey units stood between advertising billboards marketing a lifestyle only few could afford. The billboards, like the people defecating, faced away from the rail tracks. I poured a cup of contraband gin from a mineral water bottle, made a pillow of my duffel bag and stretched out on the wooden berth. A railway receipt was stuck in the slot reserving the berth in my name, Syed Qais Ali Qureshi. My father preferred M.A. Qureshi for himself. That is how he was identified as a member of the Pakistan Field Hockey team from the 1960 Summer Olympics. I had once asked him why he did not insist on the honorific 'Syed' title to be included in the plaque.

'If I had added Syed, it would have squeezed my name. This gold medal is my accomplishment, not my family's. A man earns his own medal and you must earn yours.'

4

KKK Express

'Only the djinns and *sharabis* (drunks) travel by train in Pakistan. Which one are you, Uncle?' asked the light-haired boy who occupied a berth near mine.

'I am sleeping,' I said. He had boarded the train at Kotri with his father and had provided a running commentary to anyone who was prepared to listen. I had obliged him in the beginning but I found his reference to alcohol alarming. I assumed he smelled it on my breath. I should have been more careful.

He withdrew to his corner and I closed my eyes to get in rhythm with the clickety clack of the KKK express and back to sleep. As I dozed off, I began to dream. There was a woman in my dream, but I could not pin her down to a single person, as she had the traits of many women I had known. Her identity eluded me into wakefulness, for the dream evaporated at the onset of dawn. I stuck my head out through the window. The diesel locomotive engine ploughed through the morning mist as transmission line poles framed scenes like markers on celluloid film. Snapshots flashed by – black buffaloes on green grass, maroon doors on brown houses, blue graffiti on yellow walls and a mother in a pink bodice, her head covered by a blue

25

dupatta, balancing a water urn on the curve of her waist while her two children trailed behind on the canal bank. I wanted Shereen to see this rural life of the *dihaats*, not the colours but the smell of frying parathas, turmeric-flavoured stews, the smoke from the hookahs, the chatter of birds and children and the unrestrained dialect of the village folks. But she was a city girl and had no patience for such things. The world had changed for ever.

The boy raised his hand to get my attention.

'What is it?' I asked. Part of the blame for his freshness was mine. His father was old so I had helped them with their luggage and exchanged pleasantries when they boarded.

'Nothing, Uncle, I wanted to let you know we are approaching Mohenjodaro.'

'What of it!' I said.

'It is a five-thousand-year-old city of djinns,' he smirked, and it was possible he was making another reference to my contraband gin.

'I've been there, only crumbling buildings,' I said.

'It is the oldest city in the world. Is it as old as the pyramids? But you don't know history. What are you? Some sort of a trader or businessman?'

'No, I am a … teacher.' I did not want to debate the merits of insurance with this lad or for that matter with anyone.

'You don't look like one,' he said, looking at my leather briefcase. Maybe he had gone through it while I was sleeping. Thankfully, the train pulled to a stop and other passengers boarded, so the boy got distracted.

'Where are we now?' The boy's father had woken up.

'Past Dokri,' the boy answered.

'Did you sleep?' the man asked his son.

'No, I was talking to Uncle.' It was not the fact that he addressed me as 'Uncle' but the way he pronounced it that I found annoying.

'Thank you for keeping him company. Nasir is my youngest, very bright,' he said.

I nodded, thinking that the kid deserved a couple of sound slaps.

'He is in class eight, attending Habib Public School. God willing, he will get a college degree,' the father said.

'He is intelligent, *mashallah*,' I replied. The old man was pleased with my compliment of his son. He watched the boy with pride and the boy returned his affections with a quick hug. I felt a rare jealousy at their relationship.

'Where are you going?' I asked.

'Bannu. To pick up my daughter and her little ones,' he replied.

'Is that your hometown?'

'I am from Kohat, but I married my daughter into a Bannu family.'

'You sound like a Karachiwala.'

'I am one. I have worked for twenty-five years at Javed Textile Mill. Everyone calls me Kaka. Karachi has been good. Allah has given me a mind for fixing machines. Good, honest work.'

I remained silent as he had already told me all about his job last night, but he was encouraged by the other passengers to retell his experiences.

'I bought tickets for a sleeper, so my Nasir could sleep in the train. I have worked hard all my life, never ashamed of my profession. These people, politicians, told us to vacate purchased seats. Their guards bullied us and moved us to this bogey. I have tickets – see, berth tickets? – but they are worthless,' he said.

I sympathised with him, as did other passengers. It was a national characteristic to be communal in grief.

'Kaka, as long as crooks run this country, all will remain corrupt,' spoke a man.

'And you know, Sindh is the worst with MQM and PPP fighting for Karachi,' said another passenger who was picking at his rosary. He had snored all night but had joined the conversation now.

'That is true. We all say it and we all agree on what is required to fix the country, but we carry on doing exactly the opposite. Nothing changes,' the old fellow replied.

'Let the boy sleep on my berth,' I offered. Maybe that would shut him up.

'Now there is more war, an operation is starting in Bajaur. That's why I am going. Not for a picnic or a holiday,' Kaka said.

'I pray for the safety of your family,' said a new voice. It belonged to a man in an embroidered Sindhi cap.

'Are you Punjabi?' asked the boy called Nasir as he sneaked up onto my berth.

'Yes,' I said.

'Nothing against you, Uncle, but your Punjabi army is doing *nassal kushi* on Pashtuns.'

I was too tired to be offended by this brat's accusation of genocide, but his father scolded him in Chitrali. He slunk back out of respect for his father rather than fear.

'I hope you are not offended. I try to stay away from ethnic remarks myself. My mill-owners are Punjabis, my boss is Urdu-speaking, but kids – they learn all kinds of things from TV. All this strife in our country, this hatred for each other, this did not exist when I first came to Karachi in the seventies,' Kaka said to me, apologising for his son.

'It was all because of General Zia,' the man in the cap commented. 'He destroyed Pakistan with his Wahabi Islam, created MQM and corruption.'

'Corruption always existed, but the generals have made it worse,' I said.

'I liked General Musharraf, he was a strong man with good principles,' Kaka interjected.

'He is a bastard. He sold our nation to America!' Another man joined the conversation. He had a bushy moustache and the bearings of wealth, and looked ready for a long debate on politics.

'And now your new PPP government will sell Pakistan in pieces. At least he kept our integrity,' Kaka argued.

'The only sincere leader Pakistan ever had was General Ayub. During his time, Pakistan was a rich and modern state,' said the mustachioed gentleman.

28

'Pakistan was rich because Punjabis were mistreating Bengalis.'

'Forget Bengalis, brothers, they were all traitors to the State of Pakistan; half of them are Hindus anyway, like these MQM-walas. I say if you don't like this country, go back to India.'

'Why don't you say this to your Afghan brothers? The Taliban who want to bomb our cities and put our women behind purdah.'

'It's not only the Taliban who condone violence, it is also the RAW agents from India, the Afghanistan Khad agency – they have a Shia agenda.'

'And don't forget the Americans. Raymond Davis kills two Pakistanis and the government hands him over for blood money. Shameless pigs.'

And so on and so forth, for the twenty-six hours and one thousand miles, the Khushal Khan Khattak Express ran on diesel and mutual distrust. At Jacobabad, I called Shereen, bought a paratha and egg breakfast and sat on a sunny bench to read the Urdu daily. The headlines either humiliated the current government apparatus or exploded in superlatives, to describe the bravery and sheer ingenuity of Pakistani people. The point was to demonise America, demote India and dehumanise Israel. I flipped the paper. The back pages had alluring pictures of Pakistani model Veena Malik, action shots of the tennis star Sharapova and family pictures of the cricketer Shahid Afridi. Among these were pullouts for gossips, parables, and recipes.

'We are a quantum nation,' Dr Naqvi, my university professor, would remark during our physics lectures. 'We live in duality, between *maulvis* - learned spiritual teachers - and models, Bollywood and the Taliban.'

He would then make us solve the Schrodinger wave equation. He was a good man who was killed outside his home last year for being of the Shia faith.

At Kashmore, the landscape became dreary with endless stretches of a two-tone brown edged by monotonous black hills. By the time the train passed through Dera Ghazi Khan, the billows of shalwars and the length of turbans had increased substantially. Men argued in varied dialects and baggage checks were frequent. Kaka fell asleep and the boy read a paperback copy of *The Bourne Identity*. I sneaked a final drink in preparation for arrival and read *Balochistan*, which I found to be high on Marxist bravado but low on conspiracy.

It was a fascinating read and I learned that in the 1930s the English had bombed the Waziri tribes with a Hawker Fury biplane – the high-tech weapon of that time. Their target had been Mirza Ali Khan, the Faqir of Ipi, who had led an insurgency against the British. Peace came briefly when the Federally Administered Tribal Area was formed as part of the new nation of Pakistan, but after Partition, Waziris joined the voluntary militia that fought for Kashmir. They never disbanded and were at the forefront during the Soviet war, and today they continue to fight an active insurgency against the Pakistani state.

The train was almost empty by the time we rolled into Mianwali, but the station was lined with passengers awaiting the arrival of the train. Before we could disembark, the crowds began to board the bogeys for the best seats. The more energetic men squeezed through the windows while the policemen who were standing on guard yelled and dragged a few out. I grabbed my briefcase and bag and got out as quickly as possible. I looked over the madding crowd and saw Kaka holding Nasir's hand as he struggled to hold onto his bags. Nasir looked in my direction while his father flung his arms around to keep the hustlers at bay. I walked away fast. The journey was just beginning.

5

No Place for Sufis

The concierge at Hotel Khan had a lazy eye. He leaned over the wood-panelled counter, neck cranked up to watch a TV show with giggling girls in tracksuits manoeuvring an obstacle course. Beyond him the lobby ended in a dark cul-de-sac.

'*As-salaam-alaikum.*' I passed my ID card through a cubbyhole. The concierge moved his hands but not his eyes.

'My man called yesterday about a room. Syed Qais,' I said. After a two-day communal train ride, I deserved solitude and a bath.

The concierge turned to make photocopies. A girl with wide hips and big round eyes got tangled up skipping over tyres. Someone laughed in the reception area and the cigarette embers glowed to reveal a company of men sprawled on sofas. I did not hear as much as I smelled the men. They reeked of hashish and their beards were trimmed for effect rather than for religious devotion.

'Room 121. Up the stairs, on the right.' He pushed a key through the cubbyhole and our eyes met. He was in his twenties, with Asiatic features and a wispy dark beard - probably a

Hazaran. He asked me for an advance and returned my ID. I paid for my stay with crisp thousand-rupee notes.

'Is it air-conditioned?' I asked.

'Yes, but only when we have electricity. We do have a flush toilet.'

I added a five hundred note as a tip for him. 'I have a VIP guest arriving tomorrow and will need good service. What's your name?'

'Thank you, sir, I am Owais. If there's anything you need, please let me know.' He quickly pocketed the note. 'I have been to Karachi. My uncle has a bakery in Paposh.'

'Near the Imam Bara?' I looked at my phone as the men gave my luggage a look over. Then they looked me over.

'Yes, of course. You, sir? Are you of the Shia faith yourself?' Owais whispered.

'No, I am of the Ahlay Sunnat, but my family has a special love for the Prophet.' I turned and found myself face to face with a stocky man with chubby unshaven cheeks. I expected him to start a conversation but he just stared. I looked right through him. If there was one lesson I learned from living in a boys' hostel, it was how to handle a bully.

Owais addressed the group in the Waziri dialect. Chubby's companion spat words in turn. I caught the word *mukhbir*. I had expected suspicion, but not to be called an informer on my first day here.

They argued. Owais talked faster. I was impressed, but did not show it. I was busy staring into Chubby's bulging eyes. Seconds passed, another girl fell awkwardly on the obstacle course. This time no one laughed. The programme switched to a phone commercial. I picked up my luggage and made to leave. The two men gave way and walked to the couch.

'Are there many guests staying in this hotel?' I enquired.

'Yes, we are fully booked. We have many refugees here. A new army operation has been launched. May God protect them.'

'The soldiers, you mean,' I said softly.

'Of course, the soldiers, sir.'

32

'Who are these men?' I asked, glancing sideways at the sofas.

'They are loafers who hang out here to smoke hookah. What is your business?' Owais's lazy eye wandered off.

'*Khabarnigar*,' I said. I always had aspirations to be a journalist.

*

The room was sparse but functional. The air conditioner worked, the bedding was clean and the curtains were thick enough to block the afternoon sun. I texted Riaz, took a cold shower and went to sleep with a wet towel wrapped around my waist.

I awoke from a dreamless sleep when I heard a gentle knock on the door. A glance at my Citizen Quartz told me it was 3.40 p.m. The phone rang. The door knob turned back and forth.

'Who is it?' I called out in Urdu.

'Open the door.'

It was an authoritative command. I put on clothes, looped a slipknot on the shalwar's cummerbund, and slid the bolt on the door. Two men rushed into the room and pushed me until I fell back onto the bed. One of them was chubby.

'What is your business in Mianwali?' the first man demanded. He was standing to the left of the door.

'Who are you?'

'I represent the State. This area is under strict monitoring for journalists. Where is your press card?' He had a little grey in his moustache, but could not have been older than thirty. His tall and haughty appearance, along with military mannerisms, exuded a sense of authority but this was not from his rank.

'I am a surveyor working for Buxton Tobacco,' I said, showing my trade licenses and IDs. The tall man studied them while Chubby opened my duffel bag. He ruffled through the clothes, shook out the toiletry bag, and emptied my briefcase.

The tall man picked up my copy of *Balochistan and the Great Game* while Chubby read a diary he had found in the briefcase. He chuckled.

'This is my personal stuff,' I said, making a grab for the diary.

33

Chubby slapped my face with an open palm. My head spun. The tall man barked an order. I felt like I was back in school.

'Are you a journalist, Mr Qais?' asked the tall man.

'Syed.' I rubbed my cheek. It was an extraordinary slap and had put half my face in misery. I dared not blink, in case the water in my eyes turned into hot tears.

'What was that?'

'Syed Qais Ali Qureshi,' I said.

The tall man shut the book with a tight smile. Owais was at the door. I suspected more people were crouched behind him in the corridor.

'I am Syed Mir Jehangir's cousin. What is your full name?' I asked in English. I might be a civilian but I knew how to pull rank.

'I am Captain Baz Ali Khan,' he said. This time his military training was evident.

I picked up my cellphone, punched digits, and switched to speaker mode. An eloquent female voice announced that the Minister of State for Oil and Gas, Syed Mir Jehangir, was unavailable to take this call, please leave a message.

'Would you like to leave a message or should I leave one?' I said in English.

They remained quiet. I spoke into the phone.

'Jehangir *bhai*, this is Qais. I need a small favour from you. Are you in Islamabad this week? Give my greetings to Alia and family. *Allah hafiz.*' Nobody listened to voicemails in Pakistan but it was good for theatrics.

'Sorry for the confusion. We will leave now,' said Captain Baz. Speaking English forced him to be respectful.

'Take the gorilla with you.' I pointed to Chubby.

Captain Baz swivelled on his toes and left with his companion.

'I tried to warn you, sir,' Owais said from the door, 'but you would not answer the phone.'

'Have a cold drink sent up with ice.' I closed the door in his face.

I sat down on the bed and threaded the cummerbund through the shalwar with a ballpoint pen. My face burned with the insult of what had just occurred. There was a knock on the door and an old man glided across the floor with a bowl of ice and Sprite. I added gin to the crushed ice, topped it with soda and shot off a text to Sonia. She called when I was finishing my third drink.

'I met the local goons, military walas,' I said.

'Did you tell them about the case?'

'I told them nothing. But they did search my luggage.'

'Don't be afraid, I...'

'I am not afraid.'

'I know, dear, you were always the brave one.'

I let out a bitter snort. It made my face hurt. 'Where is your man Riaz? I texted him twice.'

'I will call him. Keep a low profile. Don't die on me.'

'I am not going to fucking die. Stop saying that.'

'Fine. Talk tomorrow, okay.'

I sat on the edge of the bed and listened to the noises of the hotel. My left cheek was swollen and the eyelid bruised. I applied ice, washed it, and looked in the mirror.

I felt ashamed. I felt angry.

I drank until I fell asleep.

*

The next morning, I woke to the sounds of construction and shouting children who used the hotel staircase to play games. The lobby was bustling with distressed fathers in dirty turbans and exhausted mothers in voluminous burqas. I did not find Owais and the day concierge was frazzled by requests for bedding, food and ice. In a corner, a teenager helped men fill out application forms for Zong cellular services. These were the Internally Displaced People, the IDPs from the long war in Waziristan. These were rich families who could stay in a hotel rather than a refugee camp. Most would end up in Karachi.

35

I walked through crowded bazaars to Chowk Watta Khalil. A light breeze fluttered trash around – bubblegum wrappers, clear plastic and cigarette packets. The street had a fruity smell, hours away from a rotten stench. Crooked evergreen trees grew among shops, billboards and drab buildings. Every other block, a green minaret protruded between unfinished houses. Hanging from the rooftops was a mess of electrical wires without rubber insulation. I wondered how many of the buildings were covered for fire insurance.

At the intersection of a major and a minor street, a cluster of fruit, cellphone and appliance shops congregated. I found a juice vendor's shop and ordered pomegranate juice. There was a lively discussion going on around a cricket game. I selected a seat with a view of the main road and sat down after batting away multiple fruit flies.

'Afridi is out for a duck,' said a fat man who occupied an entire *charpai* – bed - with his frame.

'He is not a batsman any more,' added another, who sat down at my table and handed me his business card by way of introduction. He was the proprietor of a nearby mobile phone shop.

'The opening strokes set the tone. If your temperament is steady, it leads to a solid inning. But if you enter with pomp and then get out on the first ball, it's a long shameful walk back to the pavilion,' he continued. 'Do you agree?'

I smiled and agreed wholeheartedly. My cellphone buzzed and I saw that I had a message from Riaz. I told him where I was and typed a text to my daughter.

'But Afridi is a master spinner. I used to spin. It's all in the wrist,' said the large man, demonstrating spin bowling while lying horizontal.

'Misbah is better, a thinking captain and a local boy,' said the phone-shop guy.

'We lost the World Cup semi-final because of his slow *tuk-tuk* batting. It was as if he was told not to win the game.' An eager boy joined the conversation.

'He was told to lose by our president. The Indians would have started a war if Pakistan played in the 2011 World Cup final in Mumbai,' said the large man.

'The cricketers paid the price for the terrorists that went to Mumbai in 2009,' I said.

No one said anything in reply. It was something I would have said to my friends in Karachi but here it was probably inappropriate. I made a mental note to keep my comments to myself. Thankfully, the waiter brought a plastic glass brimming with ruby red juice. I took a sip as a young man greeted me from afar.

'Qais *sahab*, I have been looking for you all morning and here you are having apple juice. I am Riaz Khan Mehsud. Welcome.' He shook my hands with vigour. He was immaculately dressed in a starched grey shalwar suit and smelled like a perfume shop.

'Pomegranate juice, would you like to try?' I said.

'No, thank you, it's not in season.' He yelled orders and found a better seat. 'Miss Sonia said you met some bad locals?'

'Captain Baz and the gorilla. An ugly guy, with fat cheeks,' I said.

'That will be Zaman. They are part of Military Intelligence. You have to be careful. Mianwali is the gateway to the American war. Everyone is suspicious.' Riaz stood out among the rest of the patrons of the shop because of his close shave and rakish moustache.

'Suspicious of what?'

'Spies working for the ISI or perhaps the CIA or even the Taliban. This land is swarming with informers.' Riaz brushed away flies.

'Zaman thought I was a *mukhbir* last night.'

'That is a dreaded word. Anyone found to be a spy gets in big trouble.'

'Define trouble.'

'If you are with the Taliban, you are beaten up by the Pak Army or killed in an American drone attack, and if you are caught as a spy by the Taliban ...' Riaz ran his index finger across his throat

37

for effect. The juice from the glass dripped on my white shirt and left a purple stain.

'Beheading is a special punishment reserved for spies and informers. It spreads fear in the community,' Riaz continued, but was drowned out by spontaneous clapping because a Pakistani player had hit a boundary.

'So what is the plan?' he asked after we had finished our drinks.

'I want to meet this Major Bhatti first so I can keep out of trouble with the military agencies. Later I can get a permit to visit the godown. Do you know him well?'

'As well as anyone can. He is a man at large. Some say he is still with the ISI, but mostly he is known as the man who runs the IAS security company. They are all ex-army people and the company's run by generals. They hire a lot of people here and are well respected.'

'Can I see him today?'

Riaz looked at his watch. I kept my gaze on him. He had flat grey eyes like a Hollywood actor and was probably popular with women and perhaps men as well.

'We can try. He lives in the artillery mess near Kala Bagh, fifty kilometres up north.'

'I'll pay for the petrol.'

'That's not what I meant.'

*

Major Sultan Bhatti had a brown, knotty face and middle-parted hair. His eyebrows curved downwards and his moustache curled upwards. Both were dyed jet black. He sat behind a desk underneath a whirring ceiling fan while the air-conditioning unit blasted cold air. His white iPad was propped up on a stand.

'Welcome to Kala Bagh,' he said in the stunted English of a career soldier. I shook his warm hand and sat down in a comfy chair.

We were in a large and spacious room. Regimental photographs lined the walls and the cloth curtains were partially drawn over the bamboo nets through which light filtered on to the marbled floor. There were no flies.

'Your travel so far, good?' he asked.

'I met Captain Baz Ali Khan and wanted to clear out,' I said.

'I learned about the incident at Hotel Khan. A civilian with Marxist propaganda and a diary full of Sufi poetry is unexpected here,' Major Bhatti said with a laugh and looked at Riaz to seek acknowledgement.

'What propaganda?'

'The book you carry - *Balochistan and the Great Game* - that is anti-nationalist propaganda to support the Baloch insurgency.'

'I picked it up by chance at the train station. I am a professional surveyor.'

'He is first cousin to Mir Jehangir. Let us remember why he has travelled from Karachi. We don't want trouble,' Riaz said.

'What happened at the hotel was an unforeseen incident,' Major Bhatti said and called his orderly to bring drinks. 'We have several challenges in this region. The war next door has created a heightened sense of security.'

'I understand, but I hope there will be no more unforeseen incidents,' I said.

'I will talk to Captain Baz and explain. How long are you here for?'

'Thank you. Only a few days until I meet Malik Awan.'

'Why meet him?'

'I have to understand why he is not filing a claim for the Jandola godown.'

Major Bhatti clasped his hands and his lips parted in preparation for a sentence. He remained this way for a few seconds. A wiry man dressed in military khakis entered the room carrying a water bottle that looked like it had carried vodka in its first life. He wore a munitions belt that held a pistol. On his shoulder were patches of campaigns and courses from the SSG commando group.

'Be careful with Malik Awan. He is soft-spoken but has a hard soul. Don't let him back you into a theological debate on sharia law.'

'How do you know him?'

'I am a consultant for IAS security services. We ran security for his warehouses – I know him and his sons.'

'Thanks for the advice. I appreciate it.' I took a sip of the water. 'So is it possible to visit the Jandola warehouse?'

'Nothing to visit – the warehouse was fire-bombed. *Ka-boom!*' said Major Bhatti, gesturing with his hands.

'I still have to assess damages and estimate value of material loss.'

'It is not safe. You read the news.'

'It is the only way to verify a claim worth half a million dollars.'

'Well, it's your choice. As a civilian, it could take weeks to get a permit.' Major Bhatti's cellphone rang – his ringtone was ducks quacking.

'How do I apply?'

'At the FC regimental headquarters, at Tank. The colonel in charge is Aftab Gul. I could introduce you to him if you like.'

'Aftab Gul of the Baluch regiment?'

'Yes, you know him?'

'We went to school together. He's a good friend.'

'You seem to have lots of friends.' Major Bhatti stood up.

'They come in handy.'

'Must be the Sufi poetry.' He put his hand out but without much extension.

'It is a harmless pastime.' I leaned forward to shake his hand.

'There are no harmless pastimes in Waziristan – and this is no place for Sufis.'

40

6

Blood Money

Malik Awan's *haveli* – his mansion – was ten kilometres outside of Tank, a provincial hellhole in the middle of nowhere. The heat, the constant security checks, and the smell of diesel fumes made the journey miserable, as did Riaz's needless chatter. He had a theory on everything and was quite full of himself when it came to women. He had several online friends with whom he chatted – from Italian to Indian and even a Korean girl – all of whom were willing to marry him and provide him with a passport to a western country. But he was a good family man, he insisted. He only flirted with these women and was a good Waziri, by which he meant he would not abandon his land. 'Qais *bhai,* we are like the Scots, we are forgotten now, but we will have our day,' he repeated often.

We met with our hosts at the arranged meeting point. One of them sat in the back of Riaz's jeep and led us down a side road – into a pastoral setting cradled between craggy peaks. The country road had less vehicular traffic but plenty of animal carts and men in voluminous turbans sitting idly by the roadside. The animals and men stared at us with the same hard expressions as we drove by. The road ended at a fortified compound surrounded by a high mud wall and an imposing iron gate crowned with a hand-painted sign. The sign showed an idyllic alpine valley with green partridges, crossed swords and other talismanic symbols with the words *Subhan-Allah* – Glory be to Allah, scrawled on top. Mangled wiring extended over the walls to a power transmitter that was propped among leafy trees. Several crows sat camouflaged among the branches. In the shade were four Toyota Hilux Pickups and a platoon of wild-eyed men with dirty beards and long hair, shalwar pants tucked into combat boots and arms cuddling automatic rifles. They did what soldiers do best. Kill time.

One of the men at the gate wore a cream-coloured shalwar suit and a black turban. The turban said more than the man. It was a three-foot-wide strip of cloth with a solid black stripe running in the middle and was wrapped a few times around a semi-hard skullcap. The remainder of the fifteen feet of unwrapped silk was flung carelessly around the shoulder. The man had a dark, forgettable face set with sunken eyes under heavy eyebrows and a lengthy beard. He introduced himself as Hukum Khan and led us to a *hujra* in the main residence where the male guests were entertained. It was a long room with beige walls, which were bare but for a calendar with Islamic calligraphy and a solitary window covered by a dusty cloth curtain. The entrance was manned by guards with pump action shotguns and bandoliers across their chests. The fast-whirring ceiling fans left little headroom for their turbans.

Once we were seated on low sprawling sofas, we were served green tea, pine nuts and dried mulberries. I opened my briefcase and took out the case file and my business cards. As the tea cooled, men filed in and introduced themselves solemnly. The last man to enter was big in girth and had a white beard and matching eyebrows. He greeted the room with high exaltations and it was understood that this was Malik Awan. He sat down with the help of his walking stick, and men went to him one by one to shake his hand. We waited for our turn.

'Are my guests comfortable?' he asked, looking at Riaz.

42

'Under God's will, we are comfortable,' Riaz said, shaking his hand. Malik Awan looked in my direction. He had puffy bags under his eyes and heavy jowls. He had the air of a sage, except for his bulbous nose, which appeared to have been broken in a past skirmish.

'Thank you for seeing us. How is your health?' I asked, after exchanging salutations.

'At my age, I have many ailments. It is my Lord's punishment for a life well lived.' His tone kept rhythm with the verse he recited under his breath. 'So how can I be of service to you?'

'I am here regarding the claim on the warehouse.'

The beads on the rosary slipped through Malik Awan's fingers. 'What about it? It burned down last spring.'

'The claim was filed with Bridge Insurance.'

'I don't want to file a claim. I told Riaz Khan Masood about that.'

'That is your decision, Malik *sahab*. I am here to finish the report. Half a million dollars is a lot of money.'

'Not for me.'

'But you paid premiums for years to insure your business.'

'That does not matter. I cannot accept a dollar payment after what happened to Saifullah,' he said in a low tone, looking down at the rosary.

At the mention of the deceased, Hukum Khan raised his hand to lead a short prayer for forgiving the sins of the departed. All raised their hands in sombre silence, looking up in a meditative state. After he said *ameen*, every man present closed the prayer at his own pace by massaging his face with open palms, fingers on forehead, palms on cheeks and brushing down the length of the face to the end of his beard.

'Do you have children, Syed Qais?' Malik Awan's fingers made their way to the top bead on the rosary.

'A girl.' I waited for a patronising comment on not having fathered a son.

'Then you understand what it's like to raise a child.'

'I do.'

43

'But a son, now that is special. One day you scold him for running in the veranda without any shalwar, and the next day for running around town without a turban. That's how fast they grow.' Malik Awan closed his eyes as his fingers caressed the beads of the rosary faster. 'To raise a child in this land, one must guard against evil whisperers and informants.'

Riaz Khan cleared his throat before he spoke. 'We all share your grief, Malik Awan. I am a father myself. Your patience is exemplary. But this is our business ...'

'Riaz Khan, you as a Mehsud should know better. Still you bring this man to my home, to offer compensation for my dead son. Never will I accept that, and I say this in the presence of my Maker,' said Malik Awan.

Hukum Khan made a motion and a large-headed boy wearing a white skullcap appeared with a glass of water. Malik Awan drank it in three gulps. I wished for a rosary or a cigarette as the room went silent.

'I did not come all the way from Karachi to add to your grief. We will return the claim money to Lloyds of London.' I stood up.

'You mean you have accepted it?' Hukum Khan had taken off his turban, unveiling cropped white hair.

'A claim was filed by Malika Transport and we fulfilled it. That is the nature of the insurance business,' I said.

A trickle of sweat ran down my armpit. I walked to the window and adjusted my privates, hoping it would add to my swagger. Far away, a generator chugged. Hukum Khan followed me and stood with hands clasped behind his back. I saw a pack of cigarettes in his top pocket.

'Permit me, if I smoke,' I said. Malik Awan waved his hand and Hukum lit my cigarette. He was my height but appeared taller with his turban.

'The money can be put to good use,' I said thoughtfully.

'You want the money for yourself,' Malik Awan scoffed.

'I get my fees either way, but the claim money can be dispersed as you see fit.'

'You city folks can always find a way around religion. Islam is not a soft drink to which you can add artificial flavour. *Haram* is *haram*, and insurance, the underlying principle of which is human prowess superseding the Lord, is forbidden. Is it not?'

'The Prophet Muhammad, peace be upon Him, was a trader by profession. He paid protection money for his caravans. We have to adapt as Muslims doing business in this age of global commerce.'

'And that means changing who we are as Muslims?'

'This insurance was for cigarettes destined for American soldiers,' I said, 'the ones the mujahids are fighting. In war, returning money to the corporations of the occupiers seems shortsighted.' Malik Awan's fingers stopped on a bead. I had the attention of the room and I continued: 'Today, the Americans can bomb anywhere in Waziristan and nobody cares. It is as if the world has forsaken this land.'

'Nobody cares for Waziris, not the Americans, not the Afghan government or the Pakistan army,' a man said. There were murmurs of approval.

'They don't care, because the fight in Waziristan is not a real war, bound by international law. There are no laws here regarding civilians, loss of property or even prisoners of war. Arms dealers finance this war so they can test pilotless drones. But it still costs everybody money. Today, the Americans are in a financial crisis. Returning half a million dollars is rejecting good fortune from providence. Money doesn't care which side it is on.'

Malik Awan dropped his head and proceeded to work his rosary beads. I counted the beads as he prayed. On the eleventh bead, he looked up.

'Do you like what you do, Syed Qais?'

'It's a living.'

'Are you proud of it? Do you tell men you meet on the street that you are an insurance man with angelic powers of retribution and providence?'

I saved the thought for later digestion.

'I don't think you do. It is not your calling,' he said.

I put out my cigarette in an ashtray as the afternoon call to prayers started. I looked back respectfully as Malik Awan held my gaze.

'It is now time for prayers. You will join us,' Hukum Khan said.

'Yes, but excuse us while we perform *wuzu*,' Riaz replied.

I followed him to the toilet and joined him in the ablutions in the small sink.

'This is not looking good,' I said, washing my nostrils with water.

'You talked rationally. You had me convinced.' Riaz washed his arm to his elbows and then cupped his hand to splash water up his elbow.

'And what does the claim have to do with his son's death?' I splashed water on my face three times as Riaz plopped a foot into the sink and cleaned the area between his toes. He repeated the same with the other foot as I began to wash my elbows.

While we were entangled with each other, Hukum Khan entered and let out a short laugh, revealing his gold tooth.

'You are old friends,' he said.

'No, we met yesterday.' I smiled back at him.

'You make friends easily,' he commented before leading us to the prayer room. We were joined by the guards, who took off their carbines and filed behind the imam. The men stank of wet hair, bad breath, and perspiration. I touched my ears with hands and said *Allah hu Akbar*. I was about to recite the first verse when the man on my left motioned to me. 'You did the *Allah hu Akbar* before the imam. Do it again.'

I touched my ears again and reminded myself not to curse him during Namaz.

After the prayers were over, we were shown to the living room. Hukum Khan motioned for us to sit. Malik Awan cleared his throat.

'Our house is blessed today as we have guests. In Pashtunwali culture, we hold guests in the highest regard, even if they say

46

something that we don't like. That has been the way of my family. So with your permission, I want to share a story from the old times.'

Malik Awan counted his beads. Nobody moved until Riaz prodded me with his elbow.

'Go ahead,' I said.

Malik Awan spoke in a soft voice. 'My maternal grandfather served in the British Army under a certain Colonel Nicholas. As the story goes, he saved the Colonel's life in Burma and after that, they became good friends and shared mutual respect. Once, the Colonel visited with his wife, Lady Nicholas. She was an artist of some sort and was intrigued by the carved *darvazay* that led into this *haveli*. She asked my grandfather, how old were these doors? And my grandfather, the *malik* of the tribe, replied that they could be two hundred or three hundred years old. Hearing this, Lady Nicholas said it was a waste for such priceless works of art to rot away in Waziristan, and they should be displayed in a mansion or museum. She talked about the doors for three days – and when they were leaving, my grandfather said that if she wanted the doors, she could have them. The next day, a truck showed up and men disassembled the wooden doors. They even took the locks and hinges. As the truck went away, my mother asked, "*Baba,* why did you let them take away our doors? It is now cold in the house." And he said, "Dear, how could I stop them, they were guests. And it was only a *darvaza*, not a *dukhtar*." A door, not a daughter.'

There was a murmur among the seated men.

'The doors may have left the *haveli*, but our honour is with our daughters not with such material things,' Riaz Khan clarified the lesson. Everyone nodded in agreement.

'And now, we will have food. Please wait while we have it set up,' Malik Awan announced. I agreed to staying for lunch. Riaz complained about our delayed departure. The room emptied out and I dozed off on the sofa.

A screaming rooster woke me. I opened the shuttered door into a veranda that separated the *hijra* from the main residence.

On the right were a couple of goats in a square pen chewing grass and on the opposite side sat a toothless old man smoking strong black tobacco in a hookah, next to a pile of dried cow – pats. Behind him, a long shed housed the domestic help, and I heard the laughter of children and the smell of frying onions, mustard seeds and ghee. I lit a cigarette as a soft breeze rolled in from the hills, and noticed a boy cross the veranda. He was eight-years-old or so, and was dressed in a checkered shirt paired with blue denim jeans and had neatly combed hair. Behind him strutted a rooster, black and burgundy with a curved beak, half as tall as the boy, and almost as arrogant. I exchanged pleasantries with the old man, who murmured a reply.

'Is the rooster yours?' I asked the boy.

'Yes,' he said, staring at my clothes.

'What do you call him?'

'Surkh Afridi.'

'Does he wake you up in the morning?'

'He is not an alarm clock. He is an *aseeli* fighting cock with eight wins.'

'What is your name?'

'Qasim.'

'And your father?'

I heard a rustle of clothing and smelt perfume. I turned my head and saw a woman emerge next to the boy. Her head was covered in a paisley woollen *chadur*, which ended in a triangle above her forehead. She wore gold-coloured slippers.

'Qasim,' she said. Her face was uncovered and her eyes were lined with kohl. She took the boy's hand and led him away, but he turned around after a few steps.

'My father is Saif Awan. He is dead. The Americans killed him.'

*

Lunch was served late but had various chicken and goat curries, as well as a local speciality called the *zamarud pilau* – spinach

48

with rice. The men ate with relish, but Malik Awan only drank *shalumbeh,* a yogurt-based drink, and retired to his room shortly afterwards. After lunch, Riaz made phonecalls and I talked to Hukum Khan about war and his rifle.

'A Lee Enfield 303 calibre's got quite a kick,' I said.

'That's why it is accurate. How do you know it?'

'The instructors taught us how to load and clean it. You have to watch your thumb because a loaded magazine has to be pressed before the bolt springs back.'

'So you have used it?' he asked. He had a powerful stare and bad breath.

'A long time back. I shot the 303 on a rifle range.'

'They like the AK-47 these days, but this is over seventy years old, my grandfather's. He, too, served with the British.'

He handed me the rifle. It was clean and oiled and the aged wood was scratched but polished.

'Are you still a good shot? You want to try?' he asked.

'I can shoot, but now I am a civilian.' I handed back the gun.

'I heard that. You are the civilian with a book. May I see it?'

I took the book out of my briefcase and passed it to him.

'Written by a communist,' he said, as he looked at the front cover: it showed a turbaned warrior riding a horse over a map of Baluchistan. In the foreground was an image of the good Argentinian doctor wearing a beret with a red star.

'No, a friend. He used to live in Karachi,' I lied casually.

He took out a pair of black-framed reading glasses from his top pocket and flipped through the book. I waited with the others. Riaz entered the room and sat down. Some men stroked their beards, others scratched their balls, but nobody looked at their cellphones. After about ten minutes of silence, Hukum Khan looked up again.

'Your friend has a good understanding of politics.'

'He is an educated man,' I said.

'Are you also inspired by the *surkh inquilab*?'

'I am susceptible to causes that support social justice. Forty years ago, everyone was caught in the Marxist fervour.'

'Times have changed. You should get your friend to write about our cause. We need good writers who can speak the right words and show what it is like to live like this – in perpetual war and under the eyes of imperial drones.' Hukum Khan stood up.

'He would, if the government allowed him to come back. He is a Baluch nationalist.'

'We support the Baluch cause. The Pakistan government has mistreated them.'

'The CIA is all over Pakistan and fly drones from Miranshah,' Riaz added, but was ignored.

'Did you hear about the last drone attack?' Hukum Khan asked. He had a zip pocket on his right arm, on top of his bicep. 'It was last week, a few miles outside of Miranshah. Eighteen people dead, six of them children. Who is going to write about that? Karachi owns the media and Punjab owns the army.'

'How far is it from here?' I thought a drone could be hovering over this house as we spoke. 'Malik Awan must be disturbed by the drones.'

'No father can be disturbed once he has lost a son,' Hukum Khan said. 'You know, a drone attack leaves no body parts – flesh and bone are burned to a crisp, but wristwatches survive. We only found Saif's watch. Afterwards, when we set up a funeral for the dead, they bombed that as well. There is no humanity in Americans.'

'There is no humanity in war. Even in *khud kash* bombings,' I said.

'Or the Pakistan army. In fact, they will be waiting for us to cross the bridge,' Riaz said, getting up. 'We need to get going, Qais *sahab*, it will be dark soon.'

Hukum Khan remained seated but kept the book. I wanted it back.

'Nobody likes bombs in bazaars where our families shop. We are not terrorists, just Waziris,' he said.

'Some Waziris support the Taliban?'

'Don't believe everything you read in the newspapers. Malik Awan is well respected, and Saif was an educated man, with a wife and son. And the Americans blew him to bits without trial or conviction. They did the same to Saddam, beheaded his sons and showed the severed heads all over their news media. And they call us barbarians.'

'Many innocent lives were lost in that war,' I said, getting up. I wanted to finish this conversation.

'Only Muslim lives were lost!' Hukum said. 'Only Muslim wives grieve.'

'Maybe, but I am a civilian. All I can offer is a financial setback to the imperialists,' I said. 'Maybe you can talk to Malik Awan on our behalf.'

'As you said earlier, there are no civilians in this war, only terrorists.' Hukum Khan handed back the book. 'In Waziristan, you are one of us. Being a civilian or a terrorist does not matter. They are all the same to the drone. Have a safe journey.'

7

The Great Migraine

'It is irrelevant who wins the next election,' Riaz said as he overtook a truck on the Indus highway. 'For us in FATA', 'it is *pahtak-salari* or *tope-salari*. Do you understand?'

'You mean governance by checkposts or cannons. I know this much,' I said. Our journey back was much slower. There were many more checks by the Pakistan military as we headed back to Punjab. I was a bit charged up from my meeting and in no mood to be passive to Riaz's opinions.

'Yes. Nothing changes for us. Do you expect change?' Riaz braked hard to avoid an oncoming motorcycle.

'I do.' I gripped the door handle hard. The car had no working seat belts.

'That's because you are from the big province. Always the optimist.' Riaz merged back into his lane. 'Your people don't understand melancholy; always dancing, singing or feasting. I have never seen anyone eat as much as Punjabis do.'

He continued in a patronising tone as we drove towards Punjab. I formulated a pitch perfect response but enjoyed it for my own benefit. I had long learned not to feed into ridiculous stereotype. The rain earlier had had a pleasant effect on the population. The traffic had thinned down and the boys played cricket or volleyball on green tracts, as squadrons of birds flew between sporadic ponds. The air smelled of fertility and hope and the radio station played a Vital Signs song from the eighties. I remembered visiting this area that decade. We had driven to Kala Bagh for Zahid's sister's wedding. On the way, we had stopped at the Durra gun markets to buy pistols for comrades in the student unions and at the Bara smugglers' market to buy georgettes for our fiancées. Back then, Pakistan was the safe haven from the hot war in Afghanistan, and General Zia and Ronald Reagan were friends and fellow Cold warriors. I hummed as we stopped for the final check before crossing the Jinnah barrage. A ranger *jawan* took a dislike to my casual attitude. I was asked to step out of the car.

'This is expired.' He held my ID card between his fingers like a trump card.

'This ID is not expired.' I did my best Jedi mind trick.

'Show me where.' he snarled.

'You can't read! Give it to your officer.'

The sentry hesitated, not sure if he should slap or salute me.

'Fucking idiot,' I said. Swearing in English was a privilege of my class.

'He is a VIP guest from Karachi. Get your officer,' Riaz said.

The ranger walked away with my ID; Riaz followed him. I sat in the car, lit a cigarette and reminisced about my young wife wrapped in green georgette. Twenty years flashed by, and ten minutes later, a thickset soldier in camouflaged combat gear with shoulder patches appeared before the car.

'Everything all right, Captain *sahab*?' I asked.

'*Aap jaayein*. Welcome to Punjab.' He handed back the ID card, which would not expire for another two years.

*

53

I passed the evening watching TV channels that presented middle-class problems I had left behind in Karachi. My phone buzzed. It was Sonia.

I had hardly said hello when Shereen called and I had to put Sonia on hold.

'Hello, Shereen.'

'*Abu*, you never said you were going to Waziristan,' my daughter chided me in a tone that reminded me of my wife.

'No need to yell, dear. I will be home soon.' I was happy that she cared.

'That is so crazy. Why would you go there?'

'I stay in Mianwali. It is safer.'

'You did not even say goodbye.' Shereen mouthed the word with such sincerity that it made me consider if my mother was coercing her.

'I was in a hurry. You know I have to work hard.'

'Who's going to help with my exam preparations? I told you I needed help.'

'I will be back in a week. Promise!'

'Okay. Bring something.'

'What can I bring from here, dear? This is not a tourist spot.'

'Anything, maybe a souvenir. At least I can brag to my classmates that my father went to Waziristan while their parents can't even go to Korangi without a security protocol.'

'I will see if I can find a little present.'

'All right, see you soon. Take care of yourself. I get worried.' She cut the call.

It wasn't too long ago that Shereen had an unshakable belief in her father as 'the man with the plan'. But in the last few years, she had grown older and I had grown poorer. I poured myself a gin and called Sonia.

'Done with family?' she asked

'Yes. It was my little girl.'

'How old is she now?'

'Nearly eighteen and about to finish her A-levels.'

'I have often wondered about you as a father.'

54

'Why don't you ask her?'

'How will you introduce me? As an ex-lover?'

'That was before she was born.'

'But you were still married.'

'So were you.'

It went on like that for a while, the banter, the insults, and the casual complaints. We had not talked this long for over a decade, but soon the conversation turned to one of our earlier passionate encounters.

'I remember the night ...' her voice became husky '... upstairs in the showroom with mirrors and lights and just the two of us.'

I remembered it too. We had remained locked up in the apparel store for hours alone, before the age of cellphones and security cameras. The hotel room grew hot as Sonia cooed in my ears. I took a deep breath and loosened my shalwar.

I heard a knock on the door. It was followed by a push, and a violent shove.

'Who is it?'

'It's me,' said a jubilant voice. The lock jiggled with impatience.

I said goodbye, tightened the shalwar and opened the door.

'Drove straight from Karachi, nonstop.' Zahid dragged in a black and tan Samsonite suitcase. He placed it on the bed and opened it. Inside were carefully lined cans of Tiger beer.

'You drove from Karachi with beer?'

'I promised my cousin foreign beer. Time for a Tiger.' Zahid opened a can. I covered my eyes with my hands and shook my head.

'Something wrong, *Shah-ji*? Did I interrupt you?'

'No. Have your Tiger.'

Zahid went to the bathroom. I heard him burp as he settled his weight on the toilet seat. My cellphone beeped with a message.

U always preferred the company of MEN, xxoo Sonia.

*

Colonel Aftab Gul was the kind of man that mothers want as a son-in-law. He was mild-mannered, articulate and handsome. I met him at the headquarters of the Baluch regiment the next morning. The manicured lawns and pressed uniforms of the regiment proclaimed virility and purpose. It was a strong reminder of my school days at the cadet college. We had competed in academics and sports at school. He swam and I played squash. He had an empty mind and was guided by the certainty of his craft as a swimmer and a soldier.

'Colonel Sunflower, how are you? Old age treating you well?' I said in a jolly tone. I should not have bothered to ask. Age had treated him well. He looked the same – square-jawed, wide shoulders, chiselled face, no fat on his waist and no grey on his chin.

'What brings you here?' We hugged. It raised my esteem among the soldiers present, who had eyed my dishevelled state with disdain earlier. 'How is the family, Alia and kids?'

'They are fine. She is still dreaming of emigrating to America.'

'Still waiting on her green card?' I said. His wife's brother had sponsored the Gul family more than ten years ago. It had been a running joke among his friends for even longer.

'Yes. Make yourself comfortable. I have work to do,' he said and made himself busy making phone calls for the next few hours. In the brief moments while he was off the phone, I was able to give him my story. He was not impressed.

'I wouldn't go near Jandola without a battalion,' he said.

'I need a day pass to inspect the warehouse. I will be in and out.'

'This is a not a college excursion, but a warzone. You should think of your daughter.'

'What about your wife and son, aren't they worried about you as well?'

'I am a soldier – that is my duty.'

'I assess risk, so I must take risks,' I said as his phone rang again.

It was late morning and the room smelled of chemicals and varnish. Soldiers came in with orders and problems. Most were trivial. Like an old colonist overseeing his domain, the colonel was lonely and surrounded by idiots. A man with a long, ash-coloured beard brought tea and pieces of cake. Aftab asked the orderlies and peons to clear the room and shut the door.

'Are you here alone?' he asked.

'No, Zahid is with me.'

'Tall, dark and *ahmaq* – stupid,' he said with a sneer. The two of them never got along. Zahid was the opposite of Aftab – a backbencher, a bully and not very studious. 'These are dangerous times, my friend.'

'I have heard that all my life about Pakistan. Tell me something new,' I said.

'This time it is real. Our best institutions are failing.'

'You mean the army?'

'Yes, even the army has had a few recent failures.'

'What – the Osama raid?'

He shrugged his shoulders.

'I would say we have all failed in some way,' I said.

'Your failure is personal, but mine represents the state.'

'That's your short-sightedness. Failure in commerce supersedes martial failures.'

'Are you a commercial man now? Neither a poet nor a warrior?' Aftab said snidely. He had never forgiven me for not joining the army, as was required of a cadet.

'I am always a poet. It stays in my heart, like my personal djinn that I can take anywhere.' I thumped my chest.

He stood up with precision. It wasn't a particularly athletic stance, just rigid.

'Still playing squash?' He glanced at my expanding waistline.

'Off and on,' I lied. I had not seen the inside of the court for over five years.

The phone rang again and an officer entered. They both saluted each other. I was made painfully aware of my civilian status.

Aftab turned to me. 'Dinner tomorrow? I am busy today. My commanding officer is visiting. Maybe we will get a chance to play snooker.'

*

Back at the hotel, I found the room empty but messy. Zahid had left his clothes on my bed and the bedsheet had been pulled out from all corners, as if he had wrestled a bear on the bed. There were cigarette ashes and crumbs from various snacks all over the floor. He had gone to Kala Bagh to visit family and would come back tomorrow. I was cleaning up when my phone beeped.

Ruqiya Bibi wants 2 c u. Shall I say y? read the SMS from Riaz.

I typed *yes* and opened a Tiger beer. I spent the rest of the morning thinking of various scenarios involving this Ruqiya Bibi, widow of the suspected militant Saif Awan. Some were reasonable, others were more sensational.

In the afternoon, Riaz drove me to a Mianwali suburb with wide avenues and bungalows that mimicked the American White House with the two-pillar courtyard. IAS security guards ushered the car into one such house and I was shown into a lounge with a mezzanine floor. The room was large and the air conditioner struggled to cool the vast space. In the centre was a wicker couch with orange cushions, a glass table with a vase of imitation flowers, a crystal ashtray and a box of rose-petal tissues. There was no other furniture. By the time she arrived, I had smoked two cigarettes.

'Thank you for coming here,' she said, making her way to the sofa. Her attendant stood at the door. He wore a black *wasket*, a grey beard, and a stylish pistol-holster. I eyed him nervously.

'This is Zar Mohammad. He has been with me for a long time. I trust him. But I'm not so sure about you, Mr Qais. Are *you* trustworthy?' She sat across from me with her hands neatly placed in her lap. She was a big-boned woman but her diminutive manners made her appear particularly vulnerable.

I explained to her our predicament, the money that had to be dispersed to the claimant. She listened attentively and relaxed to let her *chadur* open to reveal a fashionably cut kurta.

'What did Baba Jaan say?'

I heard the greybeard shuffle his feet but his gaze remained above my head.

'Your father-in-law has refused to file the claim. But the warehouse is registered in your husband's name. If you act on his behalf, we can transfer the money to you.'

She nodded to the greybeard and he left the room.

'The full amount?'

'I will have to run the numbers and take the deductibles.'

'Give me an indication.'

'Two hundred thousand,' I low-balled her.

'Dollars?' she said with a smile. I was a good reader of smiles and this was genuine.

'Yes, cash or a deposit to a dollar account. But are you willing to offend Malik Awan?'

She met my eyes before she spoke.

'I want to leave Dera and be with my family in Pindi. I will take my son. Every day, Baba Jaan talks to him about Pashtunwali. As if an eight-year-old can avenge his father's death. If he grows up in Waziristan he will be killed as well,' she said.

I remained silent and let her arrive at a logical conclusion.

'What would I need to do to collect the money?'

'You need to get a No Objection Certificate as the widow of Saif Awan to accept the claim on your husband's behalf.'

Her eyes opened wider. A fat tear curved out of her right eye and ran down her cheek. She did not blink until another formed, along with a sob. I offered her the box of rose-petal tissues. She sobbed with the tissue covering her mouth. As I held the box, I knelt beside her. I could smell her expensive eau de toilette. Maybe Chanel.

'I hope you understand that I have already taken a big risk by meeting you.'

She looked down. I followed her gaze towards the floor. Her slippers had a strip of braided leather that circled the big toe and ran the length of her feet until it tied around the ankle. Her toenails were lacquered neutral. I fought the urge to touch her toe.

'I need a *jawan mard,* a real man, Mr Qais,' she murmured as she reached for another tissue. I felt her breathe as her rising chest closed the gap between us.

'I am not that person.' I stood up. It was sudden and it startled her.

'I apologise if I said something wrong.'

'Not at all. You are vulnerable after your loss, and I am too much of a gentleman to take advantage of a woman,' I touched her shoulder, 'as alluring as yourself.'

She looked at my hand. I pulled it back.

'Don't underestimate my grief. My loss is real. No one can replace Saif. With him gone, I have lost my centre.' She fixed her *chadur.*

'I understand. I lost my wife a few years back,' I said, consoling her.

'Any children?'

'One daughter.'

'I will pray for your health and safe return. *Allah hafiz.*' She walked to the door and then turned. 'Do you write poetry? You do, don't you?' She answered her own question without acknowledgment from my side, and then left.

I liked this Ruqiya *Bibi.* I liked her very much.

*

I was shown to the dining hall inside the officer's mess by a Second Lieutenant. He was a fresh graduate and had an exceptional physique that went along with his manicured crew cut and polished boots. I was guided to a long table where dinner was served on porcelain with regimental emblems. Before the meal I was introduced to the officers as the cadet who joined the civilian side. We talked of the news, the war and travelling. I ate sparsely, picking at my food with the silver cutlery and with proper manners. The food was plain but the coffee – served while we sat in a lounge lined with bookshelves and oil paintings of camel-mounted cavalries across pastoral landscapes – was delicious. The grass was always greener on the army's side.

'It is peaceful here,' I said to Aftab after the officers had excused themselves.

'It has to be, because we have to deal with the chaos of the outside every day,' he replied.

'That sounds pretentious,' I said. 'The outside is your own country and your own people.'

He closed his eyes for a moment. There was no sound apart from the shuffling of orderlies cleaning the mess hall.

'Do you know of Lord Curzon?' Aftab asked.

'No. Is he related to Lord Vader?' The façade of military life had put an edge to my mannerisms. I wasn't sure if I was jealous of them or frustrated by their detachment.

'I would not expect you to know him. You are not a military strategist. I had to learn all this to pass my exams. Continuous learning is what keeps us smart,' he said.

On another occasion, I would have challenged his hubris, but I was here to benefit from his greatness. I sipped my coffee politely instead.

'Curzon said that there would be no peace in Waziristan until the military steamroller has passed from end to end. He is credited with creating NWFP and the Indian army.'

'So, he is your father,' I said in a deep voice.

'Be serious, Qais. I am trying to teach you history. Sometimes even you can learn. As I was saying, the Waziris are different. For them, the tribe comes first. The *beradari* is what makes them resilient fighters. Take the tribe away and he becomes like any other Pakistani.'

'So how do you urbanise them?'

'That is the job of the state. The army can't take that responsibility.'

61

'Our army likes to think it can take every responsibility and excel at it.'

'Not this kind. You see, here is this shopkeeper, Umair. He used to run my tab because, as you know, our pay runs out by the twenty-first of the month. I owed him 15,000 rupees at one time. Anyway, we were ambushed once and chased the insurgents to a shack. I issued a final warning and they came out, and there among them was Umair. I asked him, "What kind of madness is this?" If I died, who would pay the debt that I owed him? He grinned, pleading his case that he was powerless when it came to the call of the tribe. "I can't oppose the Taliban and live among them," he said.'

'Can't you stop the manufacturing of guns and ammunitions?'

'The benefactors of this war are everywhere – the transporters for the NATO convoys, the arms dealers who supply the Taliban and the army. The trouble is that nobody can touch them. Their protection goes deep, deeper than the friends.'

'Friends?'

'Army lingo for Americans. Nicest guys you will meet; they respect us more than we give them credit for. After all, we are both professional armies, and our ties go back a long way. Our generals play golf and smoke cigars while they play "the Great Game" with Americans.'

'And then they found Osama in Pakistan,' I said. 'Sounds more like the "great migraine".'

'I say it was a good thing. At least it gave us clarity.'

'How can you say that? It was humiliating. And your man did not even resign!'

'You mean the chief?'Aftab said, getting up.

We walked to the billiards room where two junior officers were playing a game.

'He might have saved the *riyasat* and the country.' Aftab wrote his name down on a chalkboard.

'You seem to think highly of him. All I know is that he talks less and smokes more,' I said as the junior officers quickly wrapped up their game.

'He is a strategic and rational man, the first chief who was also a spymaster. He knows how to deal with Americans.'

'You think Americans will invade Pakistan?'

'They don't have to invade – all they have to do is move their soldiers across no-man's-land and we will be humiliated.' Aftab racked up the balls and selected a cue stick. He had always been competitive and I could see from his body language that he had not changed a bit.

'Selecting another man's cue is like fucking with someone else's dick,' I said and tried other cues. They were all the same, straight and well balanced like Aftab. I put the white cue ball right of the marker and opened with my best break.

'You know many Americans?' I asked as I watched a red ball roll into a pocket.

'My units cleared the airfields when they flew drones from Miranshah.'

'What do you think of the drones?' I missed my next shot.

'It's a weapon that I can't control. They make me uneasy.'

'Is that your opinion or also your – what do you say? – Jawans'?'

Aftab polished his cue stick. 'They know that the militants have to be dealt with.'

'What about you?' A cicada began his mating call outside.

'I know that they are an existentialist threat to the state,' he said without moving. 'But I am not the same since Black Thunderstorm.'

'What's that?'

'The Swat Operation.' He polished his cue tip with the blue eraser.

'I heard that the Taliban were pretty entrenched there.' I missed again.

'They were everywhere. So we shelled the town.'

Aftab took a long shot. The red ball fell into the far right pocket. He nudged another into the centre pocket and moved around the table with the cue held out like a fencing foil.

'It was the kind of campaign an artillery commander can only dream about. A 150mm Howitzer, a 300mm multi-barrel rocket launcher and flame-throwers to roast out survivors.' Aftab missed a shot. 'Except I never thought I would use that kind of artillery in my country and on my own kin. It left a bitter taste in the mouth. It makes you want to stop being a soldier.'

'Don't you have seniors you can talk to about your feelings?'

'They can't relate to us. We have been fighting an insurgency for ten years. They barely fought for a month and that too against a conventional army.'

We played two more games. I let him win. He took losses more seriously than I did.

'Do you know a Major Bhatti?' I asked.

'There are lots of Bhattis in the army.'

'Sultan Bhatti. He knows about you. Is he ISI?'

'*Bhai*, don't even go there. You will get killed or kidnapped. He is the point man for everything illegal.' Aftab stopped. 'Why do you insist on putting yourself at risk? Believe me, this is not wise,' he said as we walked towards a covered garage. The driver snapped to attention and opened the back door of a jeep.

'Drop Qais *sahab* in Mianwali. Stick to the main highways,'Aftab ordered the driver.

'It's amazing how they obey you. Nobody listens to me, be it at home or work.' I hugged him and made a final plea. 'I am in a rut, *yaar*. I need that pass. You know a win solves everything.'

'I will see what I can do, okay, no promises.'

'Do it quick. I am bored.'

'Go sightseeing. But keep a low profile. There is too much uncertainty. The only thing you can be sure of here, is fear.'

'What about Allah?'

'Allah checked out a long time ago.'

8

Indus Party

Hip hop party at Indus, must cum read Zahid's text.

I was bored and intrigued by the text. The last few days I had sweltered in the hotel dealing with load shedding and waiting for permission to visit Jandola. I missed my daughter, my bed and home-cooked food. I agreed to accompany him.

He was late but dressed to impress in a gunmetal grey *kurta* with silver embroidery on the lapel. My own clothes were worn out in comparison and I looked like the help.

'So who is getting married?' I asked.

'Why do you care? You are going with Zahid Fareed. Yasmeen is bringing two girls from Lahore.' He revved the diesel motor unnecessarily on the Toyota. I could tell that he was excited.

Yasmeen was Zahid's girl – his kept mistress and a whore. He had known her for a few years and gave her the protection that she needed to run her business and keep out of trouble with the law. They got along well, as both were bullies.

'Who do you know there? Do I look okay?'

'You look fine. I know the groom Malik Shahzad Khan. This is the gentry of Kala Bagh. His father used to work for the Nawab.'

'What about alcohol?'

'Scotch, gin, you name it. Beer is for the young people. Aziz, grab a Tiger for us.'

'Sir-ji, it's in the trunk, can't reach it,' replied the guard who rode in the back seat. Zahid yelled an obscenity and slammed on the brakes.

'Let it be, it will be warm and we are almost there,' I said.

He took my advice. I was one of the rare few to whom he listened.

We crossed the barrage and veered right on a side road. Beyond us lay the mountainous gorge harbouring the lake. This was the potential site for the notorious Kala Bagh Dam that would contain the River Indus. For the last thirty years, our politicians had bickered about it. The proponents saw it as the key to solving our energy needs. The opposition saw it as a ploy by Punjab to divert more water from the smaller province. Most had never visited the gorge and cared little about the city that glittered in the calm waters of the lake.

The ride took us onto a gravel road that ended in a clearing between two unfinished houses. A *shamiyana* tent with a pattern currently out of fashion in Karachi was raised on the ground. From within it came the sounds of singing and laughter of the wedding party. It was the *zenana* section and when we walked further up the street, we were escorted past a line of cauldrons and tandoors to a terrace with a smaller tent. It was enclosed on three sides by shisham trees; the fourth side overlooked the river. Dinner had been served and the servants had lined up for their dinner. The aroma of the sautéed rice and grilled meats was tempting but I was fixated on a hard drink.

Inside the tent Zahid made quick introductions. We were acknowledged and then ignored by anxious young men with soft moustaches. The older men, identified by their heavy jowls and the aged look of having partaken of alcohol for years, drank quietly in a corner. I saw the tall silhouette of Captain Baz turned towards the drinks station and watched as he poured out half a tumbler of Grant Scotch and added ice.

'I didn't know you drink.'

I cursed under my breath and turned to face Riaz.

'What are you doing here?' I asked with a weak smile.

'This is a special event for our community,' Riaz smiled.

'Do you?' I raised my glass. He shook his head.

The girls arrived half an hour later and were escorted by Zahid onto the stage with a certainty that came with experience. There were three – a sullen beauty in a shapely red dress, a slim girl with heavy brows in a white dress with sequins, and the last was Yasmeen, tall and pale in black, with a firm mouth. She introduced the other girls to us.

'Where is the groom?' Yasmeen placed her foot on the stage to buckle her black-heeled shoe. Her confidence was sensational and scandalous.

The other girls were less confident. Miss Red cowered behind Miss White and did not say a word until it was time to choose the music tracks. She worked with the DJ on the set list and took off her shoes to lead the first dance. The first track set the stage for several Lollywood favourites. It was still early and the boys had manners, the girls were nimble and the mustachioed elders continued to drink in silence.

After an hour of dance numbers and plenty of opportunities to embarrass the groom – a chubby fellow with a high-pitched laugh – the dancers took a break. Miss Red, a definite favourite with her tight dress and pouting mouth, settled into the groom's lap. Yasmeen sat down with Zahid and smoked a cigarette through a holder. Miss White found a seat next to Riaz.

'I am so tired,' she announced to no one in particular. Nobody was picky here and all the stragglers of the party encircled her. They were hesitant to approach her individually but snickered jokes between themselves in Urdu, Punjabi and English. Kala Bagh was a provincial town but these young men were globally connected and had grown up on a diet of racy Bollywood movies, mobile phones, and multi-cultural porn. I had grown up in the eighties and had to spend an inordinate amount of energy to get to see a naked picture of Bo Derek.

Miss White sang and flirted with everyone but inched closer to Riaz. It was not surprising – he had soft manners, piercing grey eyes and fine hair that fell over his forehead like a crown. They whispered to each other and the other boys were left disheartened. I closed my eyes and drifted off, having had a few drinks. When I opened my eyes I saw Riaz running his fingers through her hair.

'What shampoo do you use?' Riaz asked Miss White.

'Pantene.'

'Me too.'

'Any beer?' she said, looking in my direction. I stiffened. It was bad enough that I was old, but I did not expect to be treated like the help.

'She wants a beer. Can we get one for her?' Riaz said. 'Sima, this is Mr Qais. He brought foreign beer from Karachi.'

'That's very brave,' Sima said. Her arched brows were set close together and she reminded me of a young Frida Kahlo.

'I was travelling with SSP Zahid. He is the smuggler, not me.' I opened a Tiger and offered it to her.

'He is your friend?' she said, as she took a large gulp.

'I have known him for twenty years.' I opened a can and offered it to Riaz.

'I don't drink. Watching her is enough,' Riaz said.

She gulped the drink but with renewed interest. I had risen up in the social scale.

'Any *charas*?' She covered her mouth.

Riaz called out to a gangly kid who held a smouldering joint. He passed it and watched her. She took a long drag.

Another joint was fired up and everyone puffed, including Riaz, who finally showed a vice. The smoke hung over our heads like a cloud. Someone moved the pedestal fan in our direction. Time passed. The crowd thinned and the groom left with the mustachioed elders; being nobility he could not be allowed to soil his name in public. I drank more scotch.

'Captain is back at it,' the gangly kid said out loud. He had smoked and drank constantly but it had had little effect on him. Sima, on the other hand, looked ready to fall asleep.

I turned around to find Miss Red dancing with Captain Baz to the tune of Noor Jehan singing 'Mundaya Sialkoti'. The gangly youth joined a group of clapping revellers who surrounded the couple. Baz swooned over Miss Red with a drink in hand, his long brownish fingers draping the glass of scotch. With his black eyes and gleaming white teeth, he looked tragically handsome where as she looked dishevelled. Her mouth looked too wide, her make-up too thick, her jewelry too fake and her motions too contrived. She draped her dupatta around Baz and nuzzled against his chest.

'Take her, Captain, she is hot for you,' said the gangly kid. 'He is my cousin, you know,' he said, looking in our direction.

Baz looked over to Zaman, whose chubby frame I had recognised earlier. They exchanged a look and he steered Miss Red towards the bungalow. Zaman followed. It was a call to duty for others.

'Let's go, SSP *sahab*,' Yasmeen said.

Zahid put his hand on my shoulder and winked. 'Don't drink too much Shah-ji. Have fun. After all, you are a single man.'

I shrugged, but the signal had been given to Sima that I was to be entertained. The gangly kid sat down on the seat next to mine and asked for another Tiger.

'Sir-ji, I have never had beer this good. No aftertaste. Our fucking beer is made with Vaseline,' he said. Most of the revellers who had stayed for the party were drunk and young. It reminded me of the time when being drunk made me happy.

'Local beer is made from malt. This is pilsner made in the Philippines for the British.'

'The British know how to drink,' he said. He had straight white teeth, pimples on his face and a wispy beard.

'What's your name?' I asked.

'Feroz,' he said. 'And you, sir?'

I introduced myself and asked him how he was related to the groom.

'I am his cousin.'

'And Baz?'

'He is also the groom's cousin. Same family,' he said. 'Here, try this beer.' He held it up to one of his friends. The friend took a sip. He made a face and spat it out.

'This tastes like horse piss. Why do people drink this?'

Everyone laughed. I stared at the glimmering sequins that ran down Sima's dress.

'He scolds with his eyes,' she said.

'He is a poet, a man of culture and high society,' Riaz said.

'What do you do in Karachi?' Sima asked me.

'I am a businessman,' I instinctively checked my cellphone and saw a text from Colonel Aftab. *All clear 4 Tank, Godspeed Qais*, it read.

I looked to Riaz and raised two thumbs up. He mouthed 'FC permission' and I nodded. He winked but it was intercepted by Sima.

'*Mubarak*, you got good news,' she said.

'Yes,' I smiled. I wanted to go home. This was a long enough vacation.

She stood up, stretched, turned, and fell into my lap.

'And here is more good news,' she said. Her body was warm and her skin was covered with a translucent film of sweat and heavy body lotion.

'Can you check if Uncle is a man or a *khusra* – you never know with these Karachiwalas,' said Feroz. He was sprawled on the floor with his head in the lap of another friend.

It was all the encouragement she needed. I wiggled but she slid her hands inside my shirt. The accolades from the boys increased. She withdrew her hand and then put it on my lap. It felt as ungraceful as it sounds.

'You boys are liars. Uncle likes women for sure,' she laughed.

We kissed. Her mouth was dry with the taste of beer and cigarettes. Mine probably smelled the same. There were more cheers from the boys. I was part of the show.

'Come on, Uncle,' Sima said. I stood up uncomfortably and left the laughter behind.

Inside the house, we walked through the first open door. It was a cool room with an air conditioner, a low bed, a bottle of cold water, a blue towel, and a pack of Durex condoms.

'Turn the light off,' she said, crawling into the bed. I turned it off.

It was dark except for the light from a tungsten bulb slung on a tree outside. It cast a leafy shadow on Sima who had now stripped down to a white bra and black panties. The bulb swayed on a wire and the shadows moved, but she remained still.

I took the condom pack into the bathroom. I was tense everywhere except where it mattered. I thought of Sonia but by the time I opened the packet, the feeling was gone.

'Hurry up, Uncle, or I will fall asleep,' Sima called to me.

I returned to her and we kissed. She was a terrible kisser but she was on the clock and had a professional's reach. Within seconds, her hands were inside my shalwar. She cooed encouragements and plastered her lips on mine until I could taste more than cigarettes and beer.

'I don't think I can do this,' I said.

'You tried Viagra?' she said casually. That burned more than the whisky in my stomach. I laughed to cover my shame.

'I like you, Uncle. You should smile more,' she said.

She snuggled into my shoulder. I ran my hands on her back down her knobly spine. She had a dancer's body, slim and muscular. I was still hopeful but she fell asleep and I could hear her gentle snores. I washed up and placed a thousand rupees on her clothes and lit a cigarette.

A knock on the door woke her up.

'You want me to leave?' Sima sprang up.

'No,' I said and opened the door.

'What's happening here?' Yasmeen demanded, forcing herself into the room. 'Get up. You think this is your father's house? We have more programmes to make, more guests to entertain,' she said to Sima.

71

'Let me sleep for twenty minutes. I will make more programmes.'

'Get up now, or I will slap this sleep out of you.'

'Let her be, we are not done,' I said.

Yasmeen noticed the rupee notes placed on Sima's clothes.

'Shah-ji, let me handle this. I have done three programmes, Neeli has done two and she has to do her share. *Chalo*, get up, Sima, or I will lose my temper,' Yasmeen said.

'Fine *baji*, next time when you need my help I will remember this.' Sima picked up her clothes and marched into the bathroom.

'Don't mind this. You handle your friends, I will handle mine,' Yasmeen said, taking out a Benson. She attached it to a cigarette holder and lit it. Feroz entered the room. He had stood at the door for a while, unsure when it would be appropriate to make an entrance.

'You use a cigarette holder?' he said to her.

'I don't like the smell of cigarettes on my fingers,' Yasmeen said. 'You next?'

He nodded and Sima came out of the bathroom. She had no make-up, the eyeliner was gone – as was the red lipstick – and her hair was drawn back in a tight ponytail. Her eyes met his briefly and Sima's lips parted in a shy smile.

'Me or her.' Yasmeen pointed a long finger towards Sima.

'You,' he said.

'Let's go, we can use the other room.' Yasmeen led the gangly youth away.

I left to find food. I was hungry and asked an old attendant if he could bring me anything to eat. I could have done it myself but I knew enough about being part of the gentry. He perked up with good humour as though I had given him a big tip and returned with plates of grilled meat. I was about to dig in when Riaz sang.

'*Woh agay baray tu kuch bhi na hoga, main peeche haaton ga tu duniya hasegi...*'

'You're being funny?'

'I am singing Esakhelvi's song. You have something against him?'

72

'I have nothing against somebody named after a prophet. No girls for you?' I chomped on a chicken thigh. I could have felt ashamed for my whoring, but alcohol makes one belligerent, even when you start drinking after sunset.

'I came here to enjoy the scenery.'

'*Na shabab, na sharab, na kabab*,' I said. 'How do you get by in life without women, wine and even food?'

Riaz picked up a kebab. 'Naan has too many carbohydrates.'

'Well, one out of three is not bad.'

'I like women fine,' he said with an arrogant look. It probably made the girls fall over backwards, but I found the look silly – like that of an overacting soap star.

'But you don't find these girls attractive? I think they find you handsome.'

'Of course I do. But these girls,' he shook his head. 'Better to chat with a nice girl on the computer than fuck a whore. They like money,' he said with a polite smile. 'If I give them money, it feels like I am stealing from my family's future.'

Riaz watched me eat. With every mouthful and burp, I was losing his respect and playing into his stereotype of an uncouth Punjabi man. I could not care less. I was in a beastly mode.

'You have a ride to go home? I am leaving soon,' Riaz said. I nodded and he walked away as the only sober man in the party.

The 'programmes' with the three girls happened in quick succession. The girls remained in the rooms and the men who had not had their turn waited impatiently. Once the serial orgy was over, the girls ate by themselves.

I grabbed a few cups of tea and joined them.

'Uncle is the best,' Sima said as I handed her the tea. She had put the ghastly red lipstick back on her lips. They shared a plate of kebabs.

'Here, you take the second cup. Neeli and I share everything,' said Sima.

'Don't share me, barely enough Qais for one,' I said.

'You think too much, Uncle,' Sima laughed as she took a leg piece of chicken and stripped it clean with her teeth.

'Comes with age, not like these mountain goats.' I pointed to the men standing around.

'This is a sad lot. The older men are drunk and the young shudder in seconds.'

'And many don't like us,' Neeli said.

'What's not to like?' I said. I should have taken her. It might have worked.

'Some like to watch,' said Sima.

'They don't care about us. We are an item on the market,' Neeli added.

Sima leaned over to Neeli and whispered a few words that made her laugh. A group of young men stood smoking on the far side. One of them was showing his friends a pistol.

'Are you exchanging notes?' I asked the two girls.

'It's part of our work. That boy behind us with the gun, he has a big tool, but he does not know how to use it, ends up using his hands, as if he is making *lassi*. And that short man with the large forehead, he can't get it up.'

'What about him?' I pointed at Baz, who stood aloof from everyone else.

'The one with the hero moustache? Oh, he watches,' Neeli said.

'Is that all he does, watch?'

'Sometimes he hits,' she said.

'Did he hit you?' I asked, pointing at Baz who, noticing my gesture, started to walk to our table.

'Twice, and he grabbed my wrists.' Neeli showed me a fresh bruise on her cheek. I looked at her wrists and found pressure marks on the skin there.

'What has this bitch been saying?' Baz said as he reached the table. He slapped Neeli.

'Don't hit her!' Sima yelled.

'Gentlemen, let's not fight before the wedding,' said Feroz, who had run towards us when he saw the commotion and was now holding Baz back.

'Get out of the way, Feroz,' Baz snapped.

74

The boy held his ground. I was impressed. I had misjudged the youth.

'You like men, and that's why you hit us,' Sima mumbled.

'Here is another loudmouth.' Zaman grabbed Sima's hair. He was a lot surer of himself and his thick fingers began to squeeze her life out.

I put my hands on his wrist to stop him but he was very strong. Another boy helped. Shots were fired. Baz threw his shawl off and held a pistol in one hand and Sima in the other.

'What did you say, you two-rupee whore!' Baz shouted. I smelled gunpowder.

'Baz, it's not worth it, she is a low-class whore,' said a voice from the crowd.

'What did you say? You think I am some lowlife! Do you know who I am?' Baz said hoarsely, holding the gun close to Sima's throat. His long fingers held her by the shoulder.

It looked wrong. The bitter-eyed man in black and the shivering whore in white. It was the kind of moment that got people killed. I was too drunk to fuck, but I was right for a fight.

'You are drunk, can't get it up,' I said. 'Happened to me too.'

'You are right, it is you who has encouraged ...' Baz moved the pistol in my direction.

I dove for his gun. I miscalculated the distance but managed to topple him over. He punched my back as I fumbled for the gun. Luckily, it did not fire. In less than a minute we were out of breath and pulled apart.

'What happened here?' enquired Zahid. He had missed the beginning of the fight.

'Your friend started a fight with the nephew of the nawab.'

'It's best if you leave,' said Feroz. Baz screamed profanities while Zaman stood glaring. Zahid steered me outside. The three girls followed us back to the car.

'This is not good, Shah-ji. You have made an enemy for life,' said Zahid as he drove fast in the dark alleys, flashing his high beams. It was late but I guess he feared an ambush.

'He was going to kill her, Zahid. That would have been worse,' Yasmeen said.

'Shut up. I am not talking to you,' Zahid said.

Yasmeen sighed angrily. We drove in silence until we came to a house in a suburb. The car turned into the driveway next to a police van. At the end of the lane was a lone house.

Sima was the last one out of the car. The sequin pattern on her dress glittered and she took a moment to smooth her dress.

'Thank you, Uncle. You are more of a man than the whole lot.'

9

The Godown

Travelling drunk in Waziristan is a risky business. War and death have been the main trade for thirty years. Men here remember all wars – the Soviet shelling that went on for months and the American bombs that broke the black mountains. Ten years have passed since the last war started and Waziristan remains a very dangerous place. There are routine kidnappings, suicide bombings and public executions that continue to take place. Those done by the Taliban are reported.

'Don't roll down the window. The air outside is bad,' Riaz said.

He was right. The air outside was putrid and the heat did not help. This time we were on our way to Jandola, even past Tank, and alarm bells were going off inside my head. This was not a brave move but a reckless one. I did not need to go into a war zone with a wretched hangover and a weary heart. Not only did I get drunk, I almost slept with a prostitute half my age and fought with a captain. No amount of praying would help me.

'Bloody traffic,' Riaz said as the white pole with red stripes at the check post came down. The soldiers manning the check posts had none of the pomp and trim that one finds in cities. Even in the heat, they wore their helmets and munitions pouches, and didn't have smiles for anyone. The armoured vehicle was parked and had its gun turrets pointed at the road.

'Where's all this traffic going?' I asked Riaz.

'Afghan Transit Trade. This is where ISAF supplies go in and Afghan opium comes out,' Riaz said. 'America fights this war on Pakistan's back. All supplies go through N-55. They eat like goats. One American soldier eats and farts more than an entire village in Pakistan.'

'Cigarettes too? Like the ones in the godown.'

'Of course. All destined for American GIs. They don't even trust our water. It has to come from their country or from their suppliers. We have pimped the entire country.'

'Well, someone must be making money.'

We got out at the next check post and Riaz bought water and a packet of *miswak* sticks from a roadside vendor.

'You should keep these with you,' he said.

'Do I have bad breath?' I swallowed a hiccup that brought up last night's scotch.

'Yes. This is good for the gums and the way of the Prophet. You can't ask for more from a product.'

'I assume this is not used by American soldiers,' I said. The chewing helped my headache and the bitter bark eased my stomach. Who would have thought that holy *miswak* would be a hangover cure? I had used them when I accompanied my father for *umra*, pilgrimage. In Mecca he had prayed for a successful career for his son and a fruitful marriage for his daughter. I did not care for Saudia, but I did bond with Abu. He was an enterprising man, always starting new endeavours and making business plans with enthusiasm. I wish I had made more memories with him.

'You need a thick waistcoat with pockets,' Riaz said.

'It's bloody hot, why would I need that?'

'It gets cold at night. Delays are routine due to petrol shortages. Crossing the border is not as easy as the Americans believe,' Riaz said as we were cleared to go ahead.

78

'I have heard they spent billions of dollars building roads and schools.'

'The roads are for them to move their army into Waziristan when ours fail. As for the aid, it's mostly biscuits and condoms and they can keep that as well,' Riaz said, starting the car.

Jandola came into view as a muddy clump of buildings and commercial cloth banners. The town was surrounded by low-lying hills and in the centre was the old fort. We were stopped again as a soldier looked under the cars with an inspection mirror and made us open the boot. He was nervous and swore in Punjabi. Around him was a crowd of daily wageworkers, bushy-bearded farmers with dirty turbans, and their wives in uncommon disarray.

'The Taliban have training camps in the outlying hills. This is a dangerous area,' Riaz said as we were asked to step out of the car.

'Isn't the town controlled by the FC scouts?' I asked. An assembly of men, goats, and children stared at us blankly as we got out of the vehicle.

'They stay in the fort. Sometimes their commanders arrive in a helicopter and make grand statements,' Riaz said.

'*Bangana*, drone,' said a woman breaking out of purdah, her gray hair showing from beneath the cloth.

The eyes of the crowd wandered the sky from horizon to horizon. It was like a sci-fi movie, when an alien ship arrives over a city.

'Where?' I heard someone ask.

The woman pointed and we all saw it as a single piece of glittering metal – an elegant white swan watching over ugly ducklings.

'There is another one!' a man yelled.

The second drone flew in lower and was audible to the crowd. Fear spread like a buzz. The commotion died and the lorry engines were killed. The shouting stopped, as did the whining and the complaining. Men talked in hushed tones.

'This one's been circling for a while.'

'That's bad luck. When there are two, it means someone's getting hit.'

'Watch out for a puff of smoke, that means it has fired a missile,' said a man who had taken off his turban. A black SUV beeped indignation for being ignored – indicating an open door, with the key still in the ignition. Someone farted. I noticed a woman wrapped in a blue chadur holding her child, who sucked on a bare lolly stick.

The sound moved further away as the drones circled steadily. The army personnel shifted uncomfortably in their stance. A man started reciting the *Ayatul Kursi*; some joined in while others chanted *La ilaha illallah Muhammadur Rasulullah*.

One of the drones dipped a little and swept across towards the northern mountains. The first one remained.

'It went towards Gomal Pass. Came here to catch high currents,' said a soldier.

Some believed him while others stood frozen, with their necks cranked up. I lit a cigarette as the men settled into their routine, but the drone had taken the edge out of the crowd. The soldiers were patient and the men complained less. We left while they remained occupied speculating over the drones.

The godown was half a kilometer off the highway. We parked on the gravel and walked between rows of sheds. The rusted brown shutters were painted with the green and white Pakistan flag. There were other signs of state sponsorship. Busy shopkeepers sold food, medicine and mobile phone cards. The sheds ended and we crossed a turd-infested rocky field. There were half-dressed children, sheep, trash, urine tracts, a propane tank, flies and other signs of abject poverty all around.

'The building was over there,' said Riaz, walking towards a pile of concrete rubble.

Broken cement and girders were all that remained of the godown. The gravel bore the scorched black marks of an intense fire. The middle of the field concaved into a crater surrounded by piles of mortar. My heart raced.

'Can anyone tell us about this warehouse?' I asked aloud.

'I live here,' a kid spoke quickly in Urdu. Cries of 'me too' came from the raggedy bunch. They had crusty noses and their hands were dirty with scrapes and cuts. I sized up a shabby man with early signs of grey in his beard. He wore multiple layers of clothing.

'Do you know where the walls were and how high?'

'I will tell you, hold on. Let me pass. Here, I will show you.' He cleared the way.

The man walked us around the crater. I followed and measured the area with deliberate steps and calculated the number of containers that could have been stored here. Marine transport ships twenty foot container units known as TEU (Twenty foot Equivalent Units) with a capacity to pack 2261 cubic feet. I calculated the size of a carton and did some rough sums. It all seemed right, except there were no containers here. I asked the man about the remnants.

'It was all cleared up. The scrap has been hauled away,' said the man, walking down into the crater. 'Here, see for yourself.'

I followed behind.

'Be careful, Qais *sahab*. These girders might go through your foot,' Riaz warned me.

'Or through your *gaand*,' said the man, using a derogatory term for 'arse'.

I spent the next ten minutes crawling around and taking pictures of the fallen rubble. There were scraps of metal from the containers in it, but no signs of the tobacco cartons. They would have burned up or been ransacked, and when I did find blackened scraps of cardboard, they were of the local brand – Pine cigarettes, not the imported Marlboros. Even in the shade, the heat was unbearable and I had sweat running down my legs. I climbed out of the crater and sat on a rock among the jumble of rusted metal and mortar. From my position in the rubble, a flash of metal caught my eye.

'What is that?'

'Rubble moved by an army bulldozer,' the man said.

81

I put my hand inside and pulled at a twisted metal shard. It was wafer thin. Behind it was a cylindrical object. A welding torch had cut the upper half but the rest was stuck.

'Hey, Riaz, can you lend me a hand?' I said.

'Hurry up, please. It's not safe after dark,' Riaz said, moving towards me.

'Don't the drone attacks happen in daylight?'

'Yes, but the Taliban strike in the night. Can we go now?'

'Help me move this.' I unbent the girders and pulled out the wafer-thin metal sheet. I then slipped my cellphone through the gap and took a picture of the cylindrical object and pocketed the metal piece. My phone's battery was almost dead. I took more pictures with the camera.

'What is it?' Riaz asked.

'Not sure,' I replied.

'Can we go? I need the toilet.'

I took a few more pictures while Riaz hurried away to a corner.

Our guide grinned. 'I can show you more, Sufi *sahab*,' he said.

'More of what?' I asked. It was always an honour to be called a sufi even though I had done nothing to earn the title.

'The mee-zile,' he said, pointing to the rubble.

'What makes you think it is a missile?' I said. 'Show me.' I took my wallet out. That was a mistake. I was assailed by cries of *baksheesh*. The man took me by my hand.

'What's your name?' I said.

'I am Kazim. Come,' he said and led me away.

'Qais *bhai*!' said Riaz as he came running. 'Where are you going?' He rattled off in Pashto and grabbed at Kazim's hand, staying him.

'Riaz, relax, he is just showing me the missile,' I said.

'What missile? We need to leave. You can't trust them. The camp is filled with the Taliban.'

Kazim spat at Riaz. It was some nasty spittle and Riaz pushed him in retaliation. Kazim snarled in anger and attacked Riaz viciously. Riaz fell. The children clapped. Kazim was on top of Riaz, punching him.

I rushed towards the two men and put my arms under Kazim's armpits and clasped my hands behind his neck. He kicked but I held him until he calmed down, and then I pushed him off. He did a quick turn and dropped his chin, ready to run in.

'Show me the missile. Stop playing around. I don't have all day,' I said. I was a good six inches taller than him so he knew it was wise to back off.

Riaz got up. His top buttons had been torn out in the scuffle and his face was beetroot red.

'I hate the sister-fuckers! I am not Taliban, how dare he call me one!' Kazim shouted passionately. 'I have killed ten Taliban. My village can attest to it.'

The kids in the crowd laughed. 'Oh yes, he is a famous mujahideen commander.'

He slapped one hard, but the rest jumped out of his reach.

'Come with me. Nobody calls Kazim a liar,' he said.

I followed him and Riaz followed a few paces behind. After a row of mud houses the path climbed down to lines of plastic tarp and cardboard-covered tents. Along the way we passed feral dogs, improvised fires and crying babies with conspicuous ailments. Overhead, a Pakistani military helicopter buzzed along on its way to Miranshah. We stopped at a low-slung shack with a roof made from plywood, plastic sheets, and cardboard boxes.

'Women get decent, men coming in,' Kazim called out.

We waited until we were given a signal and he invited us to enter the shack. Inside, the paraffin lamp cast dark shadows and it smelled of faeces and onions. I was offered a stool but everyone else squatted on the dirt floor. I could make out pale faces and bright eyes. There were four children and a woman in the room. Kazim opened a pack of US-aid biscuits and asked for tea from the woman.

'I don't need tea. Show us the missile,' I said.

'My nephew is bringing the part. Have tea,' he said.

He took out a crude pipe and burned an olive-coloured opium pellet. One of the children, a girl not more than nine-years-old, watched with expressionless eyes. He offered me the pipe but I declined. He smoked it delicately, sucking in the smoke with a steady breath. He held it to the woman in the corner who took a few puffs. She then passed it to the girl, who took a deep drag.

'Fighting gives me headache. I have mental illness. This is the only thing that helps. This calms the nerves and makes everyone sleep even on an empty stomach,' he said.

I asked him about the children.

'I have three children and four from my brother. He was killed by the Taliban.'

'I am sorry to hear that.'

'It's fine. Another brother was killed in a drone attack. Now we have eleven children in the family,' he said as a child put down tea in dirty little cups. 'We are out of milk.'

Minutes passed as various children streamed in and out, some sitting on Kazim's lap or eating sugar biscuits. I rummaged through my pockets and found a pen, colourful business cards and a picture of Shereen which I showed around. One girl asked why she did not cover her hair.

'She does, but this is for her father,' I lied.

I heard a commotion outside and Kazim left to check what was happening. He returned quickly, accompanied by a small boy in an embroidered skullcap. The boy had a broken nose and dragged a cardboard box behind. Inside was a collection of metal junk and rocks.

'This is what we collected before the military arrived,' Kazim said.

'Be careful, there might be unexploded parts of the missile.' I warned everyone away as I rummaged through the scraps. I found a black metal sheet with a white label and took it out. It was half burnt but the print was clear.

MFG AC 802287
SER/LOT NO: 27099 / 090
CONTRACT DAAH01-03-c-0106
ROCKET MO
DSGN ACT 18876

GE TEMP: LIMIT 228 to 344K
FIRING TEMP LIMITS 230 TO 336K
08/2009 US

I knew enough chemistry to know that only advanced military weapon systems measured heat in Kelvins.

'You found it on the site?' I enquired and took pictures with my camera.

Kazim nodded.

'What do you think caused it?' I asked.

'A drone attack. Two missiles hit this godown during Ramzan. The military came and cleared the area same day,' he said.

'Can you keep this safe?'

'Yes, nobody would buy this from us. You want to buy?'

'No.' I paid Kazim a thousand rupees and hurried back to the car.

Riaz was furious and we drove in silence. The traffic had eased but there were still frequent checks. The drone hovered in my mind and the alcohol swirled in my stomach.

Back in Mianwali, I asked Riaz if we could stop to buy cigarettes. I had gone through a whole carton in less than a week. He agreed. When I came back from the cigarette shop, I found him talking on the phone. He seemed more at ease. On the way to the hotel, he asked me if I had gotten all I needed.

'Yes, all done,' I said.

'So there's no need to go back to Jandola,' he said, pulling into the parking lot.

'No. Thanks for driving me. I am sorry if ...' I said.

'No. It is my fault. I am ashamed. Thank you for making me stay. We did our job.'

'Yes, we did,' I said, getting out of the car.

'What are you going to put in your claim report?'

'I haven't decided yet. Acts of God and America are not covered by insurance.'

*

85

I took a long, cool shower while my phone charged. Once cleaned up, I went downstairs and found Owais and the refugees glued to the news. The tickers were crawling with flashing updates as TV hosts interviewed experts who argued among themselves amid a noisy backdrop of ambulance sirens and wailing mothers.

'What happened?' I asked.

'Another Shia massacre. Terrorists attacked a passenger bus on the way to Taftan. Up to twenty people dead. Including my cousin,' Owais said. He looked away.

I put my hands on his shoulder. He did not like that. I hugged him anyway.

'Be strong. It will get better,' I said.

He remained quiet. I had a feeling that he did not like being among Sunnis.

'You should go back to Quetta. Be with your family,' I said. I handed him my last two thousand rupees. He shook his head.

'It's not for you. I am sure others have suffered. Give it to needy families. This sectarian violence will be the end of Pakistan,' I said.

'Thank you, sir. My cousin was a good man, a tailor. You want tea?'

'No, but is there an internet cafe around here?'

'There are rental stations at the post office next door. Do you need to print something? If not, you can use my laptop.'

'I need to check my email.'

'No charge, take it to your room, it's on PTCL wireless.'

Upstairs, I caught up on the news and then checked my email. There were the usual Facebook friend requests, Russian women of marriageable age, Quranic miracles in multicolour fonts and photographs of nude women on exotic cars. I uploaded pictures from my camera and emailed them to myself. I read more news articles on suicide bombings and drone attacks, got more depressed and ended up watching more nude women before I went to sleep. When I woke up I saw several missed calls from Sonia. I asked her to connect through Skype.

Don't you have a cellphone? Sonia typed.

This is more secure.

'What are you? James Bond?' she said as the voice connected. 'Why this secrecy?'

'I went to Jandola today,' I said.

'So?' Sonia asked. I imagined her lying in bed, watching her soap operas and sipping tea.

'The godown was hit by a hellfire missile. I don't think that the Pak army has those.'

'Then how can the Taliban have them?'

'Not the Taliban, the Americans. These were launched by a US drone.'

'Are you sure?'

I said nothing.

'This is unusual,' Sonia continued.

'The third embarrassment after the Raymond Davis affair and the Abbottabad raid.'

'And you're sure about this?'

'I am positive. The crater on the ground showed a missile strike from the sky. I even saw the remnants of the missile.'

'Why would the Americans bomb a tobacco godown?'

'I have a hypothesis,' I said. 'Perhaps it was used by militants to store weapons.'

'Let's move on. That is not for us to decide or make assumptions.'

'War is not covered under the terrorism clause. That makes the claim invalid.'

'Fuck you. Don't play games.'

'I am not, but I can see Malik Awan's point of view. After all, his son was killed.'

'His son was a terrorist – the kind who blows up schools and kills children. It's good that he died.'

'Explain that to his father.'

'Forget the father; get his wife to sign the claim. That's why we've sent a pious Syed.'

'I love the way you think, darling,' I said coolly.

87

'It's my job. Now do your fucking job.'

'I will figure out a way that works for everyone.'

'That is not possible. Make it work for us and I will reward you in this life.'

10
A Suitable Punishment

The *karhai* shop was on the PAF road. There were alert security guards armed with pump action shotguns by the gate. The area was cordoned off with a fence. There was a watchtower-like structure on one side.

'What is this place?' I asked.

'The best *karhai* in the country,' Zahid said and called out to a guard by name. He in return, gave a salute.

'One of my men. Retired from the police and is now employed by IAS security,' Zahid said.

We drove right up to the front, past green lawns where families enjoyed meals under the twilight. Waiters ran out into the lawns from the base kitchen, carrying trays of food or crates of soft drinks. A small green-lit office was set at the front of the kitchen. A well-dressed midget sat behind the counter and manned the cash register. He had a handlebar moustache and mean eyes.

'Salaam, Zahid, when did you arrive?' The midget remained seated.

Zahid exchanged a few words and introduced me as we looked over an assortment of choice cut organs. There were triangular purple livers, bulbous red hearts, shrivelled brown kidneys, translucent oval testicles, and fluffy yellow brains. Zahid grabbed a heart, palmed a testicle, pinched a liver, but refused the brain.

'Brain is high in cholesterol, but the rest is good for the libido,' Zahid explained. I wondered if Sima had mentioned my failure in bed.

'I thought we were having mutton,' I said. I was tired and hungover, but I had come to Mianwali to survey the godown and eat the best *karhai* in Pakistan.

'This is just the appetiser. Relax.' Zahid led us to the seating area next to the kitchen. He had tables cleared up with a swagger particular to a policeman wearing a pistol. Soon the green wooden tables were ready. Zahid ordered a 7-Up with instructions. In minutes, I was sipping a cool gin and tonic and smoking a fierce hashish joint.

'You did it, Shah-ji. The survey is done,' Zahid said.

I smiled back. I wanted to thank Aftab. He had been a big help. But I was the one who took the risks. I was content in the twilight of accomplishment but not happy. Jandola was behind but the poverty of the IDPs and the hovering drone had disturbed my sense of achievement. A feral cat snarled from under the table and a man burped at the next table. I heard a cackle and turned around to find dozens of caged chickens staring back at me. I took another puff.

'What happened to your eyes?' Zahid asked.

'I might have caught pink eye in Jandola,' I said.

'It is a small price to pay for a mission well done. Now enjoy the best *karhai* in Pakistan.'

'Can you stop saying that? There must be more to this than just the food,' I said irritably. Zahid thought everything from Mianwali was better. 'What's the story? This place looks like a jail.'

'It was a training camp for mujahideen in the eighties. Now it is abandoned. Jahanzeb Sabzwari made a lot of money during that war but he died early. His midget son did not have his father's calibre but he had a good brain, so he opened a

90

restaurant. In the last twenty years, he has made a name for this place as the best *karhai* shop. Don't let those Gujranwala people mislead you –the best *kukar* is from Mianwali.'

'According to whom?'

'Me, I am from here,' Zahid said. He loved to talk about his family's link to the nawabs. 'My mother was a family member of the nawab of Kala Bagh, and I was practically raised in their *haveli*.' He went on about the benevolent nawabs and how they took care of the community. I was always amazed at how the feudal system extracted loyalty from their serfs. Even my grandfather, who was a local *pir* - Sufi master - in Vehari, had people who would die for him. It was absolute power but my father had broken that chain and moved to Karachi. He won an Olympic gold medal but I had not carried his torch too well – for the family or the country.

The food broke my gloominess. The salad and the yogurt were enough for a poor man's meal but the aroma rising from the woks, notwithstanding the caged chickens, worked up my appetite. The organs were spicy and chewy and that helped build my appetite further. By the time the main course arrived, I was starving. The mutton sizzled on the bone, the chicken simmered in its sauce and the peppers and tomatoes had shape and substance. We ate without inhibition – sharing naans, pulling apart meat, crossing arms over plates, plucking salad with greasy fingers, slurping yogurt from the same spoon. Within ten minutes, we were mopping up the remains of the *karhai* from the greasy wok.

'Was it worth it?' Zahid asked me, looking satiated.

'Possibly the best meal of my life. For once, you will get no argument,' I said.

'You deserve it, Shah-ji,' he said.

We enjoyed a last cigarette. Zahid asked for the bill; I made false attempts to pay. I had no cash. He paid. On the drive back, I dozed off.

I woke up when the hotel guard opened the gate to the carpark. I was about to step out of the car when Zahid grabbed my shoulder.

'Wait, Shah-ji,' he said.

A pair of headlights flashed briefly. Doors slammed. Two men walked briskly through the gate. They were dressed alike in dark shirts and brown trousers that bore the emblem of IAS security. One carried a rifle, the other a shotgun. The hotel guard slunk away into darkness. Two more figures walked towards the carpark, one tall, and the other stocky.

Zahid parked the car and stepped out.

'We need to talk,' I heard Zaman say. Baz stood a few paces back.

Zahid walked over quickly. I followed behind.

'So let's talk,' Zahid said. 'You want to come inside?'

'Your friend has dishonoured Baz Ali.' Zaman pointed with a truncheon. He was also dressed in the uniform but Baz wore a shawl over his shalwar suit.

'If it is an apology you want, you can have it. I am sorry. I was drunk.' I held my hands together to show that I was asking for forgiveness.

'Let me talk, Shah-ji,' Zahid said.

'I have no quarrel with you.' Baz walked past Zahid towards me, but Zahid held him back by grabbing his arm. Baz looked back furiously. They were both tall but Zahid had more bulk.

'He is with the police,' I said. I was tired and I had a pink eye. I did not want a cockfight to add to my woes.

'This is not a matter of law but of honour,' Baz said. His one hand remained under his shawl.

'Your plaintiff is here, but you can't touch a hair on him while I am here.' Zahid's hand opened the button that trapped his pistol in the holster.

Nobody moved. Time froze. The men stared at each other in silence. In moments like this I have often thought about what could happen next if the situation had de-escalated. But the silence made me nervous.

'Let's go up to my room, brother,' I said.

'Stay here. And I am not your brother,' Baz growled at me.

'At least let's go inside and talk this through. We can sit in the ground-floor room,' I tried. This place was a hangout for the guards. Baz exchanged a look with Zaman and we walked in, past the concierge desk, and towards the room behind the stairs. The rest followed.

I turned the light on. The room was dusty. It was stocked with extra bedding and broken furniture. Zaman, Baz, and I sat down on the chairs. The wiry IAS guard with the Kalashnikov leaned against the wall and held the rifle by the strap so that the barrel swung between his legs.

'In the land of Maliks, honour is everything. Baz Ali Khan's cousins and brother were at the gathering and were insulted by this pimp's *bazaar* language.' Zaman slapped the truncheon on his palm and continued with his speech. Zahid placed his pistol on the small table. Then he took off his watch and placed it next to his wallet, phone and his spare pistol magazine.

'Therefore, a suitable punishment must be found.' Zaman stopped behind my chair. I heard his leather sandals creak under his weight.

'What's that for?' Zahid enquired, pointing to the wooden truncheon with a smile.

'What's so funny?' Baz asked. His breath came in short rasps.

'It looks like you want to fuck Shah-ji to restore your honour!' Zahid laughed.

'What do you know about honour? You son of an Arayan whore,' Zaman said.

I heard the muffled noises of a TV and cats fighting in the alley. Zahid's face froze midway on a laugh that never reached his eyes. His nostrils flared slightly.

'Is that not true? Your mother was Habib Niazi's keep and you are dirty laundry from a one-night stand. The nawabs raised you as family but now you conspire with this man to insult the nawabs, *namak haram* that you are.'

I smelled hashish on the second guard with the shotgun. He had a pockmarked face and sunken eyes. He stood with his feet apart and the swagger of a man who is not afraid to shoot.

93

'That's enough, Zaman,' Baz warned. 'We are not here to insult Zahid.'

'He insults himself by siding with this old man. Who would want to fuck him? He is already shitting in his pants.' Zaman hit my neck with the truncheon.

I fell from the chair on to the floor. The sharp pain in the nape of my neck brought tears to my eyes. I probably looked worse than I felt when I met Zahid's eyes. In that moment, I knew nothing good was going to come from this but I did not care.

'Never trust a man with two first names.' I wiped the blood off my busted lip.

'What was that?' Baz said. He still had his holster buckled shut.

'I was not talking to you,' I smiled. It was a cruel smile.

The first shot was from the H&K and it hit the guard with the pockmarked face through his neck. A stream of blood shot out as he whirled and fell dead. Zaman's entire swagger disappeared in less time than it takes a bullet to leave its chamber. He got shot multiple times in the face. His head broke and splattered on the walls and blood speckled the floor. The body fell with a heavy thud. I charged the wiry guard holding the AK-47 and pushed him against the wall.

'He will kill all of you.' I struggled with the guard. 'Stop this now.'

'Give me a clear shot, Shah-ji,' Zahid said. The guard's eyes twitched with anger. He followed his instinct to lift the rifle's barrel. Zahid hit him on the shoulder and the AK-47 fired into the ground. Zahid shot him twice more in the torso then ejected the spent clip from the pistol.

Baz stared at Zaman's body on the floor. His skull had been shattered and the exposed brain was on display like a diagram in a biology textbook.

'How are we going to explain this to the police?' Zahid pointed the pistol at Baz.

'I don't know,' Baz said. 'You didn't have to kill him.'

'This pistol is not for show. When I take it out, I kill. I don't take second guesses.'

'What about me?' Baz asked. He was in shock but he still had rage in his eyes.

'You are from the nawab's family. I would never hurt you.'

'But what about all these men?' I said.

'Zaman came here to start a fight. I killed him. Baz was never here. It is best for everyone,' Zahid said.

Baz stood up slowly. He walked backward a few steps but then he turned and walked out.

Somewhere, stray dogs howled and somebody screamed from one of the floors above. Zahid called the police. I covered the bodies with bedsheets and locked the room. I told the concierge to wait for the police and promised him money to cover the cleaning. I smoked a pack of cigarettes over the next few hours. It kept the smell of death away.

I had seen dead bodies before. I had washed my father's cold dead body, closed Jameela's eyes after they had rolled under the lids, and seen hundreds of burned bodies in fire claims. But violent deaths followed Zahid. I remember carrying the slack body of the unfortunate carjacker who had stopped Zahid near Goli Mar. He had shot him through the car window. Now three men were dead and covered in dirty bedsheets. And they died because of my alcohol-inspired heroics.

The police arrived in an hour and Zahid explained the scene. 'It is no hassle,' the inspector told Zahid. They knew each other. I waited as they picked up the bodies in stretchers and took them to the morgue. I did not even know the name of these unfortunate men, except Zaman's. After everyone had left, I went upstairs and found Zahid watching TV.

'Shah-ji, do you still have the gin?' he asked.

I gave him gin to wash down the blood he had spilled.

*

After a few hours, there was a knock on the door. A soldier in uniform informed me that Major Bhatti was waiting for me downstairs. I looked at Zahid.

'Only you, sir,' said the soldier.

I followed him down to the parking lot. There was still a police van outside but the noises of the city had made the death scene less conspicuous. Zahid had already sorted out the case with the local police and my name was not on the report and there had been no FIR registered.

The soldier led me to a white Suzuki jeep with Government of Pakistan licence plates. Two more soldiers stood by it. One was short-haired and wiry and sported an SSG commando patch and the other was squat with grey sideburns and a bushy black moustache.

'Let's go for a drive,' Major Bhatti said from inside the car.

I got in. He was freshly shaved and smelt of aftershave. The wiry soldier got into the driver's seat and fixed his rear-view mirror. Our eyes met; his were behind dark glasses, and mine were red with conjunctivitis.

'Where are we going, Major *sahab*?' I asked.

'Rahbar, let's drive to Lake Namal,' he said.

We drove through the cantonment slowly. The silence was irritating and there was little traffic this early in the morning. A right turn took us to the numbered water syphon on the canal and the refugee camps on the banks. The sun burned the morning fog off the lush fields, which were spotted with lonely black buffaloes. We left the highway and drove on gravel tracks amid pointy brown hills that looked like teepees from a western movie.

At the top of a plateau was a vista of the lake. We stopped here and Major Bhatti took out a steel flask and a wooden hiking staff. He did not offer the coffee and I did not ask for it either. The soldiers stayed in the car as I followed him up the trail. I followed as best as I could. He wore tan hiking boots with bright laces while I was in street sandals.

'So what are you going to do about being an accessory to murder of three IAS security guards?' he said as we stopped at the first vista. I tried to make out his expression but he was backlit by the sun and it made his visage look like a dark blot on the scenic panorama.

'I did not kill anyone. It was …'

'You know IAS is all ex-army. Friendships mean a lot to soldiers. We all know each other. If we can't protect our own, then how can we ask these men to risk their lives?'

I remained silent but my stomach gurgled.

'All these men sign up so that they can support their families. IAS is known for taking care of the families of guards who die in action. Except this is not an official police case because of your friend Zahid. But that does not mean it is not personal.'

I started to speak but Major Bhatti held his hand up in a gesture for silence.

'They want to put you in a safe house. Zaman's colleagues will make mincemeat out of your internal organs and not a bruise would show on your body.' He lit a cigarette.

By now I was looking down. I did not want him to see the fear in my eyes.

'I know that you are not a killer. You have spent your life hiding behind Zahid. But in a warzone, the rules are different. He needs to leave the district by tomorrow morning or he will become a missing person. Am I clear on this?'

'Yes, sir,' I said and immediately hated myself for saying sir.

'Good. I like you, Qais. You are a smart man. No wonder Miss Sonia speaks so highly of you. She said, "No Qais, no cash",' he said with a quick smile that flashed on and off in a second.

I gave him a weak smile. In the last few days, I had seen drinking, dancing, whoring and murder. I had seen poverty and misery, experienced fear, loneliness and physical pain. Now here I was on this beautiful vista, but I feared for my life.

'We need to get these soldiers suitably compensated. Otherwise you will be a wanted man for the rest of your life. Even in Karachi, they will find you. I give you less than a year to live.'

'But Zahid killed them.' I felt a pang of regret for betraying my friend.

'They don't know that. And you are an easier target. You must pay blood money,' he said.

'How much?'

'Twenty-five lakh for Rahim and Ghulam each. Fifty lakh for Zaman.'

'I don't have that kind of money,' I said.

'You will,' said Major Bhatti. He threw his cigarette butt in the sand, where it smoldered in the dry bush. The fact that all he wanted was money made him less frightening, less potent.

'Would that money cover Zahid as well?' I asked.

'Worry about yourself.'

'Both or no deal,' I said, meeting his eyes. It was not a strong stare but it had steel.

'Okay, but get the money quickly,' he said. 'Now what did you find in Jandola?'

'A few random bomb parts. Doesn't make a difference. I will seal the case as planned.' The pitch and the pace of my speech gave away my lie.

'What do you know about Saif Awan?' he asked.

'Not much. I met his father.'

'Saif was a top-notch rabble-rouser. He became an overnight sensation after his belligerent video. The next Nek Muhammad.'

'Wasn't Nek killed in a drone attack?'

'Yes, one of the early drone attacks. Saif was inspired by the likes of Nek Muhammad. They were both tall and commanding men. You know the type.'

'And now Saif has been killed in a drone attack.' I caught my breath as the trail angled up.

'They are precise weapons and kill the right people. Yes, civilians die, but that is collateral damage in war,' he said. 'I am a realist. Drones are here to stay. We need them to keep these Taliban, at least the really bad ones, on the run. Ideally, the Americans should give us the drones so that we can kill these terrorists ourselves.'

'Yes. Nobody cares when the Pakistan Army kills Pakistanis.'

Major Bhatti studied my face like an artist studying a profile he is about to sketch.

'Are you a patriot?' His voice trembled slightly as he said the word.

'I went to a military cadet college.'

'So you understand the need to save the *riyasat*. We are not Iraq. We have to manage our backyard long after the Americans have withdrawn.'

'That is your business.'

'War is my business and these days it is not going well. The world is tired of this long war. After the Abbottabad raid, the whole world has been watching Pakistan. One spark could launch an American invasion. Did you take any pictures at the godown?'

I nodded.

'I need the SD card and if you have copied the pictures, please delete them. Americans watch all electronic communications. One leak on this and it can force the government to take drastic measures. You must understand.'

We walked to the jeep. The soldiers were still waiting but had the air conditioner on. We drove down the track and another army jeep followed us.

'Protocol?' I asked.

'A precaution. I am on their hit list.'

'You are the second person who has said that to me this week.'

'Who was the first one?'

'Colonel Aftab.'

'He is on the Taliban list, I am on another list,' he said conspiratorially.

Nobody stopped our little convoy and we breezed through checkposts. At the hotel, they waited until I came back with the SD card that had the pictures. I handed it over to Major Bhatti. He threw it carelessly on the seat and held up three fingers.

'You are a patriot and so you get a second chance. You have three days to get the money.'

*

There was no power in my hotel room. I was now a pariah here even though I had tipped the hotel staff generously. The staff were afraid of Zahid and did not come up to the room. Fortunately, Zahid was not in the room when I came back. I missed Karachi, coffee, and sweets. Any kind of sweetness would do, so I called home and lied to Shereen and Ammi about my success. I told Ammi to deposit the post-dated cheque from Anthony Lobo. I was completely out of money now. I took a shower, applied eye ointment for my conjunctivitis and went to the mosque for Friday prayers. I ignored the sermon but caught up on missed prayers. I promised no more drinking or whoring. I had promised both earlier but it was the thought that counted.

Riaz was waiting in the hotel lobby when I returned. I told him everything that had happened and how I had three days to arrange the *diya*.

'I can't stay here. I need to leave. Is there another place outside the city?' I asked,

'Let me find out. You have money?'

'Yes, I should have it by tomorrow.'

He promised that he would find another place. I walked him to the car and saw an IAS security jeep in the parking lot. It was the men who had come with Major Bhatti. I discreetly pointed them out to Riaz. He looked worried and hugged me, then asked me if I prayed regularly.

'When I can,' I said.

'Then somebody must be praying for you.'

*

'You would never believe what I have been up to,' Zahid said.

I ignored him and he went to the toilet. I heard his weight settling on the commode seat, the sounds of prolonged farting, water splashing, a couple of flushes, a faucet being turned on, and then, conversations on the phone. The way he giggled I could tell it was not his wife. He came out grinning.

'You will never guess what I did today,' he repeated.

'Let me guess. You killed men, drank gin and fucked whores.'

That wiped the smile off his face.

'What is wrong with you?' he asked, peeved.

'You killed three men last night and you are asking what is wrong?'

'You fought an army captain over a whore. I finished what you started.'

It was irritating to see how calm he was. It was almost as if he needed killings to be human.

'I have never killed anyone who did not deserve it. I saved your life. Next time you want to be heroic, go all the way.'

He left the room and I watched TV. There was a report on the river Indus flooding – more than two million refugees in a single sweep, and entire villages wiped away. The next reports were on a suicide bombing at a volleyball match, a drone attack on a tribal council and a highway accident that killed even more people. International news was no better – shootings in America, turmoil in Arab countries, rapes in India, cannibals in China. I switched to a history show where a white-haired, clean-shaven Dr Hansen talked about the end of the world according to the Mayan calendars. The world was spiralling out of control. I put a pillow over my head and fell into an uneasy sleep.

I woke up with a feeling of nostalgia. For a moment, I was in my childhood home in Karachi, watching Hindi movies on the VCR – my head on *Ammi*'s lap, feet touching my sister, hand caressing an aunt's elbow – protected by deities more powerful than all demons. This bliss was broken by a TV programme that was showcasing a rock ensemble led by a Punjabi folk singer. Zahid swooned, his eyes closed.

I had known Zahid since the time we shared hostel rooms. I used to read him Ibn-e-Safi detective novels aloud. He became my friend when the bully Akbar and his minions stripped my clothes and wrote obscenities on my butt with a ballpoint. I fought them off until I cried and Zahid told them to stop. Akbar did not listen and ended up with a dislocated shoulder.

101

'*Balle balle, shawa shawa*,' Zahid sang. 'Did you sleep well?' he asked me after the song finished in a crashing crescendo.

'I have conjunctivitis. It's contagious. You should go,' I said, applying ointment on my eyelid.

'I filed a police FIR for last night's event. Your name is not on it.' He poured out the last of the London Dry Gin into two cups and added Sprite to the drinks.

'You have to leave Mianwali tomorrow. Clear out of here,' I said, looking at the ice crackling in the warm gin.

'Why?' he said with a smile.

'You are a marked man. Did you notice the Suzuki Potohar?'

'You are a silly little man.' Zahid swirled the ice in the gin. I could almost taste it.

'We are both marked men. One of the men outside wears a Special Services group patch and that means he is trained as a commando. They would have killed us by now if it was not for the deal I made.'

'I have never run away from a fight. MQM has a contract on my head, the Taliban, the Baluch – they all want me dead,' Zahid said.

I put one hand on Zahid's shoulder and touched his chin with the other.

'*Jani*, this is not a gang fight. This is a war.'

'But I came here for you,' he said.

'You bloody bastard, you came here to party at the mouth of Indus. I can take care of myself,' I said. 'You attract trouble like a bitch attracts stray dogs.'

Zahid paused and looked at his phone. I didn't really want him to leave.

'I do have things to do. One of my colleagues in narcotics just had an assassination attempt on him. DIG wants all heads back for an emergency meeting,' he said.

'Exactly. Do your job. I am all done here.'

'When will you be back?'

'I will fly out of Islamabad next Wednesday as a VIP,' I said with a sinking heart.

'Cheers then to a successful mission.' Zahid raised his glass. The ice clinked again.

I said cheers and picked up the cup, thinking: I will make it up to Allah some other day.

11

Lakh in my Pocket

The next day, Riaz lived up to his word and arranged a hostel room at a local college. He knew the principal and introduced me as an author researching a book who was willing to pay for the accommodation. It was a few kilometres outside Mianwali but it had a reliable generator, good Internet access, and clean toilets. I was given a visiting professor's room, which was large and lit with fluorescent tubes and furnished with a large bed, a working table and a couple of chairs. The windows opened to a view of the crooked hills of the salt range.

I kept in touch with the world but avoided phone calls. Mrs Saif had added my number to an SMS list and would send me random anecdotes from poets and philosophers. In the midst of spirituality, she would slip in a text about her plight and how she needed to escape from Tank. I replied that I was negotiating with the insurance companies. She asked how much of the claim she would get, to which I told her to call me directly later that afternoon.

'Two hundred thousand dollars,' I said.

'But that's not even half the insured amount,' she said.

'There are deductibles that have to be applied. We can't use a bank transfer and also have to attest to the final claim amount. It's technical but it means I have to pay off insurance people. They are like flies on a speck of honey.'

'How would I get the payment?'

'Cash in US dollars. Would that work?' I asked. Few in this world will have a problem with US $200,000.

'Real dollars, not fake currency,' she said in a hopeful voice.

I laughed. A sigh would have been more appropriate.

'On my honour, Mrs Saif. Hand-delivered to you. Don't you trust me?'

'I trust you, Mr Qais, but ...'

'Yes?'

'It is nice to hear your voice, Mr Qais. It reassures me. *Khuda hafiz.*'

That was the easy part. I called Sonia.

'I settled the claim,' I said.

'What's the final payment?' she asked.

'Three hundred thousand dollars.'

'Did she sign?'

'She will sign the NOC. But the payment has to be in US dollars.'

'You are a son of a bitch. What game are you playing?'

'I am not playing games. Mrs Saif wants the $300,000 in cash. No bank transfer.' I was lying to both of them but it did not give her the right to call my mother a bitch.

'You want $300,000 in Waziristan? Have you lost your mind?'

'I am not in Waziristan. I'm in Mianwali. Completely under the control of the federal government.' I mocked her accent. There was silence on the other end. The line was crystal clear and the hostel was quiet. I waited.

'I don't think we can do that,' she said.

'Don't you trust me? After all I have done for you?' I asked. I had done a lot for her, but I had never reminded her of those things before now.

'What have you done for ...' In the middle of her sentence, Sonia realised where I was going with this. It was a moment of weakness and she knew that I was hiding something.

'I will talk to Anthony. Let you know on Monday. If he agrees, I will bring the cash.'

'That's a bad idea,' I said. I could not afford a delay. I only had three days.

'Why not? That way I can keep an eye on you,' Sonia said.

'This is no place for a woman. Especially a Christian.'

'Call me Sania, the Muslim Sonia. We have done it before.'

'Times have changed, and this place is more *fundoo*. Let's meet in Islamabad.'

'That sounds complicated. I will bring security.'

My hands trembled and I took a deep breath.

'Qais, are you there? Come on, I can do it. I will even wear a burqa.'

'What's the point of that? You should think of your admirer.' I gripped my wrist to calm the trembling.

'My admirer can ride back with me,' Sonia said.

'With the guards?'

'Once we are done, I will send the guards back by bus. It will be the two of us. We can pretend we are married. Would that suit you?'

It suited me fine. To hell with prying drones, hairy Taliban, and the bloody money I owed to Major Asshole. We had spent years playing hide-and-seek with the world, creating stories within stories and now we had our own Alif Laila. It was time I made new memories with Sonia.

The next day, I worked and prayed hard. First I prepared an No Objection Certificate attested by the Assistant Deputy Commissioner of Mianwali stating that Mrs Saif Awan was authorised to collect the claim as the beneficiary of her deceased husband. Then I typed an imaginative claim report for the incident. It included photographs that showed the debris of the walls that had fallen inward – a simple function of flipping the image – as well as scarred propane tanks superimposed on the original photos and a detailed explanation on how a negligent smoker had caused the propane tank to explode. I appropriated language from a report written by a foreign surveyor who had investigated a gas explosion at the British Oxygen Company plant in Karachi. A comprehensive but tight report would not be challenged. I proofread the report, felt proud of my work, and went for a walk.

It was autumn and time for the equinox. Squirrels scampered along trails that skirted the hills surrounding the campus. A flight of geese flew overhead, possibly heading for the warm lakes of Sindh. As the call for prayers echoed from the hills, I hiked back to the hostel. Outside the front entrance, I saw a white jeep with IAS security at the corner opposite the mosque where students assembled for the Asr prayers. A guard stepped out and surveyed the area. I joined the students. The soldiers remained outside. They did not pray. They just watched.

*

The college student body was composed of drab young men and hijab-wearing girls gathering in the cafeteria or the computer lab. The conversations were thematically similar at both venues – one black-bearded boy talked about downloading Pink Floyd's *The Wall* while another showed Veena Malik's pictures sporting a fake ISI tattoo on his smartphone. At night, I walked the halls and marvelled at the labs and facilities. This was a co-ed college and it was remarkable that girls from the tribal areas studied computer science fifty kilometers from Waziristan. It's only when you have a daughter that you recognise how hard it is for them to get higher education in Pakistan. I did not want Shereen to be wedded into an unhappy marriage by her aunts. I wanted her to get the best education possible. My earned lakh would cover that. The stolen lakh could give me a second chance.

The next morning, I called Aftab. I could not get hold of him and left him a message. When he returned my call, I told him I needed to see him.

'*Yaar*, it is going to be tight. I have news for you too ...'

'It's important, I am in trouble,' I said.

I did not need to explain more. In an hour Aftab arrived in a private car. We sat inside the vehicle and smoked while I told him what was going on

'I warned you to be careful. This is a bad situation,' he said.

'Can't you talk to him? Isn't he your junior?' I pleaded.

'Different command structure. ISI is like a secret society. Our brigade has no access to their business. I can't get involved in this mess right now.'

He gestured for a cigarette. I gave him one and he smoked it like he always did, like a novice, puffing his cheeks to keep the smoke from entering his lungs.

'Alia's green card came. We are supposed to be in America within two weeks,' he said.

'What? The miracle happened?' I queried.

'I have one year left in retirement and benefits. I don't want my CO to know. I will take a vacation. I must visit America and get my passport stamped.'

'I understand.'

'No, you don't. My CO is mad at me for dumping a vacation on him at the last moment and Alia is on my case for delaying our departure.'

'Congratulations on becoming an American.' I could not keep the sarcasm in.

'Stop it, Qais. You know my heart is not in it, but I have to do it for Alia and the boys' sake. It's a better life for them. What have I ever done for her? Moved her from one army base to another for the last nineteen years.' Aftab threw the cigarette out of the window.

'What will you do in America?'

'I don't know. Probably work at a petrol station.'

'You will be fine. You are very talented.' I opened the car door to step out.

'Would you do it, Qais, if the chance came to emigrate to America?'

'Yes. And don't ever trust anyone who says otherwise.' I ran up the steps of the hostel. When I reached the top floor, I looked down. Aftab's car was still there. So was the white jeep.

*

I did not hear from Sonia until Monday afternoon. She said that Anthony had agreed to pay, as long as the documentation was covered.

'I need that report,' Sonia said.

'When can I have the money?'

'What's the hurry, Cash? I am flying to Islamabad on Thursday.'

'I don't want Mrs Saif to change her mind.'

'I am sure you can manage. Now email the report,' Sonia said and hung up.

I looked out of the window for the white jeep. It was still parked under the shade of a walnut tree. Two men were outside talking on their cellphones while looking at the window of my room. Major Bhatti's three days ran out today.

I gave Major Bhatti a missed call. He called back.

'Do you have the money ready?' he asked.

'Miss Sonia is bringing the claim money. She will not have it before Friday.'

'You were supposed to have it today.'

'I need more time. Cash is not easy to arrange.'

He remained silent. I watched the two plainclothes commandoes walk back to the jeep. They were relaxed and shared a bag of roasted nuts.

'Come to my farmhouse on Friday and bring the money,' he said.

'Can't we meet in town?'

'No, bring the money to my place. It's called Duck Hunter's Lodge – outside Tank, across the river on the DI Khan road.'

I went down to the students' computer lab and paid one of the tech assistants to scan the documents. Shereen called while I waited. She had had a row with her grandmother.

'I don't want to live here any more,' she said.

'What stupidity is this? Tell me what happened.'

'Shahrukh said you are responsible for *Ammi*'s death. He said if *Ammi* had had proper care, the cancer would have been discovered early. I told him to F-off.'

'Why do you care what that fatso says? He is not the sharpest kid.' But I felt proud of her.

'I don't care. Nobody insults my dad. But *Nani* was there and instead of defending you, she said that I should respect Shahrukh. Why the hell would I respect him? We are the same age!'

'I will call *ammi*, just relax, *beta*. She is worried about *duniya dari* – our standing in society.'

'Whatever. She respects their money,' she said. 'So when are you back?'

'Sunday, *inshallah*.'

'Come back quick, *Abu*. I have lots of things to do with you,' she said.

*

Friday morning, I missed breakfast, not because of a hangover – I had been clean for a few days – but due to a cramped stomach. It was raining by the time Riaz came by the hostel. Sonia had landed in Islamabad the night before and was getting the cash from a moneychanger. I hounded her on text, asking her whereabouts every hour. Finally we intercepted her at a PSO petrol pump on the Islamabad-Talagang road. She pulled up in a midnight-blue Land Cruiser and was covered in a plain brown chadur. Two armed guards rode in the front. I sent her an SMS.

Do you have the bag with you?

Yes.

Take a picture and send it.

She sent a picture of a tan bag placed between her feet and I could see her painted toes. I walked to the Toyota.

'Don't show your nail polish to the Taliban,' I said, climbing into the back seat.

'I don't plan on meeting the Taliban. Unless you have turned,' Sonia mumbled. The guards pretended not to register our English conversation.

'I will take the money to her,' I said. The smell of jasmine distracted me from the business at hand.

'*I* want to hand the money to her,' she said, and clasped the bag handle. Her lips glistened with gloss. 'I want to make sure it gets to the claimant.'

'The claimant does not want to see you,' I said.

'It's not your money, asshole. I am ...'

'You stupid bitch. I am the one risking my life. All communication runs through me. I call the shots. This is the way or I am going back to Karachi in a Daewoo.' I opened the car door. My stomach torqued in pain. I winced and it made me ugly.

'Stay here,' Sonia whispered.

I felt for my cigarettes.

'Don't smoke in this car. It is a loan from a very important person in Islamabad.'

'I know important people as well. I don't ask them for favours,' I said.

'Why don't I take you to her house with the guards? It is safer, no?'

We drove in silence towards Mrs Saif's house, Riaz leading the way. Sonia was busy with her cellphone. When we arrived in the locality, we parked the car outside the unpainted house. I put my hand on the bag.

'I shouldn't be too long,' I said with a smile.

'Communication runs through you because everyone can press you to their advantage.' Sonia poked a finger into my torso. I wasn't fat everywhere but she knew where. I could not suppress a giggle.

'You have fallen for this Mrs Saif, haven't you?' she asked.

I walked away, not looking at her, a smile forming on my face.

I was received by Zar Mohammad and immediately asked for the bathroom. He pointed towards a door with disdain. I

111

could tell he spent lots of time practicing that expression in the mirror. I closed the door and opened the zipper bag.

The bills were wrapped in plastic. There were six packets. Each bundle was made up of $100 bills. I had never seen so many dollars in my life. I opened two packets and placed the wads inside my vest. Two packs on each pectoral muscle and six across the stomach. I walked outside with a lighter bag.

Mrs Saif arrived in a blur and I quickly gave her the papers to sign. I also asked her to add a thumbprint and took a copy of her ID card. Then I unzipped the tan bag and took out the bundles and laid them across the coffee table, around the crystal ashtray. Even the venerable Zar Mohammad leaned over at the sight of dollar bills.

'Does this make me a millionaire?' she said in awe.

'No, a million is ten-lakh,' I said. My stomach cramped even more intensely.

'Don't the Americans have a word for a lakh?' She put the bundles into her satchel.

'No. Aren't you going to count the money?' I asked, sweating under the burden of the hidden lakh in my vest.

'I will take your word for it.'

I managed a smile. She sure had a lot of class.

12

Jasmin Noir

I walked out of the half-constructed white house to the main road. Sweat ran down my back and I looked around for Riaz's jeep but could not find it. The American dollar bills were a burden on my body and soul. For a second I felt an urge to give back the dollars to the widow.

'Over here,' Riaz said. He was standing by the midnight-blue Land Cruiser. He had his Ray Bans on and posed in front of the car like a fashion model.

I walked towards Riaz and noticed two armed men approaching from the side. I quickened my pace and asked Riaz to get back in the car.

'Relax. They are Miss Sonia's guards. Why are you so nervous? Everything is going according to plan,' Riaz said.

'It's so humid. I am melting. Where is Sonia?'

'She is in the car.'

'I will see you in the jeep,' I said to Riaz.

I climbed through the rear door.

'Did she sign?' Sonia said.

'Yes, here are the documents,' I said. 'They are all in order.'

Sonia looked them over. I reached for a cigarette.

'Please don't smoke in the car,' she said.

I ignored her. I needed it that bad.

'Anything else?' she asked.

'No. I will see you in Islamabad,' I said. 'I will ride back with Riaz.'

'Son of a bitch,' she said and punched my shoulder. 'Are you trying to steal my money?'

I opened the door and walked out.

'Where are you going, Qais?' Sonia called after me.

I called to Riaz to start the jeep.

'Fucking asshole,' I heard Sonia say as I got into the jeep.

'Most unladylike of her,' Riaz said. 'Where are we going?'

'Major Bhatti's farmhouse – Duck Hunter's Lodge. I will give you the directions.'

'Okay. By the way, she is following us in the Lexus,' Riaz said. 'How much do you think that car is worth?'

'Let her follow, it will be her doom,' I said. It took all my restraint not to curse.

We crossed the Jinnah Bridge over the Indus. I hoped this would be the last time I would have to take this journey and that I would make it back safely to Karachi. Sonia called my phone but I did not pick up and looked at the text from the Major.

At Caltex, get off road. Drive dirt road till u c saeed battery. Then, river road to Duck Hunter's Lodge.

We did as we were told and drove past the Indus tributaries. This was marshland and wild goose habitat. The farmhouse was alongside the river and was cordoned with a high wall. Guards opened the front gate and we drove into the compound. Sonia's Lexus followed us in. Major Bhatti was standing at the entrance of the bungalow. He was smartly dressed in black pants and a grey windcheater.

'Who's with you?' he asked as I emerged from the car.

'Miss Sonia,' I said.

'Does she know about your debt?'

'No.'

114

Sonia stepped out of the car. Under the chadur, she wore a sky-blue long shirt with embroidery on the lapels and sleeves. She moved her white oval sunglasses to rest on the top of her head.

'Hello, Major Bhatti,' Sonia greeted him and then complained about the heat in an elegant accent. 'The car's air conditioner was not working.' She continued in this manner until she had moved between us. Then she announced: 'I must use the bathroom.'

We were led across a manicured lawn on a pathway lined with budding jasmine bushes into the farmhouse. Military men and vehicles were in view and to the left was a field littered with clay from broken skeet. Once we were inside, Sonia was shown to the bathroom.

As soon as she closed the door and we heard her lock it, the rest of us looked at each other with suspicion.

'Do you have the money?' Major Bhatti asked.

'Yes,' I said patting my chest.

'Let us go into the study. It is private.'

Brocade curtains covered the windows and kept the study dark. It smelled of cigarette smoke and mothballs. There was a library table in the middle with maps, ashtrays, and Major Bhatti's iPad. The bookshelves were lined with thrillers by James Hadley Chase, Alistair MacLean and Ian Fleming. I had just sat down when Sonia came back.

'So, what are we here for?' she said with a dazzling smile.

'Cash has not told you?' said Major Bhatti.

They all looked in my direction. I took off my shirt and then the money vest. I placed the bundles on the table one by one.

'This is my client's money,' Sonia objected.

'Not any more,' said Major Bhatti. 'It belongs to the martyrs' family.'

'What martyrs?' She kept a steady gaze.

'The ones murdered by his friend Zahid. This is their settlement.'

'Zahid – that beast! He was here?'

115

'He killed three men and Mr Qais is an accomplice.'

'Zahid is a criminal, but I am surprised at Syed Qais.' Sonia emphasised my pedigree. 'I would have never guessed that he could cheat a widow.'

There was a cloudburst and rain pattered on the patio outside. I looked outside.

'In the land of Maliks, dues have to be paid; even the Americans pay for their convoys. If he had not complied, his life would not have been worth the plastic these dollar bills are wrapped in.' Major Bhatti stuffed the bundles back into the vest and hung it in the closet. Everyone's eyes were on the closet as he shut it.

The first explosion sounded like a cellar door being slammed. It was muffled but throbbed through the flooring.

'What was that?' Sonia asked in alarm.

'Thunderclap?' I said hopefully, but the second explosion was followed by gunfire.

'That is not thunder,' said Major Bhatti as men rushed into the room and unlocked another closet. Inside were guns of all kinds. Sniper rifles, SKS and G3 carbines. Major Bhatti called out to a man called Rahbar.

'What the hell ...' Sonia said.

Major Bhatti picked up an intercom device.

'Hold them off – it is your job,' he ordered. 'Keep them outside the walls. I will be out soon.' He grasped a rifle.

'What's happening?' I asked.

'Trouble, big trouble. Do you know how to handle a rifle?' he said. 'The front gate is blocked by a tractor and the militants are going to scale the wall. We are surrounded and outnumbered.'

'Did you call for help?' Sonia asked, fumbling with her cellphone.

'I have to use the radio. No cell service here, it is blocked,' Major Bhatti said and handed me a G3 rifle. I checked the magazine.

'Where are my guards?' Sonia asked.

116

'They are at the front gate. At a time like this, private guards will run for their lives. Next time, get IAS guards,' Major Bhatti said with a smile. 'Don't worry, I will take care of you.'

Sonia touched the gunmetal barrel of his rifle.

'Thanks. Should I carry a rifle as well?' she asked.

'Maybe it is best if you carry a pistol,' he answered. I admired his calmness but I hated his existence.

There was another rapid burst of gunfire outside. The intercom buzzed. Major Bhatti asked Baig to answer it and went into the inner room to use the military radio.

'Hello, yes, how many of you are there? Okay, if they start firing let me know and keep the line open,' Baig said.

The guards were nervous and ranting in Punjabi. One man said that we should surrender as the Taliban often behead soldiers. He covered up half a sob. He sounded like one of the guards who came with Sonia.

'Baig, keep it under control.' I heard Major Bhatti talk into the intercom. In the other hand, he held the radio.

'I understand, sir, but we have civilians here, and they are using RPGs and rockets. Air support would scare them off, but the storm will not blow over till tomorrow morning. We can't hold out all night.'

Riaz stared out of the window, watching the rain. He had stayed quiet all through.

'Are you going to take a weapon?' I asked him.

'I don't want a weapon or a uniform. If I wanted to fight, I would be outside,' Riaz said, looking at the rifle in my hand. 'There's no use fighting. We will not get backup in time.'

Major Bhatti returned in a raincoat and boots.

'Where are you going?' I asked. Outside, the wind howled and rain pattered on the patio.

'I have to be with my men. You stay here with Miss Sonia. If anyone enters, shoot to kill. Baig, get your gear.' Major Bhatti packed a 9mm Glock, put on a beret and picked up his rifle.

'What about the rear?' I asked.

'Don't worry, I have guards posted.' Major Bhatti paused before going outside, where a jeep awaited him. Two soldiers had thrown off the tarp that covered a heavy machine gun.

'I have no intention of turning my guests over to the Taliban. If these savages want a fight, we will give them a fight. We are the true mujahids,' Major Bhatti said as he left.

Rapid gunfire broke out again. I asked Sonia to pray.

'For what?' She looked at her cellphone.

I sat down with the rifle across my lap. The rain hit the fields and the scent of soil and flowers rose from the earth. It triggered childhood memories of muggy Karachi nights and summer weddings with silk-clad aunties and cauldrons of saffron-flavoured rice. On the way, my father would stop at a traffic light and buy *motia* garlands for my mother, who would wear them until the white flowers withered away.

I stood up and walked to the closet and opened it. The money was still there. I closed the closet and saw Sonia looking at me. I smiled.

A fierce explosion in the front rattled the windows. The smell of cordite filled the room. I went deaf momentarily and then looked outside. Two black figures crouched near the boundary wall had hoisted up a ladder. I sized them up through the riflescope as one climbed down like a ninja.

'Shoot, you idiot,' Sonia whispered.

I took my eye off the scope to see Sonia staring at the wall with her mouth half open. I had survived forty-two years of my life without killing a man and I did not want to start now. I rattled off a few aimless shots to impress her.

Another explosion shook the room. A Toyota truck had stopped outside the guard shack. A soldier manning a .50 calibre machine gun fired a round. A black figure ran across the field. Bullets whizzed across and towards the boundary wall, lighting their path, amid the raindrops and the crack of lightning.

Major Bhatti stumbled out of the truck. He helped a man out of the vehicle and with the aid of his men, carried him into the kitchen. I could not see his wound but I could see that he was bleeding from the torso.

'Can I help?' Sonia asked.

'No, Rahbar is a medic. Turn out the lights and bar the doors,' Major Bhatti instructed. He looked worried and had lost his beret. His hair dye ran down his sideburns.

I helped the men stack a table against the door. He whispered that this was useless.

'They have RPGs. They can blow these doors right through,' he said.

All the lights were turned off and we sat near the front doors. All was silent except for sporadic gunfire. In between, we heard the chatter in Pashtun walkie-talkies. The conversations got louder. I heard more shouts.

'I must talk to them,' Major Bhatti said. 'Rahbar, turn the lights on.'

Major Bhatti moved the table that blocked the door and opened it with caution.

'You are a brave man,' Sonia said to him as he walked out.

'It is my duty, madam.'

Major Bhatti carried a white undershirt in his hand. He came back in ten minutes.

'We have lost radio contact with the rear post and they have captured the guards upfront. They are threatening to execute them if we don't agree to their terms,' he said. 'I don't want to lose more men.'

'What are their terms?' Riaz asked.

The tungsten bulbs flickered. All I could think of was how he lost radio contact.

'They want the insurance people,' Major Bhatti replied.

'I told you it would not be this easy.' Riaz turned to me.

'Why do they want us?' I asked Major Bhatti.

'They say you abused Malik Awan's hospitality and connived with his daughter.'

Rainwater poured from the rooftop down the drains.

'They want to put you in front of a tribal *jirga*,' Major Bhatti continued.

'What about Mrs Saif?' I said.

'She left for Peshawar. They want you, Riaz and Miss Sonia.'

'I have nothing to do with this. You must tell them,' Sonia said.

The thunder outside was extra loud. We all jumped except Major Bhatti. He remained steady and heroic. That was supposed to be my job in front of Sonia.

'I will go but Miss Sonia must stay,' I said to Major Bhatti.

'I have done no wrong. I will go with you,' Riaz said, getting up.

'That is a wise decision. We can arrange the ransom with the elders. These tribals are not unruly during the day,' Major Bhatti added.

I left for the bathroom. I had become a prisoner of my own lies. I needed a wash to see the hero I was trying to be. When I returned to the room, Sonia was waiting for me.

'I don't want you to do this,' she said.

'Don't be stupid, I can talk my way out of this.'

Sonia's eyes and fingers were locked with mine. I pulled her close and kissed her. It had been over a decade since I had kissed her. Her memorable smell and taste fired off neurons in my brain that had long been dormant. I felt a sense of loss for all these years that we had lived separate lives because of trivial grievances. She pushed me back and then unbuttoned the front of her long shirt.

'What are you doing? Someone will come.' I rushed to lock the door. I was ready to do whatever was needed to receive whatever gift she wanted to impart before I walked away as a hero.

'Just hold on.' Sonia took off her shirt to reveal her black lace bra. Her brown stomach was still trim, except for a few folds, and her breasts had filled with age. I pulled her back and kissed her. She breathed a few sighs before breaking away.

120

'Later.' She put on the money vest and pulled the shirt back on, over the top of it. 'This will be your ransom,' she said, patting her chest.

'Now you are worth millions,' I said. 'What happens when Major Bhatti finds the money missing?'

'I will tell him Cash took it with him.'

I hugged her again and held her close. She wriggled out of my grasp.

'Wait. Sonia. One more thing,' I said.

'Yes?' she whispered.

'What perfume are you wearing? It suits you,' I said as I covered her with a chadur. I had never covered a woman in my life. Not my wife, sister or daughter.

'Jasmin Noir, by Bvlgari,' she said. Even in this moment of haste, she had to mention the brand. 'Do you like it?'

'Yes, it suits the mood,' I replied as we walked outside.

In the patio, I found Riaz, Major Bhatti and more men waiting for us. I turned back to see Sonia.

'Tell my daughter that I will be home soon,' I said. 'Don't forget me.'

'I will never forget my first love.' Sonia rested her head on my shoulder. 'I will get you out, Cash. I promise.' She covered up a sob.

I pushed her away.

Her tears had left a damp spot on my clothes. It spread as I walked out in the rain.

13
Taliban and Other Wild Men

'*Raza, raza,*' shouted the tall silhouette from the Hilux.

I hesitated at the edge of the flowerbed. The backlit silhouette had two horns sticking out from his head. The compound wall was maybe thirty feet away and beyond it were the marshes and the river road. The urge to run took over and I shifted my weight restlessly.

'Move it.' A short figure shoved me forward.

The horned silhouette called out again. I looked back at the Duck Hunter's Lodge. The rain had subsided and all the lights were out. There was no one outside except a battalion of screaming cicadas. The fragrance of jasmine was overpowered by gunpowder and diesel fumes.

I walked towards the vehicle that had spewed the diesel fumes. Brawny hands pulled me to the flatbed. The back of the cab was covered like a wagon and the silhouette was covered like a Taliban. He was tall and wore bandolier belts around his torso and a backpack from which protruded pointy rockets that gave him his satanic outline. Riaz climbed in after me, followed by the short figure. He closed the tailgate behind him and thumped the fender as he held a large rifle in the other hand. The Hilux

122

took off with a jerk and we drove out of the compound wall past the gate where two more dark figures jumped in. It took a right turn onto a paved road.

The Hilux speeded up, sliding in the slick rain and hard gravel. There were no check posts and we were not stopped even once. It was a moonless night but the driver drove without headlights. I grasped a roll bar while resting on a wooden plank. I made no attempt to talk to Riaz, who also swung back and forth, holding onto the roll bar. We waited for the ride to finish, bearing the pain and the jolts of the vehicle in silence.

Dawn brought relief. The man with the rockets uncovered his face and hummed. He was young and looked Hazaran with a sallow complexion and a wispy beard that was long on the chin but spotty on the cheeks. He scratched his thigh, revealing a dirty-yellow prosthetic leg. I was trying to figure out the melody he was humming when the car stopped at a cul-de-sac. Our captors jumped out of the car and then asked us to step out carefully. They quickly covered the vehicle with camouflaged tarp and unloaded supplies. Two men carried weaponry bags in tandem as another slung a leather strap around his shoulder to carry fuel canisters. The short figure grabbed two propane tanks. I offered to help but I was ignored and he ran up the hill, his rifle jangling against the metallic tanks. He was followed by the limp rocketeer.

'What do we do now?' I asked Riaz.

'Maybe they left the keys inside the Hilux,' he said. I went to the car and was about to lift the tarp when I heard the short figure yelling excitedly. He had taken off his headscarf and came sliding down the scree with his rifle pointing towards us. I expected him to fire by mistake. The rocketeer turned to look and then continued limping up the hill.

I raised my hands and gestured to Riaz to do the same.

'What are you doing?' said the boy in Urdu. 'Follow us up the hill.'

We followed him. Halfway up the hill was a makeshift camp. It was on the tree line, on a flat plateau with a sheer cliff on one side and a slanted ledge that ended on the canyon side.

123

There was a dank hut built with corrugated sheets and more camouflage tarp. A power generator chugged nearby and a pot boiled on a stove. A man held his phone in the air to check for signal. One man said, '*Bangana*,' and pointed to the sky.

'Where do you see it?' I asked, but my attempt to make conversation was ignored.

We were pushed inside the muddy hut, which smelled of onions and sweat. Nobody spoke. They uncovered their faces and sat on the floor. There were only four men and one boy, and they had stormed Major Bhatti's compound all by themselves.

'What do they want?' I asked Riaz in a low whisper.

'I don't know,' he said and raised his voice. 'Where are we? And where is Hukum Khan? We were promised we would meet him. We came here of our own free will,' Riaz continued.

The men stared at us with expressionless faces. One man kneeled next to a wooden plank balanced on buckets. It acted as a makeshift table for Qurans, prayer rugs and a laptop. He turned on the laptop and waited for it to boot up.

'I don't trust them. We should stay vigilant,' I whispered to Riaz.

We watched them in silence. The computer booted up after a long time. It was an old Dell laptop and made plenty of beeping noises. Then the man tethered his cellphone to the computer and smiled. He was slow and methodical. I dozed off.

It was a short nap. I was woken as Riaz handed his phone to the boy.

'Empty your pockets out,' the boy instructed me.

He was the only person in the room and his folding stock Kalashnikov was slung from his shoulder and across his chest. I exchanged a look with Riaz. The boy pointed the gun towards my face.

I emptied my pockets but kept my eye on the barrel. I threw the things on the floor.

'Do you want trouble? I can give you trouble,' the boy said sharply and cocked the rifle. It was an ugly-looking thing with a collapsible skeleton butt.

'I was following your orders,' I said, emptying my pockets.

The boy pocketed the money and asked for the phone's pin code. I gave it to him. He looked at the strip of Restoril and the tube of Polyfax ointment.

'What are these for?' he asked as he emptied my wallet.

'One is for my condition and the other is for an eye infection.'

'You are sick?'

'Yes,' I said.

'You keep them,' he said, handing over the medicine.

'Thank you. What is your name?' I asked.

'Tariq.'

'I am Qais and this is Riaz Khan Mehsud. Are we going to meet Hukum Khan?'

Tariq slapped my Nokia battery into a serialized battery charger connected with wires to the power outlet.

'We travel at night, so you can rest,' he said.

'Can I go to the toilet?' Riaz requested.

'Stay indoors,' he said. 'We are under surveillance.'

It was not until the time of the evening prayers that we were allowed to go to the toilet outside. Then we lined up for prayers and made loud proclamations of *Allah Hu Akbar Sunni*. After the prayers, Tariq spread out a plastic mat under the shade of a gnarly tree and uncovered a pot of rice. He added dried meat on top and handed out metal bowls. The other men started eating but kept their faces covered with scarves and sunglasses.

'What is this?' I asked. The food was tasteless and formless.

'*Londi* pilau,' Riaz said.

'Is that man a Hazara?' I chewed the gristly meat.

'No, probably Uzbek,' Riaz answered.

'Stop talking.' Tariq silenced us and we finished the rest of our meal quietly.

After another few hours of boredom and silence, we were told to get up and were escorted down the trail. The sun had set and it was almost dark. The Hilux was uncovered and Rocket Man got into the passenger seat. He ordered the other men to blindfold us.

'Yes, Commander Badar.' Tariq took out black cloth bags to cover our heads, but he was too short to reach us. He tried to figure out his next steps. A smile formed on my lips. He hit my thigh with the butt of his rifle.

'On your knees!' he yelled.

I dropped to my knees. I heard Commander Badar shout from the vehicle: 'This is for your own safety.'

We drove for a few hours but this time we were on populated roads and passed lively towns. I heard horns and music and smelt the odour of fertilizer and camel dung. We were definitely in an urban setting with many turns and stop signs. After another hour, the vehicle stopped and men got out. I heard the grating sound of a gate's drop-bolt dragged across concrete and we rolled into a driveway. Someone grabbed my hand and helped me dismount. Riaz and I were led upstairs, past a kitchen and into a room. Tariq removed the bags from over our heads.

'Where are we?' I asked him.

'You are here,' Tariq said, pointing to the ground. 'Stay long as our guests.' He closed the door and left the room.

'Where are we?' I walked around. The light in the room cast a red hue on the walls.

'How would I know? I am not a compass.' Riaz sat down on the bed, which was piled with blankets. There was nothing else in the room apart from a low stool. A door led to a bathroom with running water.

'What do we do now?' I wondered aloud.

'We sleep,' Riaz said.

Buzzing flies, the pungent smell of urine and Riaz's snores made sleep impossible. The door remained locked; the room was windowless but the bathroom had a high window. I dragged the low stool to the bathroom and looked out of the opening. The window was too small for a man to fit through, but I had a view of a green-lit minaret. It was quiet outside and I assumed it was past midnight. I put the stool back and offered the optional *tahajud* prayers. I still could not sleep after the prayers and kept drinking and pissing water all night. In between I stared at cracks in the ceiling and cursed my luck. All the double-dealing, debauchery, greed and lust had led inevitably to this situation. I had been kidnapped by the Taliban. Fear ran through my body, draining all my courage. I took a Restoril and drifted off to sleep in the early hours of the morning.

Fajr prayers woke me, reminding me of my imprisonment. I rushed to the bathroom to look out of the high window. In the soft light of dawn, I saw the lonely minaret and some craggy hills in the background. Riaz slept soundly for a few more hours and woke up when Tariq entered with tea. The scent of loose black tea revived my senses and courage. I thanked him.

'Do you have a cigarette?' I asked politely.

Tariq took off his skullcap. Inside was a pack of Pine cigarettes. He lit one and took a long drag before blowing the smoke out with a long hiss.

'How old are you?' Riaz asked him.

'I don't know,' Tariq replied.

'You have parents?'

He shook his head again.

'I have a son in Mianwali, his name is Faisal. He is four-years-old,' Riaz said.

Tariq remained silent.

'Qais sahab is a big man in Karachi. His cousin is a minister.'

'Is that true?' Tariq took a long drag. I was envious of his lungs.

'I don't know about "big man", but I have a family as well. A daughter,' I said.

'What use are they?' Tariq said, cutting me off.

'To make more of us,' I replied. Tariq's face was deadpan.

'They give birth, men can't do that,' Riaz explained.

'That's all they do, I have no use for them,' he said and tossed the cigarette on the bed. I picked it up. He gathered the cups back on the tray and left. I checked to see if the door was locked. It was.

'Odd boy,' I said, smoking the cigarette.

'He is a *kuchi* orphan raised in a refugee camp. He knows nothing about women or fucking,' Riaz said. 'We are lucky, Qais *bhai*. We had mothers who raised us with love.'

'Do you miss your mother?'

Riaz let out a sob unexpectedly.

'She died. I miss her very much,' he said, covering his mouth with his hand. 'She was my protection. I have been incomplete since she died.'

'When did she pass away?'

'Last year during Ramzan,' he said. 'Do you have a mother in Karachi?'

'Yes. She is alive and well. But I wish I were a better son to her.'

'I am sure you are a good son.'

'I don't know. I argue with her a lot. I still can't afford a ground-floor apartment for her. Even with her arthritis.'

'You are a good son, otherwise why would you come to this *kumbakht* place,' Riaz said.

I finished the cigarette. The tobacco and the tea helped my brain, and Riaz's sensitivity gave me emotional strength. It was clear that I was going to be responsible for both of us.

I spent the day snooping around the room, looking for objects that could serve as a weapon but found nothing except a pair of D-size battery cells. I heard hawkers and rickshaws outside. Inside the house, cellphones rang, doors slammed and feet stomped.

That evening after the sun had set, we were surprised by a visit from Hukum Khan. Badar accompanied him, along with a short man who was dressed in a burgundy shalwar suit. After exchanging salaams, Riaz and I broke into long-drawn appeals stating our innocence.

'Shut up and sit down,' Badar said. 'You are in the Islamic Emirates of Waziristan.'

'Why are we being held? What are the terms of our release? Have you contacted Major Bhatti?' I argued as I ignored his order.

Badar shoved me. I fell on the bed and hit my head on the wall. I rose, only to be pushed down again. He was twice as strong as I was, even with a prosthetic limb.

I coughed. Hukum Khan asked for water. Tariq filled a cup with tap water from the bathroom. I drank the water. Then Hukum Khan began speaking with a tone of elevated importance.

'You will have to stay in this room until we inform you of the next plan. You are under the eyes of the drone. This area is under curfew during the day. If you go outside, you will be shot. At night, it is full of Taliban, but also informers; if they get wind of the presence of strangers in this house, it could lead to a drone attack. If that happens, we all die.'

'I came here as Malik Awan's guest. I demand to be released,' I said. I sounded terrible.

'Syed Qais, you are a rich man. Your family will pay a ransom,' Hukum Khan grunted.

'Your information is wrong,' I said. 'I am poor. I live in an apartment with an ailing mother and a daughter.'

Hukum Khan took out a brown rosary. It looked suspiciously like Malik Awan's, but maybe all Waziris carried this brand.

'You were supposed to pay Major Bhatti money. Where did that money go?'

'It is with the insurance agent as a guarantee for my release. I can get it,' I said.

'How much is it?'

'One hundred thousand dollars,' I answered.

'That is nothing. In this time of inflation, it will buy a dozen rockets. We need more, otherwise you could be on trial in front of a *jirga* with Riaz.'

'I am ready to face any *jirga*. I am a Mehsud. My tribe will stand by me,' Riaz said.

'Well, you must think of something.' Hukum took out the rosary and counted the beads.

Time passed. Nobody said a word. I wracked my brain. I owned no property, only my wife's jewelry, which was probably

129

overpriced to start with. I was a conman to my business associates, and to ask my friends or relatives would be shameful.

'There are rich businessmen in Karachi. You would know where they live, their children's schools, their factories and offices, how much cash they have in their house,' Hukum Khan said.

'You want me to be a traitor to my own family? Never. Not if you put the sun in my right hand and the moon in my left,' I said, aghast.

'You quote the holy Prophet?'

'I am from his lineage.'

Badar moved his weight from his good leg to the prosthetic. I knew what was coming, but I did not want to step back. He slapped my face with a full palm.

'Watch what you say. Do not insult the Prophet with your ill-educated attempts,' Badar said. He then hit the other cheek with the back of the same hand.

'He is a Syed by name only. I don't have patience for his kind,' Hukum Khan said.

I waited for the door to close. I bet Badar's hand would hurt later, because my head was reeling. I closed my eyes but that did not help. The fan whirred above. I would have cried if I were alone.

'That was a pompous boast,' Riaz said, sitting on the bed.

'Something my grandfather would have said,' I said.

'But you made it sound convincing. You believe in that?'

'My grandfather told us that Syed were the princes of the ummah.'

'When did you stop believing?'

'The day I washed my father's cold dead body.' I popped off my last Restoril pill.

I drifted into sleep and into dreams of my childhood. Carefree afternoons when we ran through orchards, swam in canals, bathed in tube wells and picked fruit from trees, vines or bushes. The farmland stretched for miles around the bungalow where Dadaji lived with his two wives, and the sons who had not yet

130

moved to cities. The shrine was outside the village but Dadaji was acknowledged as a living saint. His followers kissed his feet and would have died at his whim. I remember him as a stocky, white-bearded man slicing mangoes for his grandchildren. As the custodian of the family shrine, it was his job to serve his disciples and descendants.

I was awoken by the sounds of a commotion. The door was flung open and two men grabbed Riaz. He fought them and tried to wriggle out of their grip.

'What is the meaning of this?' I demanded as the men dragged Riaz out.

'Let me go, you heathens, where are you taking me? Let me go, I beg of you,' Riaz sobbed while he clawed at the doorframe. The sobs turned to screams, but I remained frozen.

It was a few minutes before I had the courage to walk out. Two armed men stood at the staircase.

'Where is Riaz?' I asked.

'The *mukhbir*?' one of the men responded.

'An American spy,' said the other man. His eyes gleamed with excitement.

'That is impossible.' I backed into the room – and then I heard a scream.

I showed fear and like dogs, these fighters sensed it. One man punched my stomach. I hit the doorframe and buckled over. I had no energy to do much else and they dragged me down the staircase. I caught a glimpse of the patio through the lattice pattern.

In the veranda, the midget in the burgundy shalwar whipped Riaz. He stomped his foot to gather strength as he cracked the whip. Every crack led to an ominous yelp. After ten lashes, Riaz fell. The midget jumped on his toes, poised to attack like a mongoose but somebody called out and he had to hand over the whip. Everyone deserved a turn.

More whipping and whimpering followed. The midget pressed Riaz's torso with his sandals as another masked man kicked him. Riaz's screams were now muffled.

'He's done,' said the laughing midget.

The men caught their breath but they were not done as the midget had said. I was pushed onto the patio.

The first crack of the whip left a fiery line of pain on my neck. Before I could sense the full impact, the second blow struck, and the third and the fourth – fiery fingers that thrashed my skin. I recited Durood Shareef in praise of the Prophets from Ibrahim to Muhammad. My recitation included high-pitched yelps. I fell. The whipping stopped and the kicking started.

I did not see stars but the canvas in front of my eyes changed colours. From yellow to black and red, and I felt like a villain in the old *Batman* show. Badar let the midget Robin kick with his tyre-tread sandal soles. A solid object connected between my shoulder-blades. I heard a crack and screamed. I recognised my screams through the haze of pain. It filled me with shame.

I passed out.

I woke up alone from a dreamless sleep. I sat up as drool ran out of my open mouth. Fear and fever crept through my body. I hurt in multiple ways – I felt all at once intense throbbing, sharp burns and hard aches. I could have had a concussion and perhaps a broken rib. I cursed Sonia. She was the conniving bitch who got me into this mess. Once I got tired of blaming her, I blamed myself.

I heard footsteps approaching; they stopped outside. The door swung open. Lights were turned on and men entered the room. Someone kicked my stomach. I curled up and received a few more thuds.

'The only reason you are alive is because Hukum Khan sees use in you. Otherwise I would have riddled you with bullets as you hung from a tree,' Badar said.

I said nothing but made short, snorting noises – anything to swallow the cloudburst of sobs that threatened to shame me. My stomach twisted around as I lost control and let out a sob.

'He is crying. These *munafiq*, Shias and Sufis are Islam's worst enemies. Allah is watching us all and he knows who is righteous.' Badar closed the door.

132

My father had always warned me about the righteous. 'These people have a hole in their heart that they fill with belief. *Iman* and *khudi* are what makes you complete. There has to be a balance.'

But Dad was an Iqbalian and had no idea how to deal with these Wahabis. That was not a challenge for his time. As for me, I was not a saint or an Olympian. I was a cheat who had made a habit of conning widows – like Ruqiya Bibi and like the wailing villagers with bangles up to their elbows and children in tow – the unfortunate ones whose husbands had died in the Millat tyre factory fire. They had expected the charming Shahji to get them fair compensation. But they got nothing and I made a hefty commission on a fraudulent claim report I filed on behalf of the factory owners.

The worst part was that I could not remember what I had done with that bloody money.

14

The Mukhbir and the Munafiq

'The Islamic Emirate of Waziristan is neither Islamic nor an emirate,' I said.

Footsteps stopped outside the door. Riaz stopped scratching the welts on his shoulder. It was a week since the whipping and we had passed the time praying, drinking tea and scratching each other's backs.

'This is the time of *Jahalia*, when the Arab tribes lived in the dark ages with no writing, law or sense of nationhood. The Prophet, peace be upon him, brought all to the righteous path through peace and just warfare. The biggest battles he won were by the force of his personality.'

The door unlocked and Tariq entered. I knew he was eavesdropping as he was flat-footed and dragged his feet in a specific way. This speech was for his ears. I was hoping for empathy.

'Secondly, to have an emirate you need an emir and a proper army, not a hotchpotch of ill-tempered fighters who have no respect for any laws known to man or God.'

Tariq put down a metal pot wrapped in terry cloth.

'*As-salaam alaikum*, Tariq *beta*, what food have you bought us?' I propped myself up, using the wall as support. Pain was a constant companion but I always saved a smile for Tariq and called him 'son'.

'Bhindi,' he said, uncovering the pot.

'*Zabardast*,' I said and broke a piece of naan to taste the soggy okra. We were served one meal a day between *Maghrib* and *Isha* and spent the entire day starving.

'This is peasant food,' Riaz complained. 'Too much salt and cumin and this meat is not fit for a dog.'

'Then starve.' Tariq took a metal plate and hit Riaz over the head. He was fast and not afraid to hit, and we had long since given up the idea of trying to take away his AK-47.

'You are a landless peasant. My tribe will avenge this dishonor – I am a Mehsud,' Riaz said through tears of pain. He had recovered his pride but not his appetite. His condition was deteriorating and the purple gashes on his back had changed to yellow boils. I feared an infection.

'You are about as useful to your tribe as an old donkey,' Tariq said.

'Even a donkey has its use. Forget about him,' I said. 'Did you bring the medicine?'

Tariq took off his skullcap and took out a brown glass bottle of Amoxicillin 250.

'Wah, Tariq's *zambeel* produces more surprises,' I said.

'What is *zambeel*?' he asked.

'Umro Ayyar's *zambeel*. You know the adventures of Amir Hamza?'

'Look – this stuff expired in 2009,' Riaz complained.

'It is penicillin, so it is made from mould. Can't be worse than the pus you keep squeezing. Take a pill,' I said.

Riaz took out a pill and went to the bathroom to drink water. Tariq lit a hash joint and I took a puff. No doubt this was the reason for my constant diarrhea, but it helped to smoke.

'Is it a Muslim story?' Tariq asked.

'Of course. Sahib-e-Qiran Amir Hamza was the Prophet's uncle, a great warrior who destroyed armies and sorcerers. His faithful companion was Umro Ayyar, a vagabond, charlatan and magician. He had no loyalty except to his sheikh, Amir Hamza. He carried a *zambeel*, a magical basket from which he could pull out anything that he desired, and a Suleimani *topi* that made him invisible.'

We smoked and I told him a tale that I had concocted from what I recalled of the chivalrous duo. The tale involved princesses, giants, and fairies living in the meadows of Kohkaf.

'"I was a great magician, Umro, but alas - you have killed me," said Saamri *jadoogar* as he turned to dust.' I ended the tale with the death of the great magician-warrior.

'That was good,' the boy said.

'They were good and chivalrous and righteous. This was a time when the world would turn to a Muslim scientist to save them from a calamity or a Muslim general to save them from injustice. But now ...' I paused.

'What now?' Tariq asked.

'We Muslims fight and kill each other over little things. We forget that we all believe in one Allah and one Prophet.'

We heard footsteps outside and Tariq picked up the pot.

'Come back again and I will tell you another,' I said.

He came back the next day and I adapted stories to his heroic ideals. I had always wanted to be a storyteller but my daughter had no time for such things; she read Harry Potter, antiquated tales of medieval princes held little interest for her. But Tariq did enjoy them, and in turn he became comfortable spending time with me and answered my questions. We had figured out that we were near Datta Khel, a small town in North Waziristan. The house was called the Red House and served as command centre for 'The Asad Brigade'– a specialist fighter group made up of Uzbeki fighters led by Badar the limp rocketeer. The housemaster was a midget named Abdul Qudoos who spent his time either licking Badar's balls or beating us for no reason. There were several other men in the house but they either covered their faces or kept away from us. At night, vehicles would arrive and park in the compound of the house and there would be feasting, but during the day the house was quiet.

Every night I had trouble sleeping. I was done with all the Restoril and although my panic attacks had subsided, I was bored and found Riaz's company unbearable. I pleaded with Tariq to bring in reading material. Eventually, he found a stack of old newspapers and magazines and gave them to me. I took the pile and sorted it into categories – newspapers, magazines, jihadi literature, promotional brochures, and schoolbooks. Then I started with the newspapers.

'Any cricket news?' Tariq asked.

'Do you play?' I smiled. The papers were a few months old but I read all the news that I had ignored when I was home.

'Back in Karachi. Long time back.' Tariq said it with all the conviction of an aged man.

'You visited my city?'

'I lived in Gizri and collected plastic bags. You know where that is?'

'I live close by.'

'On Thursdays, we went to Shah Ghazi for biryani and sea view.' He smiled at the memory. The rifle that rested across his lap pointed towards the wall.

'Where are you from?' I asked him, wrapping up the newspaper. I could always read them later.

'Pararot, a village on the Herat-Kandahar highway.'

I stayed quiet. I wanted him to continue but did not want to seem too interested.

'I left Karachi to see my brother. In Chaman, the army caught us and put us in jail. They mixed glass with lentils and we cut our mouths eating the food. They wanted us to die.'

'Why did they arrest you?' Riaz enquired.

'Because we were refugees they called us terrorists. When we refused to die, they transferred the young ones to a refugee camp. It was there that Kaka found me,' Tariq said.

'Who's Kaka?' I asked.

The door opened and the midget entered. He did not have his turban on and I could see his close-cropped hair. Usually he came in to beat us for no reason but this time he was accompanied by

137

two burly men with their faces covered. They grabbed Riaz by the shoulders and dragged him out of the room. Hukum then entered, dressed in starched white with his turban perfectly upright.

'I see you have recovered,' he said. 'Nothing broken?'

I stood up, careful not to wince in pain. His visit did bring a flowery scent with it which I welcomed, as the putrid smells of our room had put me in a permanently sour mood.

'Tariq said you cried a lot. You carry a lot of pain,' he continued.

'I have an eye infection. They shed water easily,' I said testily.

He picked up a magazine called *Zarb-e-Momin*. On the cover was a troop of soldiers stepping through snow. The caption read: *Yesterday we saw Russia break, now we will see the same for India.*

'You agree with our cause?' he asked.

'I told you before. I am a civilian.'

'You are a *munafiq* – a hypocrite – so you can play either side. A wolf only respects a lion's iron slap; lions do not impress with the logic of a sheep,' he said. 'May Allah forgive us for our sins.'

I was not sure if I was the sheep or the wolf. It was clear, however, that he considered himself a lion.

'Where have they taken Riaz?'

'Don't worry about the *mukhbir*. You know he is guilty of spying for the Pakistan army.' Hukum Khan looked for a reaction but I remained silent. 'He will be put on trial tomorrow morning. You should worry about yourself.'

The two men came back. They wore clean clothes that were stretched and smelled of perfume. I tensed up, expecting to be dragged downstairs for a beating.

'I need the names of people who can pay a ransom.'

'My family will pay a hundred thousand dollars,' I said.

'I need a list of rich people.'

'What will you do? Kidnap their children?'

'Don't worry about them. We treat them well,' Hukum said.

'I worry about everyone. It is what makes me different from beasts, *ashraf-ul-makhlooqat*.'

138

'This is no time for your *munafiq* philosophy. I need five names with addresses. I am leaving tomorrow for Karachi.'

He left the room. Tariq gave me a pen and a child's copybook with a Barney the dinosaur cover.

I began with a list of people I hated. There used to be many, but right now even my worst enemies including Anthony Lobo did not deserve to be kidnapped by the Taliban. But I had to come up with names and so I wrote down names of people who would be heavily guarded. When Hukum came back, I handed him a torn page from the copybook.

'It's an impressive list – a provincial minister, a regional council member, an SSP of police and a textile businessman. Who would have thought that Syed Qais would rat that easily?' he said, reading the list. 'Are these addresses correct?'

'As far as I can remember,' I said.

'We will run checks. If they turn out to be good potentials, we might want more information. Now where is the money you were supposed to give to Major Bhatti?'

I gave him Sonia's phone number at her office.

'What is the name here?'

'Miss Sonia, she has my money,' I said.

'She is Christian?'

'Yes, Catholic. We have them in Karachi,' I said with a sardonic smile.

'I am not against other faiths. It is the *munafiqs* and *mukhbirs* within our faith that poison the religion. Still, you trust her to stand by you. I am surprised. You seem to have more faith in her than your own fellow men.' He left the room.

The fact was that I did not trust Sonia. The more I thought of her, the angrier I became. She was the architect of all my pain. She had ruined my youth with her deceit by sleeping with Vicky and then marrying my friend, and now she had trapped me in this hideous plot. Who knew, she was probably in cahoots with the Major, and together they were sharing my ransom money.

Later that afternoon, the guards brought Riaz back into the room. He immediately limped straight to the bathroom to

139

clean himself. When he came out his eyes were swollen and his face was beetroot red. He collapsed on the bed and fell asleep. When he woke up, he started to cry. I asked him what had happened.

'These men are beasts. May Allah punish them for their sins,' he wept.

I put my hand on his shoulder and hugged him. I had a fair idea of what had happened.

*

I did not tell Riaz about the trial but Tariq did. When he heard, he bolted for the door.

'Stop or I will shoot,' Tariq yelled.

But Riaz was already out of the door into the corridor. He ran into the two burly men who were in the next room. They grabbed him by his hair and dragged him back. Then one of them stuffed his mouth with the dirty blanket and hit him.

'Make them stop,' I said to Tariq.

Tariq shrugged. I yelled into his face as the man punched Riaz.

Tariq asked them to stop but they punched Riaz a few more times, ran out of breath and then left. I took the bedding out of Riaz's mouth and I washed his face with water.

'Come with me,' Tariq said, grabbing my hand.

I rested Riaz's head on the pillow and followed Tariq onto the veranda. He lit a cigarette.

'Syed Qais,' he said, addressing me like Hukum Khan. 'Riaz is finished. His life is hanging between the index finger and the thumb.' He pinched his finger and thumb together.

'What does that mean?'

He looked astonished. He was a child who repeated conversations that he overheard without knowing their exact meaning. He was surprised that I did not get the reference.

'You too will be found guilty. You have enough sins,' he said.

'Allah is my judge. What is the punishment?'

He turned away. I was more concerned about what the punishment was than why.

*

'Obviously beheading,' Riaz said the next morning. We were served milky tea and fried eggs, Tariq also left a plate covered with tin foil and a pipe with an opium pellet.

'Why obviously?'

'They want to make an example of us. Do you know what they did to Colonel Imam?'

'Who's Colonel Imam?'

'He is the father of Taliban, an SSG commando who trained Mullah Omar. He was captured in 2010 and Hakimullah Mehsud posted a video of himself shooting the colonel three times in the head. This is what they do to people who are sympathetic to their cause.'

'Didn't they kidnap a Pakistani-British journalist with him?' I recalled.

'But they killed his driver and released the journalist.'

'See – we are like the journalist, we will get our ransom,' I said. The hot yolk burst like an orange sun of happiness in my mouth. This was a treat after all the terrible food I had consumed since my kidnapping.

'What are you talking about? We are insurance men in the service of western companies. We have connived with the woman of a Pashtun household and could be tried as informers.' Except for his bloodshot eyes and unshaven face, Riaz still looked like a soap star.

'*Mukhbir* we are not,' I said.

Riaz looked away, and for the first time, I doubted his intent. Could he really be a *mukhbir*? It was possible. That would mean the worst for him.

'Or *munafiqs*. Either way, they will find us guilty. They can shoot us and get it over with, but they will probably behead us.' Riaz continued with examples of different methods of execution

141

as he rolled the green pellet between his index and his thumb and then dropped it in the pipe.

'They want us to forget our miseries,' Riaz said and lit it. He took a drag and passed it over as the smoke curled up inside the pipe like a question mark. I took a drag and put my back against the wall. Smoking was not just a pastime but also a way to overcome all the bad smells and memories.

'What would be your last wish?' Riaz asked.

'What do you mean?'

'If they ask for your last wish, what would it be?'

I had never thought of such things and it was a cumbersome process. My head was heavy with opium and fatigue.

'I know what mine would be. To sleep with my wife,' Riaz said. I smiled.

'Not for sex, which is good, but for how she feels. Her body is smooth and curvy and the way she speaks is very alluring. Her family is from Mardan and they speak the hard Pashto and switch the letter *shay* to the letter *khay*. It is beautiful to hear her pronunciation. I miss it. Allah as my witness, that is what I miss.'

He went on to describe his wife as a woman of exceptional patience and beauty. It was inevitable that I thought of my wife. We had been married twelve years before she died but during those years we had a system for initiating lovemaking, a touch, a glance, a smile and a final nudge. It was a simple act without an elaborate ritual of courting, a finely honed process that took years to develop. How I missed my family and the company of women! I promised myself that if I survived this imprisonment, I would marry the first willing woman I found. I would never touch a whore or alcohol ever again. I would take my mother for hajj. This time for real, I promised Allah.

*

Early next morning, an hour before dawn, I was woken up from an opium-induced sleep. The two burly men in their crisp

142

uniforms told us to do *wuzu* and clean ourselves. Riaz asked for permission to pray and the men nodded without saying a word. He went through his prayers solemnly and ended with ceremonious *salaams* to his two guardian angels.

'I have made my peace. I am ready to meet my maker.' He folded the prayer rug.

'The trial has not begun. I will fight for you,' I said.

'Please don't. You will only make things worse. You have been a good friend in the time I have known you. If you are set free, see my family. Tell my wife that I loved her very much ...' The rest of the sentence was lost in a sob. 'Syed Qais, make sure my family gets their due,' Riaz said.

I nodded.

'When Faisal grows up, you will be there to tell him that his father was a good man, that he never drank or stole from anyone,' he made me promise.

The men walked alongside Riaz and held his hands. Even they had found manners today.

'Tell him that I, Riaz Khan Mehsud, was not a traitor to my tribe,' he said. 'And that he must avenge my death.'

The men took Riaz away and closed the door. I heard several footsteps walking up and down and the sound of furniture moving. I felt ashamed for doubting his integrity earlier; Riaz was my companion and a friend. This depressing place had made me doubt everything I had learned in life. It had made me a shameless and a fearful person. I stood next to the wall, shivering. When the door opened, I let out a small cry. But it was only Tariq.

'Do you wish to see the trial?' he asked.

I followed him through the dark corridor to the latticework wall, which showed a view of the fluorescent-lit veranda. The veranda was covered with tarp.

Sombre figures stood on the side, deep in conversation. Their faces were covered and they wore turbans or caps. I recognised Hukum Khan among them. Riaz was in the centre of the patio, next to a man in a white robe who held a Quran in one hand. He held up his hand and the chattering stopped.

143

'Bismillah ar-Rahman ar-Raheem. Today is Hijri date 1432, the seventh day of Dhu al-Qa'dah, a month in which warfare is prohibited in Al-Islam, but I am forced to decide the fate of our captives,' said the white-robed man.

The trial continued in Pashto and Arabic. There was no secrecy to the trial and no witnesses were called. Hukum Khan spoke but was made to stop when he bore witness to the drone attack at the godown that killed Commander Shahin. The inquiry then turned to Riaz. He was asked questions but most of his replies were cut off. In effect he was blamed for spying for the Pakistan army and the American masters. It did not take long to reach his verdict.

'According to the sharia law, in the Islamic Emirates of Waziristan, I, Qazi Abdul Akhund, after careful consideration and in accordance with the law of the holy book of Quran, pronounce the death sentence for the *mukhbir* Riaz Khan Mehsud for the martyrdom of our soldiers.'

The guards tied Riaz's hands and covered his head with cloth. Badar rolled up his sleeve.

'Do it before *Fajr*,' the qazi said and walked away. Hukum Khan shook his hand and then came to where I was standing.

Hukum raised his finger for silence. 'Pray for your friend,' he said.

The men standing on the veranda left. Riaz stood alone with the two burly guards. The midget took out a cellphone and started recording a video. A tall figure emerged from the shadows. His face was covered but I could still make out the limp from the prosthetic leg.

'How can you let this happen? You gave us your word!' I cried out fiercely.

'Take him to his room,' Hukum told Tariq.

Tariq nodded his head but nobody moved. One man toppled Riaz to the ground but he managed to get up on one knee. The other men pulled him back down by his shalwar and the first jumped on top. I heard grunts as the men pinned Riaz down.

'You have to stop this, Hukum Khan!' I held him by his lapels.

144

'Take him, Tariq,' he said. But the boy remained fixated.

Badar recited the *kalma*. His voice rose as with his right hand he grasped a dark knife between the index and the thumb.

'You can't stop it, can you? You have no power over them,' I said.

Badar caressed the naked throat with his left hand and raised the knife towards the sky.

'*La illahailla Allah Muhammad Rasul Allah,*' he chanted.

Riaz gave a final shove and the men sitting on top of him rocked as though on a carnival ride.

Badar proclaimed a louder *kalma* and ran the blade across Riaz's throat.

The men jumped off and Riaz's body twisted with spasmodic jerks. The executioner kept the head pulled back by the hair until the blood flowed out and the tremors left the body.

Badar worked the knife, cutting around the neck so that it was only connected to the body halfway. Once finished, he wiped the blood off the knife. He only had blood on his hands; his clothes were spotless.

'Separate the head from the body,' I heard.

The midget appeared with a curved, sickle-like weapon and struck it hard at the neck. He picked up the severed head and passed his cellphone to his mate who shot the rest of the video that the midget had been recording. He then put the head in a sack. Others dragged the headless body away, leaving a bloody streak.

'*Khawarij,*' I said. I repeated it louder.

'Stop it,' Hukum said.

'The *khawarij* left the middle path and will burn in hell,' I roared

'Be quiet.' Tariq grabbed my hands as his nails dug into my shoulder.

'*It is all the same to them. Whether you warn them or not. They will not believe,*' I quoted from the *Surah Yaseen*. 'Mark my words. You will all burn in hellfire. It's a Syed's curse – don't treat it lightly.'

145

It was the superstitious act of a desperate man, a last appeal to an indifferent deity. I repeated the verses, but I choked as my words turned into sobs.

But I continued. I wanted Tariq to believe in the power of this curse. Even if he was the only one who did.

15
Mullah, Martyr and Monster

'Save me, Syed Qais, save me,' she said. A fleeting glance from a green *pari* and I am running after her, down a garden pathway with a boy's stride. She is almost within my grasp.

'Wake up. We are leaving,' I heard a voice say. As she looked back with a mocking smile, I woke up and saw Tariq's round face. He shook my head like a tin can.

It was a forewarning to sort out my thoughts and my possessions; the former were infinite but the latter I could count on my fingers: a pen, the Barney copybook, *miswak* and a sweet candy. All trades made from services rendered to the Taliban. None of them involved sex.

'Where are we going?' I mouthed the words. The left side of my face was heavy but that was the least of my worries. I had fought off infections only to uncover mechanical ailments like cracked ribs, sprained muscles, and a state of constant fever.

'Toilet,' I mumbled and set off, careful not to slip on the dark pools of liquid waste that were leaking from the oil drum in the bathroom. It had not been emptied and the waste was layered with feces and vomit. The fact that Riaz's shit had outlasted him made me throw up, but this was part of my regular lavatory process. I heaved until there was nothing left except bile. I washed, tightened the shalwar's cummerbund, and slipped on my sandals.

'Hurry up,' Tariq said and I followed him down the stairs. I had not walked out of the room since Riaz's execution. There was no banister and the walls were unfinished. Each step threw my head in a spin and sent a jolt of pain up my spine.

'Why do you call it the Red House?' I asked as we waited by the front door. My sandal covered a drain. 'Is it because of the blood spilled?'

'Our car is coming,' he said, ignoring my question.

'Where does it go? Even after it is washed with water, blood cells find each other. They stick together. That's why blood is thicker than water.'

'What nonsense,' Tariq said, shaking his head. The supernatural disturbed him.

'The drains are clogged with the blood of men. That attracts demons and flesh-eating djinns. My grandfather could command *jinnat*. They loved his recitation,' I said as a car horn beeped. 'I have the same gift.'

Tariq turned and punched my chest. It was a routine punch without malice.

'They are here,' he said.

'Of course they are here. *As-salaam alaikum*. Lords of fire, show your presence.'

Tariq took a step forward but I raised my hands and called to angels and djinns. I expected something to materialise. Opium is a wonderful drug.

Badar waited outside in a new camouflage jacket in a commercial Toyota garlanded with plastic flowers, tassels and mirrors. One headlight was red and the other green and both were decorated with drawn brows and eyes with long lashes and dilated pupils. The overall effect was disturbingly sexy, like a captivating *hijra*.

I sat on the padded bench next to Tariq and another covered fighter. At the street corner, we picked up a scowling man and two women in yellow burqas. It was morning and the roads were terribly silent. We breezed through abandoned checkpoints. I had expected to be moved at night when the roads were less travelled, the soldiers barracked and the drones blind. A few kilometres and then a few more; my fever burned higher as we went around hills but never lost sight of a particular snow-covered peak. At a village, the other three passengers disembarked and then I drifted off into a fever-driven fantasy.

When I woke up, the whole day had passed. The Hilux had slid to a stop and Tariq was already out of the vehicle. I stepped down from the car, still caught in a hopeful dream, and took in the surroundings with disbelief. I had not been outside for weeks and the fresh air, open skies, and the tree-lined slopes of the mountains reminded me of scenic landscapes from commercial bank calendars. It was as if I had arrived at Koh Kaf.

'Where are we?' I asked.

Tariq unloaded a dusty duffel bag and walked away.

A mud wall punctuated by a stubby lookout tower and a hefty iron gate enclosed this particular fairy meadow. A brown building had been built into the side of the cliff and matched the hue and colour of the mountains. It looked like a brown shoebox with slits cut in to keep crawly critters breathing. Next to it were smaller boxes with slits and chimneys and finally a dome beside a sandy graveyard. A ledge extended to an area where figures were lined up for prayers.

'Let's join our brothers in prayer,' Badar said and hobbled towards the ledge.

His enthusiasm after the soul-crushing ride was irritating. I grumbled as I followed the limping executioner and flat-footed boy soldier. My irritation brought back a sweet memory of my mother. No matter the gravity of the situation, her first reaction had always been one of annoyance. For the first time in days, I felt like myself.

149

The imam said *Allah Hu Akbar* and carried the followers with him. The recital was short but pitch perfect and the chorus of *ameen* after the *alhumdulillah* reverberated across the valley. The spirited prostrations and the clean air lifted my spirits and cleared my mind.

After the *salaams*, Badar joined the imam in the front row. They embraced and Badar kissed his hands. They talked, holding hands and exchanging smiles. Once, the old man touched Badar's long hair and the executioner blushed. The rest of the prayer party – teenage boys in white skullcaps – continued their individual prayers but watched Badar with adoring eyes.

I finished the remaining *rakats* and then recited *surahs* aloud. It wasn't pre-planned but it was something that I felt like doing.

'Syed Qais, come and meet the imam,' Tariq said after a few minutes.

I had reached the limit of my *surah* memorizations and was reciting the name of Allah.

'Al-Jami, Al-Ghani,' I said, standing up.

Tariq prodded me but I continued aloud. At the ninety-ninth name, As-Sabur the patient, I offered my greetings.

'You have good *tajweed*?' the imam asked me. He had a badly dyed beard and kohl dripped from his eyes. 'You learned it from a *madrasa*?'

'No. My grandfather stressed elocution as the key to unlocking the power of the Quran. I was on the path to be a *hafiz* but tragedy struck.'

'This one is the *munafiq* and a born liar,' Badar said.

I looked down. My hands trembled and I could not bear to look Badar in the eye. I was equally afraid of him and of my own rage.

'We are all liars in this world, for this world is not real. One must prepare for *Akhrat*,' the mullah said. 'Bring tea for our guest.'

He reached for my hand and I jumped back in fear. He smiled and grasped my right hand and held it. It was an old hand but it was warm and I swooned from his kindness. We walked to a wooden bench that overlooked the forested valley. A fair young boy came running with a hot pot and two cups. The mullah introduced himself as Nazeer. He asked careful questions and I answered truthfully. The tea was sweet, the air smelled of pines and the wind bristled my beard.

'You are a man on a search,' Mullah Nazeer commented.

'For freedom,' I said. A hawk unfurled its wings and took off from a tombstone.

'To do what?'

'Go back to my family. I left an ailing mother and a daughter, in search of financial profit. They don't even know if I am alive. It would mean so much to me if ...' I stopped. I did not want to choke up and it was not the right time.

'Something else,' he said. 'Beyond leisure, family, or profit there is a worldly purpose in all of us.'

The hawk had taken off once more, across a pink sky and the jagged, snow-covered mountains. I shivered and shook my head.

'Ghazigar is a special place. Stay as our guest and you will not be harmed.'

We watched the sun disappear behind the western peaks. As the light waned I was escorted past silhouettes and heard the chatter of children and their nagging mothers. Inside, the shoebox building was brightly lit and the floor was covered with blankets and dirty bedding. It smelled and felt like a boys' dormitory and I made out some scowling faces under embroidered skullcaps. Tariq found two places next to each other and dropped his duffel bag on the ground.

'You want to do your ablutions?' he asked.

I nodded and was shown to a communal washroom. I washed myself as the boys stared. They wore man-size sandals but child-size clothing and their faces had an odd asymmetry – flat noses, extraordinarily large heads, exceptionally rotund torsos, bowlegs and ragged scars on their cheeks. Once I'd finished cleaning up, I slipped into the bedding and dozed off.

151

I woke up in the middle of the night. It was pitch dark inside the room. The boys were whispering to each other, and outside I heard shouts and the sound of vehicles and gunfire. I asked aloud if it was safe.

'Don't worry. It is the mujahideen. They train at night. You will meet them tomorrow. Be nice to them,' said a voice.

I heard a rustle and got slapped on the face. Then I heard laughter and I hid inside my blanket. It was like my first night in the hostel at my cadet school. I had hated that as well.

*

The next morning I woke up drenched in sweat. The room was empty and shafts of sunlight stewed the bedding, loosening musky smells. I attended to my toilet and then ventured out. The smaller buildings were humming with domestic activity and I could hear the boys in the seminary building reciting the Quran. I caught up with missed prayers. Around mid-afternoon the mosque filled up for *jamaat* led by a teenager. After the prayers I looked for Tariq and found him talking to a young man with one eye stitched shut.

'Where were you? I missed you, *beta*,' I said.

Tariq spoke to the one-eyed man who winked back at him. He was slightly built and had a haircut that reminded me of the Beatles.

'What do you need?' Tariq turned to me. I noticed that his rifle no longer had a magazine.

'Food and good company,' I said.

'I will find you when it is time for food. You slept through dinner and breakfast.'

'Where are we going?'

'I am going to the *mukhabarat*.' Tariq quickened his pace.

'Can I come along?'

He did not reply so I followed him. We walked past mud huts where babies cried and mothers scolded, amid sheds littered with old tyres, car batteries and oil drums. We came to a camouflaged building with satellite dishes and antennas on the rooftop. Outside the building, a goat shared leafy greens with a donkey that was tied to a post. The air smelled of goat droppings, grease and diesel fumes. The one-eyed man was bent over a Honda generator.

'We might have work for you,' Tariq said. 'Wait here.'

I heard a grating noise and the noise of vehicle horns. The iron gates were dragged open across the gravel, revealing farm tracts surrounded by pine forests. Overhead, electric lines swung between wooden posts leading towards civilisation.

'Are you good with machinery?' the man asked in Urdu.

I did not reply.

'I am talking to you, Punjabi,' he said. His beard covered burn scars but he had a trusting, pleasant face.

'No, not very good. I can read and write. I am also good with computers,' I answered. He shrugged his shoulders.

'It is impossible to get mechanical help here,' he sighed. Even with all the marks of war on his face, he looked good-humoured.

'I can learn,' I said.

'Maybe,' he said, and went back to his tinkering.

An hour passed before I was called. The office was comfortable with an Afghan carpet, a wide desk, and a wicker couch. Two men with laptops sat cross-legged on the carpet. Between them the fair boy sorted bullets into piles. Stacked against the wall were rifles, crutches, and collapsible wheelchairs. In a corner was a squat safe with a TV on top and a photocopy machine. Behind a desk, Mullah Nazeer talked on a satellite phone in Pashto. No one sat on the sofa.

I waited and ran my fingers through the carpet, which showed a battle scene with tanks and helicopters. People came and left. Tea was served a few times. The one-eyed mechanic came and sat on the floor and gave instructions to others.

A phone rang and I jumped in fear. The fair boy stopped counting and laughed when he saw my reaction. It was a childish laugh – he couldn't have been over ten-years-old. He had green eyes and beautiful features.

The one-eyed mechanic yelled at the boy. 'Zain, I told you to pile the 762s for missions. Keep the Chinese round separate for target practice.'

'Is he of any use to you, Sabir?' Mullah Nazeer asked, pointing in my direction. He cradled a walkie-talkie with a long antenna under his freshly dyed black beard.

'He says he can write,' said the man called Sabir.

'Can you read this?' Mullah Nazeer held out a page to me.

I took the piece of paper. I found the writing legible but the assembly of words made no sense. It was like a free-flowing poem but read like a shopping list.

'I can read but it makes no sense,' I said.

'Rightly so. It is in a code of my own making. Handwritten and personally delivered by a trusted courier. The Americans watch everywhere. Can you make readable copies of these? They must be legible like print,' he said.

I nodded and was given a sheaf of paper and a fountain pen. I spent the afternoon making the required copies. Once I had finished, Mullah Nazeer examined my work.

'This will do for now,' he said. 'Come back tomorrow. We will find more work for you.'

*

The next day I copied more handwritten notes onto a magazine-size sheaf of papers in Nastaliq script. I did the same the next day. It was delicate work, sloppiness was not an option, and anything outside of the margin would mean a slap or a shove. The physicality was not meant to hurt but to humiliate a forty-two-year-old man. Sometimes the TV would be on and I would hear Pakistani advertisements for cooking oils and mobile phones. Other times I overheard disputes over tactics, money and other petty rivalries between the Taliban. I wrote and I listened and I learned.

The Taliban had no centralised command structure and relied on independent mullahs to stay relevant and inspire the field

154

commanders to work together. Mullah Nazeer was one such mentor and from the likes of the brash fighters who visited the seminary at odd hours, it seemed he was a successful one. He edited a magazine called *Zarb-Ghazi*, which had coded instructions hidden in personal letters, poetry by anonymous Taliban as well as narrative essays on strategy and outreach for the social jihadist. The bulletin was photocopied and hand delivered to the commanders who were referred to by their field names like 'Baz', 'Zulfiqar','Badar', and 'Shaheen'. Some of the inspirational essays were read aloud during sermons at the seminary. They all had aspirations to be field commanders. But most did not enjoy the stature of a field commander. Taliban preferred their leaders to be tall and fair-skinned, and their path usually led to martyrdom as a suicide bomber. Still, their loyalty was utmost and they were governed by rules that none of them questioned. Each day they thanked Allah for their dastardly existence. Each of them had a story about how they had lost a limb or a family member. It was common to have a prosthetic leg or an eye patch, and the fighters wore them as a badge of honour.

In the afternoon, the mullah took a nap on the couch while we sat outside in the work sheds. Sabir had a few apprentices who helped him. He tasked them with constant work but also entertained them with stories about his missions.

'I lost my eye on the road from Kabul to Bagram. We called it Bagh-Shaitaan,' he said. 'It was heavily mined.'

'Was it Americans?' I asked.

'The mine was Soviet but I was chased into the Devil's garden by the Americans. The shrapnel hit me in the face. It carried with it the fires of hell.'

'You are lucky.'

'It is a good thing Allah makes us forget the pain.'

'And now you are the mechanic.'

'And I run the dispensary. Mullah Nazeer trusts me,' Sabir said.

'Also, he can't be a fighter because he can't aim a rifle,' Tariq said.

'Dickhead, I can shoot better with one eye than you can with two.' Sabir flexed his index finger. He had two missing fingers from his hand as well.

'I can beat you any day – when do you want to try?' the boy challenged.

'It is forbidden to fire weapons during the day,' Sabir replied.

'If you compete, I will join in. I bet I can beat Tariq,' I said.

I wouldn't have dared to challenge Tariq in the Red House, but working in the *mukhabarat* had given me the clout to do so. The nightly antics of hiding my pillow or stealing my bedding had stopped too and the students treated me as an equal. They were uneducated in the literal sense but had skills peculiar to their craft. They knew the seasons, they could navigate by stars, remember codes and secret passwords. They trained hard on obstacle courses that required crawling, climbing, jumping and swinging off ropes. They had little compassion for the amputees and would ridicule them for their handicaps. But they played together, sometimes jousting on motorcycles and other times swimming in the water reservoir. Without their turbans and shirts they were frightfully young – with lean bodies, longish hair, drooping beards and ballooning wet shalwars. Their jumping and splashing in the foaming water of the reservoir reminded me of gay porn that my friends shared on emails with disclaimers. There were other indications of *humjins* affection among the students, especially at night when their whispers ended in sensual yelps. I wasn't particularly bothered by it as long as they kept their flotsam and jetsam to their own bedding.

In the office I took on more work – making photocopies, sealing envelopes, cash accounting and dictation. I had become an integral part of the magazine staff and enjoyed freedom of movement, but I remained a prisoner under watch. I made it a habit to go for a run around the compound after morning prayers. The gate was always closed and the trails that led down to the valley were under constant observation from the lookout towers. I stayed alert for a way to escape but saw no option. Even though escape seemed futile, I was happy that I had at least managed to recover my health and get into a training regime of running, lunges and squats. I had no racket but I imagined playing squash against a wall. One morning, Zain watched as I played an imaginary game of squash against the back wall of the shoebox building. He giggled incessantly until I got annoyed.

'What's so funny?'

'You look like a dog chasing his tail.'

'I am training.'

'You are soft-headed. That's what Bilqees said.' He lit a joint and offered it to me.

'Who's Bilqees?' I ignored his offer. 'I only know Gul Khanum, the mullah's wife.'

'She wears a dark blue burqa. She knows Urdu.'

'What did you tell her?'

'I told her that you are Pakistani and know many things.'

'Is she married?'

'She is a widow. She brings bad luck to all her husbands. They all die.'

'She can't bring me bad luck if I talk to her.'

'Why would you talk to her? What benefit can a woman give you?' Zain asked.

'I hope you find that out one day,' I said as the morning fog cleared. I could not help but be intrigued by the fact that the women noticed my poor self.

That day at the *mukhabarat*, Mullah Nazeer dictated a long list of items for the upcoming Eid festivities. He then specified a budget for each category. It was a long list.

'We will have guests visiting. Purchase rice, confectioneries and other supplies you deem necessary for the dispensary. Students who have memorized the Quran should get a new *libas*.' He handed Pakistani rupee notes to Sabir.

'Anything for you, master?' Sabir asked.

'*Khas ittar,* if you find it. Also, please make a list from my *khanum*.'

I added it to the list and gave it to Sabir. He looked at the list and frowned.

157

'What's wrong?'

'It is hardly legible,' the mechanic complained.

'Why did you do that, Qais? Do you not know how to write?' Mullah Nazeer turned to me,

'It was long list. I ran out of space in the end,' I said. 'I will rewrite it.'

'No time for that. Just go with Sabir. Can I trust you not to try anything foolish?' he asked.

'On my honour,' I replied.

'Take Tariq with you as well, and keep an eye on him.'

I followed Sabir to the female quarters with Zain in tow. He called out ahead and the half dozen women sitting on plastic tarp covered their faces. Mullah Nazeer's wife's face remained uncovered as she sorted through a pile of clothing. She was small-framed with a youthful voice but had a weather-beaten face.

'Why is the Punjabi here?' she said, giving me an enquiring look.

'He is helping. My eyesight is not well,' Sabir said. He said more, but I did not understand.

'I can't tell him personal things. It is shameful,' she said. 'Can you take the list?'

Sabir gestured for me to move back and I stepped back with Zain. The women talked among themselves. One midnight-blue burqa separated from the group and emptied a basket full of pine nuts into a plastic bag. The burqa had no sleeves but had a hexagonal grill that floated like a protective djinn. I asked Zain if that one was Bilqees, the Taliban widow.

'Yes. She is bad luck,' he said.

I watched as she walked into the house and returned with more pinecones. I imagined what she would look like underneath the shroud. Was she heavy? Did she have curly hair? What was her skin complexion like?

That afternoon we rode to Hassu Khel, on a clear November day. To the villagers and the drones I looked like a Taliban fighter with a thick beard and a keffieh, except I was unarmed and older. We stopped at a one-stop shop where I read off the list and the shopkeepers packed everything in plastic shopping bags inclusive of beauty and pharmaceutical products. Sabir haggled on the final price, then paid in cash. We then stopped at a scent shop, where perfumes with names like 'Sexy Saeed' or 'Blue Nightingale' were packaged in colourful bottles. I scanned the cellophane-wrapped boxes. If I had money I would buy Jasmin Noir for Bilqees, the Taliban widow who called me softheaded and brought bad luck to her husbands. I sat down on one of the restaurant benches that overlooked the village square.

It was a small town with a mosque, phone shops, pharmacy and a supermarket. On the far side of the gravel road were long steel girders and labourers who were mixing cement. A billboard advertised money transactions through a national bank. A man in an embroidered cap had erected a wooden plank under the shade of the billboard across from the restaurant. It had coloured balloons in rows that looked like inflated condoms. He offered an air rifle to passersby for target practice.

'Here is your chance to show your marksmanship,' I said to Tariq. He ran up to Sabir to ask him for money. They argued briefly but Sabir was in a good mood and paid the vendor.

'Who goes first?' the vendor asked.

Sabir took the gun and dropped down on his right knee. He then peered at the target with his good eye and fired. He got all three that they had agreed upon. He handed the rifle to Tariq.

The boy loaded the pellet and shot the gun. He got only one, and handed the gun to me.

I aimed and hit a white balloon, then a yellow one, but I missed my third shot on purpose.

'In the land of the blind, the one-eyed man is king,' I said. 'You win, Sabir.'

'Let me try as well,' said Badar. Other fighters accompanied him to the town area. The town folk stopped what they were doing and stared at the battle-hardened, longhaired band of Uzbeks.

Badar grabbed the air gun and fired without getting down on his knees to the level of the rows of balloons. He fired twice but missed both times. His companion whispered to Badar, who cocked the AK-47 that slung from his shoulder. The vendor stepped back and we braced ourselves for a volley of shots.

'Commander Badar,' Sabir said. 'Have food with us.'

The waiter from the restaurant placed a plate of grilled bits of lamb on bones on the table.

Badar laughed and threw the offending air rifle to the vendor, who caught it, picked up his board and walked away quickly.

'I am a rocket specialist. I can't aim with a small gun.' Badar sat down and ate up the *tikka boti* in rapid succession.

'The barrel was probably bent,' Sabir said.

His men ordered more food and gathered around exchanging war stories.

'I have fought in five *tans* – Chechistan, Dagestan, Uzbekistan, Afghanistan and Pakistan.'

Someone asked him if he had killed an American. He opened a flap pocket on his jacket and took out a plastic card.

'Here is a blood chit from an American soldier,' Badar said.

The card was passed around. Everyone looked at it, but I passed it on without a glance.

'Do you not want to see the blood chit?' asked one of the Uzbeks who noticed this.

'I have seen him execute.' I wanted to add 'unarmed men', but didn't.

'Wallah, it is not an easy job. To be an executioner, I must have a strong heart, and show no mercy. Because if I falter, my hand trembles, it will be sloppy and the victim will suffer. It is not my job to make anyone suffer,' Badar said. 'Only Allah can cause suffering.'

I bit my tongue, literally.

*

After Eid prayers, Mullah Nazeer slaughtered a fat, fluffy sheep. Other commanders followed with enthusiastic slaughtering and the sheds reeked of intestines and blood. The day was spent cleaning the meat and preparing the meal. Everyone helped as more fighters arrived. At *maghrib*, a bonfire was lit in the clearing and charcoal grills were placed at the back. Some fighters performed the *attan* dance accompanied by clapping and shouts but no music. The feasting was jubilant with roasted sheep, grilled meats, mounds of rice, and rich *halwa*. After the food, Mullah Nazeer greeted all the commanders who sat around the fire in their *pakols* and heavy shawls. I sat in the back with the seminary students. Conversation started with a series of questions posed to the mullah. Mullah Nazeer articulated his response on the Pashtun destiny.

'War is Afghanistan's holy burden. We are destroyers of empires, and this land is the graveyard for the British, Soviet and American empire. We fight for *azaadi* and our religion allows it. This is the holiest of all wars – a generational war where the opportunity to fight evil is clearly defined.'

There were murmurs of approval.

'Did we oppress the Americans, enslave them, kill their children and destroy their homes? They and their puppets are like the pharaohs and they will be destroyed. Who knows the difference between a Muslim and a Mu'min?'

'A Muslim prays five times. A Mu'min fights,' a man said from the back.

'Mu'mins are those who have taken *shahadat* and are martyred. A true warrior possesses *firasah* – that is what we achieve. But only if we can escape the deception of Dajjal that keeps us tied to this world. This world is finite. The West says you only live once, but Mu'mins say that we will live again, though we die only once.'

The fire crackled; it was a clear night with an almost full moon. When I was a child my grandmother told me that if one observed the moon carefully, we could see an old woman

161

knitting on a spindle. I could see her today, except now I knew that her features were just craters on the lunar landscape.

'Master, please tell us about paradise,' Sabir requested.

'You all know what pleasures await Mu'mins. Janna is filled with beautiful women with fair skin, long eyelashes, slender limbs, and fruitful bodies that are clean of sin. And you are at will to do whatever you desire.

'Today you think of women like these Indian and American *filmi* prostitutes. They are nothing compared to what you will have in heaven and you can sleep with them with the stamina of forty men. One after another.'

Some boys giggled. Others shifted uncomfortably in their shalwars.

'But before all this we need true faith to release us from worldly attachments to all that is material. Mu'mins live in this world, only to prove their worthiness to their creator, *Allah Subhanahu Wa Ta'ala.*'

He recited more verses in Arabic.

'Before the Last Hour, there will be great liars, so beware of them. When the most wicked member of a tribe becomes its ruler, and the most cruel member of a community becomes its leader, and a man is respected through fear of his evil.'

'Who is the wickedest of them all?' asked someone from the dark. The voice sounded like Hukum Khan's and my ears pricked up.

There were many shouts. Zardari, Karzai, Kiyani. Far away, jackals howled in the hills.

'Do you hear the call of the jackals? They will scream for mercy in the Almighty's court. May Allah guide us,' Mullah Nazeer said.

The fighters scattered into smaller groups. Mullah Nazeer remained in conversation. I saw Hukum Khan's turban in the dark. He was talking to a fighter who wore a flak jacket and a *pakol* cap. I said my salaams to other students until Hukum Khan noticed. He finished his conversation and I grabbed his right hand and greeted him as an old friend.

162

'Syed Qais. You are looking better. Walk with me,' he said. He took out a pack of cigarettes and offered it to me. I took one and he lit it for me. I made casual conversation about his health. He nodded and smiled but looked worried.

'How is your struggle?' I asked.

'It goes,' he said.

'Do you agree that it is the Pashtun's burden to continuously fight holy wars?'

Hukum Khan stopped at the edge of the cliff. The valley below was dark and silent. Far away I could see dull flashes in the night. It felt like shelling.

'I have seen too much war. I pray to Allah to lift this blessing and let us have peace.'

'How is Malik Awan?'

'He passed away,' he said. 'Saif's death was too much for him.'

'I am sorry if I caused him grief. How is Ruqiya Bibi?'

'She is in Islamabad. I don't blame you. She made her own decisions to leave her home.'

I waited a few minutes. The starlight was bright and a satellite moved across the sky.

'What about my status, Khan *sahab*? I am still an unfortunate civilian caught in this mess.'

Hukum stubbed his cigarette out with his sandal. 'Are you not comfortable here?'

'I am, but this is not home.'

'We never reached agreement with your contacts.'

'You were asking for too much money. Did you talk to Major Bhatti?'

'You should not put your hopes on him. He is the one who handed you over and made a deal for his life,' Hukum said. His gold tooth glittered in the flames of the bonfire.

A few seconds passed. I forced a laugh to cover my confusion.

'You did not know that, did you?' he said. 'You made a deal with the jackal. The Major lied to you and us. You are not worth a ransom. Nobody wants to pay for you. Nobody misses you. Including Miss Sonia – she does not even return our calls. We

163

believe your family has been taken care of by the insurance people.'

'What does that mean? They don't know that I am dead.' I did not want this to be true. What about Shereen? She had already lost her mother and now she was all alone.

'It's easy to convince the police. A disfigured body with your ID was all they needed.'

I looked away, perhaps to hide the tears. He put his hand on my shoulder.

'You belong here now. This is the life Allah has chosen for you. Be content.'

16
You Only Die Once

By mid-November there was snow on the mountains and the weather turned dry and cold. The fighters left to be with their families in their native villages or in big city neighbourhoods like Sohrab Goth and Karachi Company. The strategists stayed behind to plan next year's spring offences and so the coded letters continued, as did the magazine publishing and other outreach efforts. I had been a guest of the Taliban for over two months and I could now speak, eat and sleep with them – but I still lived every day in hope of being rescued.

Not all fighters had left. Sabir and Tariq had stayed behind. They were not bad company; Sabir had done his matriculation but he was ignorant of history, geography and logic, yet he argued constantly. Usually it would centre on the common grievances of the Muslim *ummah*, the loss of caliphate, the Balfour Agreement, the State of Israel and the loss of Jerusalem. The world conspired against Muslims and they were weak because they had lost their way and did not practise sharia. I offered Saudi Arabia as a functioning sharia state.

'That is true,' Sabir said.

'But you agree that their princes are corrupt.'

'It is a big country, there are good and bad princes. Not all fingers of the hand are equal,' Sabir held up two fingers and a thumb. He had lost the two little ones in a mishap. I laughed.

'Why do you laugh?'

'Your fingers look equal. With apologies, I don't make fun of it,' I said.

We all chuckled then. I told him I had been to Saudi Arabia for *umra*.

'You did not do *hajj*?' he asked.

'I was young, maybe only the same age as Tariq,' I said.

'You are a lucky man to go that far.'

'It's close to Pakistan.'

'How can that be?' Tariq asked. 'It's above Europe.'

'No, not at all.' I drew a map on a piece of paper from my notebook. I pencilled in latitudes and longitudes and labelled the countries.

'This is Europe, and America, and here is Asia with India, China, Iran and Saudi Arabia. Here is Pakistan and Afghanistan.' I shaded the area. 'And we are here in Waziristan, right?'

Tariq ignored the question and pointed the muzzle of a rifle at the map.

'America has an ocean, and even India, Saudi, Iran, Pakistan, but no ocean for us? *Afghanistan bandh hai*. From all corners, surrounded by enemies. Not fair,' he said.

'Mongolia is land-bound but Ghengis Khan conquered the world,' I told him.

'But he was an infidel and killed Muslims,' Sabir said. 'Bad example, like my fingers.'

'Our Prophet, peace be upon him, is the best example,' Tariq said.

'Yes, of course. He loved everyone. Men,' I paused. 'And women.'

'What do you mean by that?' Sabir questioned.

'Well, he married eleven times, so he must have liked women. He had a daughter – Fatima. I too have a daughter and she is studying to be an engineer.'

166

'If my daughter wanted to study, I would forbid it,' Tariq said.

I asked him if he had ever gone to school.

'For two months only. I couldn't handle it.'

'Better for a gun. He is a soldier. Some day he will be a great martyr,' said Sabir.

'Sabir, Gul Khanum wants you,' Zain called out from afar.

Sabir got up sheepishly. 'I must go and help with errands,' he said.

'He is turning into a woman himself,' Tariq whispered as Sabir walked away.

*

With the fighters gone, the women had relaxed and walked around the compound with more confidence. They freely asked Sabir *bhai* for help with the domestic chores. I would watch them solemnly and exchange greetings with them, but they ignored me. In the afternoon, they would walk down into the valley to collect firewood and pinecones. I had learned to recognise them in their burqas, especially Gul Khanum and Bilqees, the Taliban widow. It had become an obsession for me to find out what she really looked like and I would find excuses to sit at the ledge with Zain and wait for their return. Usually she was accompanied by other women but often she straggled behind.

One afternoon as I sat there humming a tune, I saw Bilqees climbing up alone. When she came within an audible distance, I greeted her by name.

'How did you know me?' She slowed to catch her breath.

'Your burqa is different. It has flower buds on the trim.'

'You should not look at women like that. That is not the way of a good Muslim.'

'If I don't ever look at women, how will I find a wife? I have no elders here. Only me to take care of myself,' I said.

She took a yellow-sleeved hand out and uncovered her face. It was a pleasant face, oval in shape and fair in colour, with small eyes and fine eyebrows.

167

'You think I am stupid,' she said. 'I know men and their tricks.'

'No tricks. I like you.'

'What good is that?' She clasped the cloth between her teeth so it half covered her face. I noticed a black tattoo on the top of her hand that looked like a candelabra.

'Is that the last of the pinecones?' I asked, continuing in Dari.

'Yes. Season is done,' she replied in Urdu.

'Where did you learn Urdu?'

'Hindi movies.' She walked past. 'You are from Karachi?'

The climb in the cold had brought colour to her cheeks, and her lower lip quivered as she spoke. She could not have been older than thirty.

'Yes, a long way from home. A poor man trapped here,' I said.

'You don't look poor.'

'How can you tell?'

'You have a white beard but good teeth. You must have been rich once,' she said.

She then covered her face and spoke sharply to Zain. Then she walked away with the basket. I finished humming the Kishore song. I had not felt this upbeat for months.

*

Zain and I spent more time on the ledge but I did not get a chance to talk to Bilqees as it had gotten colder. He had taken a liking to me and we spent time singing or playing childish games. One evening we were balancing flat pebbles on top of each other when I heard Mullah Nazeer calling out to him. I immediately stepped back and stood to attention.

'Continue. Nothing wrong with playtime,' Mullah Nazeer said.

I placed another pebble on top. It was Zain's turn and he set the next one carefully. I placed another one but on the next one the pile fell down and he laughed. It was a clear, carefree laugh that echoed through the valley.

'What I admire about these loafers is their youth.' Mullah Nazeer handed a hashish strip wrapped in cellophane to Zain.

168

'I established this madrasa so that I could remain close to their innocence. I left my hometown when the first call for jihad came during the Russian war. I fought with Ismail Khan of Herat. But after that war I found out that city life was not for me and I established this school near the graveyard of my commander.'

'You have been a warrior all your life?' I asked.

'One would not have thought so. I was born to an old couple, thin and disease prone, but I survived many wars and calamities.'

The boy stuck a matchstick in the pellet of hashish and roasted it in the steady flame of a lighter. He then ground the mixture in his palms and forced it into an empty cigarette. He could have been cast in a Lulu biscuits advertisement, but here he was rolling joints in Waziristan.

'They all make wars in their own way. The Soviet did not understand our country and the Americans think too much. Like you.'

'I am of little use here,' I said.

Zain handed the tightly rolled joint to Mullah Nazeer.

'You have a good mind we can use for jihad,' he said, coating the joint with saliva.

'Don't you think we have enough warriors here?' I said.

'Never enough. I sired two sons. But lost both as martyrs,' Mullah Nazeer said.

'And your wife?'

'One died from a disease. Then I married a widow,' he said and lit the joint.

I praised him for following the *sunnat* of the Prophet. He liked that and we looked at hawks catching up-draughts over the distant hills. The joint was passed.

'You too can marry a widow. Your sons could be mujahids,' he said. 'Maybe a woman from our family?'

I coughed. Was this a trap? Had my talks with Bilqees come to his knowledge? My intentions were never that serious but I had to take this opportunity.

I looked at Zain. He winked. I cleared my throat.

169

'Maybe a widow like Bilqees.'

'How do you know her?' Mullah Nazeer said sharply.

'Just what Zain had mentioned. That she is a widow and brings bad luck to her husbands. I only have good intentions,' I said.

'What nonsense. She is a widow of two martyrs. It might be a good match. After all, you are of good stock. Not a pathan but still fair for a Punjabi,' he said.

'How can I even attempt such a thing?' I moved closer to him.

'You pay to make her yours. She was married to Nooruddin for two lakh rupees.'

'But I have no money.'

'It's a future commitment. Once you marry her, you become part of our *biradari* for life. But I am not sure we can trust you yet.'

'Perhaps I could be trusted as a husband,' I said. 'And as a father.'

'Possible. I will consult my *khanum* on this,' he said.

I thought about what this meant – freedom from this passive captivity, a chance to see Shereen and maybe another marriage. It seemed complicated, but I could only hope.

*

Next day after noon prayers, I ran to the ledge. I wanted to see if Bilqees would go down to the valley. It was a clear day and I saw aircraft passing the sky with their jet streams. On the horizon I spotted a lone white drone. It flew towards the ridge and hovered low, and I heard its motor puttering like motorcycles in the skies.

The drone circled slowly into tighter circles and was joined by another. I became uneasy and was walking back towards the buildings when the gate opened and three Toyota pickups entered in a swirling dust cloud. Fighters stepped out, brandishing weapons and white flags. It was the Asad brigade led by Badar and his Uzbeks. I heard them shouting commands.

'The *bangana* struck the compound at Spinzada,' I overheard.

'Did they kill him?' Sabir asked.

'It was a cowardly thing to do. Many brave fighters were martyred,' Badar replied.

'We don't know, we left as soon as we could,' another fighter said.

'So you came here to put us all in danger,' Sabir said.

'They will not hit this compound, you have women and children here,' Badar said.

'Nothing to do now. Just mingle with everyone else,' Mullah Nazeer instructed and went into the *zenana*. '*Khanum*, come out. I need to talk to you.'

Two fighters climbed to the roof to keep a lookout. The men were nervous and agitated. They had no weapons that could counter an imminent strike. Another drone appeared from the western horizon. There were now three drones circling the valley.

An hour passed. It was around 3pm and everyone kept their eye on the drones: my neck was hurting from watching them and their aerial manoeuvers. Sensing somebody behind me, I turned to find Zain motioning towards the valley. I followed him to the ledge and saw a dozen burqas climbing down the trail. They were led by Mullah's Khanum.

We were halfway down when I heard a loud boom. Someone had fired an RPG at a drone but it did not even reach the height of the deadly thing.

'It has fired!' I heard a shout. Two white jet streams left the drones. There were more shouts. They fired more rockets and their Kalashnikovs. I heard a loud roar as rocket motors punched through the sky. I ran like an Olympian.

The first explosion was deafening and all subsequent sounds were muffled. A gust of air blasted through the valley and the pressure exploded all around me. I heard a zinging sound that bounced inside my head. The second blast swept a wave of debris, dust, and mortar down the valley. The force of the explosion blasted the concrete; rock and gravel shot outward.

171

Simultaneous explosions merged into a wall of sound. I fell down on my face. Darkness descended in the form of soot and smoke.

I kept down till I felt another body next to mine. It was Zain. I did not hear him but felt his tremors. I recited verses as more explosions shook the ground like the skin of the dhol drum. I counted six explosions. The drone could fire many more missiles. The pilots who flew these machines with joysticks called the targets 'bug splats'. Once their shift was over they would go home and watch *American Idol*.

After a while the explosions stopped and then the screaming started. I eased my grip on the boy. He stood up and looked at the smoke that rolled into the valley like black fog. Zain ran into the black soot. I ran after him.

Haphazard fires burned around the scorched graveyard. There were more explosions from the propane cylinders or perhaps from a weapons cache. The shoebox building burned with black soot and a putrid smell filled the air. It was a smell that can never be forgotten – the stench of roasted human flesh. The ground was littered with bodily debris; an arm here, a head there, a headless corpse elsewhere, a burnt woman with sandaled feet and a half body mangled in broken mortar. It was hard to tell animal remains from human or child from adult.

I stopped looking at the horrors and filed away details that would have been irrelevant to anyone except an insurance surveyor. I had spent twenty years retracing fire claims that had engulfed factories or warehouses and here I was at the scene of an incident as it unfolded. Except Ghazigar was uninsured and the people would not be filing a claim with God or government.

The settlement had forty people and an unknown number of fighters. Some men upturned charred bodies to locate relatives. One man documented the mayhem by making a video on his cellphone. Another man accused him of defiling the dead. Others joined in. An argument began and soon a fight. It was time to leave.

I sprang across rock, rubble, and death. A dead man lay in my path. His finger gripped an SKS rifle. I had not seen him before but I pried loose the rifle and slipped a hand inside his vest. His body was warm but his heart was still. I extracted his wallet and found it filled with rupee notes and an Afghan ID in the name of Jan Muhammad Arish. I pocketed the wallet and ran down the hill holding the rifle like a squash racket. I was back in the game.

A man limped down the path using his rifle as support. I pushed him from behind and he fell down. I kicked the rifle away and faced him.

'Are you going to kill me?' Badar asked. His breathing came in short gasps and his hair was matted with blood.

'You killed Riaz,' I said.

'Who?' His face filled with confusion.

'You cut my friend's throat like a goat and you don't even remember his name!' I screamed at him. My heart was beating furiously. He said nothing.

The rifle felt heavy and potent in my hand. I squeezed the trigger. A burst of bullets went flying over his head into the valley. He rubbed away the blood that trickled down his forehead.

'I told you before, I am an executioner. It is my duty to take lives,' he said. 'Whatever happens, I am bound for heaven. You are a *munafiq*, a man with no morals, a false Syed.'

I fired again. This time the bullets found their mark.

I heard no echoes and felt no guilt. There is no high ground in hell.

17

Once Upon a Time in Waziristan

'Follow me and I will lead you to Pakistan,' I said.

It was high noon and the stragglers of Ghazigar looked bewildered. The drone had destroyed the village, mosque, and the graveyard of the mujahideens. Mullah Nazeer was dead, as were his kin and students. But I was free with a rifle in my hand and a spring in my step.

'Why should we follow you?' Tariq questioned. He had lost his gun and cap.

Every moment was precious. I looked up at the sky. I had read that drone pilots frequently targeted the rescue teams. They called it double tapping. I did not feel like being tapped even once.

A woman's scream brought my gaze back to land. I saw Tariq sliding down loose scree and falling headfirst. I followed him down quickly and grabbed him by the shoulder and turned him over. His face was covered in blood and dust.

'You need medical care,' I said. He ignored my remark and waved for others to climb down. Gunshots echoed through the valley. A fight was breaking out. One man, whom I recognized as a Talib from Ghazigar, walked towards me.

'Stay back,' I warned, and cocked the SKS rifle and pointed it at him. He kept walking in a daze and I fired a shot. He stopped with a look of surprise on his face. I wondered if he had seen me shoot Badar in cold blood.

'Who has a gun?' I asked, pointing the SKS at the stragglers. I asked the men to raise their hands. There were four men, five women including Bilqees, and five children. I ordered them to go down the trail.

'There will be angry men coming. You better hurry, Punjabi,' said a man as he passed.

We walked a few kilometres through the fields before the valley narrowed and the tract turned into a forest bordered by a stream. We took a break and drank water and washed ourselves.

Tariq sat on a boulder. I waved to him. He leaned forward and toppled over.

'Idiot.' I balanced the rifle against a tree and walked across. I rolled him over and saw that he had passed out. I was not a medic but I could tell that he had a concussion.

'Tariq, *beta*, wake up,' I said.

There was no response and I yelled out to the men for help.

We dragged him to the streambed. His face was swollen and the crown of his head was damp. I soaked my turban in water and put it on his forehead.

The roar of vehicles filled the forest. We all froze and waited until the motors were turned off. The villagers fidgeted as doors slammed and men trampled through the brush.

'Get down on your knees.' The command was followed by a volley of shots. The zinging sound from the missile strikes was still trapped in my head. I cursed under my breath.

The adults gathered around the cowering children. I tied the turban around Tariq's head before kneeling down. Men in camouflage jackets broke through the brush. They checked everyone for weapons, including the women. Once they had verified that we were unarmed, the leader uncovered his face.

175

He was dark for a Pashtun and had a thick moustache and hazel eyes.

'All clear, Captain Haider.' He waved at the men who stood on the ridge. They were tall and had scarves wrapped around their faces. The stragglers murmured. The soldiers conducted a perimeter check and found the SKS rifle.

'We need food and water, we have not eaten for days,' someone said.

'Whose rifle is this?' shouted the dark Afghan.

Nobody said a word. He asked again. One of the stragglers pointed in my direction.

'The Punjabi's,' he said slowly.

All eyes turned on me. I still held Tariq in my arms. The two foreigners descended through the brush. They weren't fast but they were deliberate. One of them was a white American and the other was dark like an African. The white American stopped a foot away from me and took off his sunglasses, revealing striking blue eyes. He had close-cropped fair hair and wore body armour over his shalwar suit. He said something to his companion in English.

'This is our follow-up?' the African replied as they walked over to where I was standing. He was even taller and his body armour made him look like a WWF wrestler.

'How the fuck would I know,' said the other American. 'I guess it is time for us to exploit and analyse.'

'You. Are you Punjabi?' he asked in Dari. His gun held at waist level.

'I am a businessman from Karachi,' I said in English. 'I was kidnapped by the Taliban and held for ransom.' I pointed towards Ghazigar.

The blue eyes stared back. He did not understand my accent. I said the same, slower and with better enunciation.

'Is that your rifle?'

'I just picked it up. I am a civilian.'

'A civilian with a gun,' said the dark militiaman who was now standing next to the American.' You have ID?'

I took out the ID and handed it over. My hearing was still damaged.

'How long were you imprisoned?' the fair man asked.

'This is not your ID,' the dark militiaman said.

'My name is Qais. I was kidnapped in September,' I said.

The sound of a helicopter made everyone look at the sky. The dark Afghan militiaman threw the ID on the ground and retreated under the canopy of trees with other soldiers. They stood a few feet away and talked in military jargon. I picked up enough to understand that this was a covert mission. The helicopter circled around but never came into view. Eventually, the sound drifted away. I picked up the ID and put it inside my pocket.

The Americans regrouped and gave orders to the other soldiers. I had a lot more to say.

'Excuse me, are you an American marine?'

The dark Afghan stepped in my path. His face was inches away and his eyes were bloodshot. He grinned like a baddie from a spaghetti western.

'*Kya hai*? What was that?' he said with a chin jerk, speaking Urdu like a Karachi gangster. The rifle's stock dug into my stomach.

'I talked to him,' I said.

He elbowed my stomach. My knees buckled and he swung the rifle. My shoulder took the hit. I fell like a tree on my face. He pressed his knee into the small of my back and slipped plastic handcuffs onto my wrists. His mouth smelled like a latrine. I heard shouts as I spat out dirt. The handcuffs cut my wrists and made my fingers immobile.

'Pasha, this one can't even stand up,' said a tall militiaman. He prodded my groin with his boot. I rolled over and found a tree to lean against and stood up. I felt angry and humiliated. I had had a gun and a chance to run away, but I got caught. This time by Americans sent to kill Pakistanis. Fuck my luck.

'Let's go,' said the darker militiaman named Pasha.

It was hard going up the path with my hands tied behind. The trail was through thorny trees and foliage. I was lashed by

177

branches that others cleared out of their way. Blood trickled from my forehead into my eyes and cobwebs clung to my beard. I could not see and eventually yelled out to Tariq. I got no response. Then I called Bilqees.

'You want me to carry you, Punjabi?' She slowed down.

'I can't see. Please clean the cobwebs off my face,' I said.

She took a sharp breath but then reached over to clear my face. Her dry palms scrubbed my cheeks as her fingers parsed my beard. She even cleared the cobwebs from my eyelids. I felt blood rushing down my torso. The surprise on my face made her look down.

She stepped back. I blushed, ashamed of this unexpected arousal.

'What's going on?' yelled Pasha.

'Cut his hands loose, he can't make his way through the bushes,' she said.

'Hurry or I will leave you with your *majnu*,' he said.

'He is not my lover.' She moved ahead as she clutched the burqa's front pleats in her hand. I followed her with a persistent stir in my loins. A short climb and we were on flat ground where two commercial pickup trucks were parked. They had Pakistani licence-plates. The soldiers regrouped.

'What are they saying?' Bilqees asked me.

'I can't hear them,' I said.

'The children can't survive the jungle at night. It is freezing and we have no provisions. We are thirsty and hungry,' one man said to the soldiers.

'He is right. Give us something to eat and drink,' said another man.

There were more consultations. I was separated from the group and the blond American gave orders for the tribesmen to be loaded up into the vehicles.

'We will drop you on the other side of the valley, near the high village. After that you are on your own,' said the tall militiaman, chewing a matchstick between his teeth.

178

There was a mad scramble as the women moved toward the vehicles. The children followed. I saw Zain get in with Gul Khanum and Bilqees. I was glad that the women had survived.

'Take him as well, he needs medical care.' I pointed to Tariq.

'I am fine,' Tariq slurred but nobody listened, and the men helped him into the vehicle.

The loud racket of a whirring helicopter was heard in the valley. The sky was still lit but the light was fading fast.

'It's the opposition,' said the black American. 'Get under the canopy.'

The helicopter did a final sweep and flew away to the mountains. The vehicles left, leaving me with the Americans and Pasha.

The four of us hiked up spindly ridges that cut through the mountain range. Its trails spread outward like spider legs into deep ravines. The Americans led the way, pointing with their halogen flashlights as we skirted gravelly trails and large boulders. It was a steep incline but I used my thighs wisely. It gave me pleasure to see Pasha breathing hard. It was a moonless night and the wailing wind and the howling jackals made the supernatural seem ever present. But the devil is the last thing you fear when crossing the Pakistan-Afghanistan border.

Somewhere, a phone vibrated.

'Fuck,' said the African militiaman.

'Congratulations, motherfuckers! We are in range of Afghan telcos. Whoa!' said the blond American.

I saw his shadow slip on the scree. His hand grabbed at my shalwar. I held my ground, sinking low to plant my feet.

'I can't hold on much longer!' I yelled.

'Hold on, Jack, I am coming,' said the African. He grabbed me first and pulled me back along with the fair-haired American. I fell on the ground and caught my breath. The man named Jack fell beside me and breathed deeply. That made him mortal.

Nobody said a word as we rested. Then Jack stood up and touched my shoulder.

'Thanks,' he said.

'I was just saving my shalwar,' I said with a smile.

He motioned for me to turn. I did, and he cut off the plastic handcuffs.

We continued hiking for twenty more minutes until we came up to a crude campsite. Jack posted a lookout and fell asleep between the gravel and the boulders. I did not sleep long as the ground was cold. I woke up at first light with aches and an urgent need to go to the toilet.

'Do it behind the boulder,' said Pasha.

I did my business and returned to see the two Americans sprawled on the ground, overlooking the valley that led to a dry riverbed. I climbed down and heard an angry hiss. I froze.

'I see a muj', one o'clock. Maybe a sheep-herder, but he is dressed in black. You have a clear line of sight,' said the African as he looked through his binoculars.

Jack put a piece of chewing gum in his mouth and looked through his sniper scope. The barrel had a dull metallic finish but the stock was black plastic. Every time his jaw moved to chew, the muzzle twitched with intent along with him.

A few minutes passed and I crouched behind them.

'What are you looking for?' I asked.

'That's Ghulam Khan Kelli,' Jack pointed. 'We will wait until the pass is clear.'

'I see movement over there. They are running quick, not civilians. Two clicks to the right,' said the African.

'I see a rifle, probably an AK. Great for saturating the area with bullets. What will he do?' Jack responded. A bird chirped and a small animal scurried in the sagebrush.

'Wish we could nab the coward.'

'You will never catch a Taliban alive,' Jack said, moving one eye from the rubber socket and wiping his sweaty brow with the side of an index finger.

I watched the black figures as little specks climbed into vehicles and drove away in a dust cloud. Over the horizon I saw a helicopter patrolling the area.

'Those dipshits know they are going to die and they have accepted it,' said the African, putting down the binoculars. He had stripped down to a t-shirt and I stared at his neck muscles and back tattoos, and at a scar on his shaven head that resembled a question mark.

'You know why, because it's better to die in jihad than to continue to get butt-raped by a stinky mullah in a Paki madrasa,' said Jack.

'My winning strategy includes going wherever the enemy is and killing them in their sleep,' said the African.

'That's a fair fight,' Jack laughed.

All three of us returned to the campsite. I walked between them and the African took out his phone. He read a few things and chuckled to himself.

'Hey Cap', do you know why a hipster is like a haji?'

'I can't imagine,' Jack said.

'They both shave their balls but not their faces.' He laughed at his own joke.

At the campsite, Pasha had made a hot meal without a fire and poured sticky porridge into tin cups. Jack took one cup and ate with a spoon. Pasha handed me a cup but no spoon. I was starving and scooped with my fingers.

'You should wash your hands before eating,' Jack said.

'I have no spoon,' I said. To think that a foreigner would lecture a Muslim Syed on cleanliness was embarrassing. But I was starving and wiped the bowl clean.

'Keep it. That's yours,' he said, packing brown powder into a glass jar. All his actions were slow and deliberate.

'Are you a marine?' I asked.

'Nope.' He poured hot water into the contraption and kept it on the ground. Then he took out a yellow cigarette pack from his pocket. He opened the pack and carefully took a cigarette out and lit it. I followed the action until he blew out the smoke. He then offered me one.

'Thank you. Are you a Green Beret?'

He looked at me curiously.

181

'I have seen many movies about special forces, like *Rambo* and Chuck Norris's movies,' I added.

'I am a ranger.'

'And the African?' I said. The cigarette was densely packed and hard to smoke.

'He is not African. He is American and his name is Wade. He is my spotter,' Jack said with a frown.

'Sorry, I was not sure how to describe him other than African or black.'

'Just stop. What's your name?'

'Qais, but my friends call me Cash.'

'Where did you say you were from?' He pushed the metal down and the muddy water flowed up the cylinder. He poured himself a cup. He did not offer me one.

'I am a surveyor and was kidnapped by the Taliban. My family could not afford ransom, so I was imprisoned for a long time,' I said.

'A surveyor?'

'Insurance loss adjuster.'

'Like in *Double Indemnity*,' he said. Wade emerged from behind a boulder.

'You know insurance?' I said with a smile.

His mouth parted in a self-assured sneer. In daylight, without his sunglasses and helmet, he looked young. He was probably twenty-five, but he had the confidence of a man who could and had done many impossible things in life.

'I am a family man with a daughter,' I said. 'Are you married?'

'Hell no, I haven't met the right stripper yet,' he said. 'Let's get moving.'

We moved down the ridge with Pasha leading the way this time. The warmth spread through my body and I followed. He had seen me talk to Jack and asked me about the conversation.

'What did you talk about?' Pasha enquired as I lowered myself down using a boulder.

'Just an introduction. He told me his name is Jack.'

'We call him Captain Haider. That's what you should call him.'

182

'Why do you call him that?'

'You listen to me, I am the one responsible for you. What is your real name?'

'My name is Qais Qureshi.' I told him a quick version of my ordeal as I followed him down the slope. We came upon a clearing and found a mud house built into the side of the cliff. The outer wall was pockmarked with bullet and mortar rounds. The two pickup trucks that had left us last night were parked here. There was camouflage netting all over the clearing.

I heard barking and two large German Shepherd dogs came running towards us. They jumped up in joy on seeing Jack and Wade. These dogs were large – with heads as big as my own and fitted with four-inch canine teeth.

'Don't be afraid, but stay very still,' Pasha instructed, although he too was uncomfortable.

I stood still as the first dog gave me a sniff and thrust his nose into my crotch. My balls were inches away from his nose and it took a lot of self-control not to run. For the second time in twenty-four hours I wished I had worn underwear.

'Damien, Shadow. Here,' Wade called. The dogs ran back into the house.

It was dark inside the cottage, with slants of light cutting through boarded windows. Up a narrow staircase on the top floor was a room with a TV, gaming consoles and plastic chairs. There were a few more Americans and ferocious dogs in that room. They greeted each other gruffly but cooed to their dogs with variations of baby, booboo and baba that would have made Elvis proud.

'Hey Captain Starfucker, you still wearing the mandress?' said a lanky red-faced American. He had thinning, long fair hair and wore a camouflaged but nondescript uniform.

'Jared, did you get lost in a war zone? I thought you would be back at Khost,' Jack said.

The men took off their body armour and were soon in their boxer shorts. They had smooth hairless skin adorned with tattoos and some freckles. The soldiers talked like they did in

Hollywood movies, exchanging insults and jokes. They did not talk of missions but argued about sports and music or preferred brands of shoes and sunglasses. Not once was religion or politics mentioned. Neither did they talk of their families.

A little while later, Pasha came up and asked me to follow him downstairs. This is where the militiamen had made camp. I heard the chatter of children and women as we descended. My spirits lifted at the thought of seeing Bilqees again. Others things rose as well. I was ecstatic and embarrassed.

'Are they here – the women and children?' I asked Pasha.

He pointed to a corner where Tariq lay, curled up. His face looked flushed and I could tell that he had been beaten. I walked over to him.

'What happened?' I asked.

Tariq turned his head away. I felt it and found it bloody from the wound.

'What did he do to you?' I yelled in Urdu.

'I fight Taliban and this one is a Taliban,' Pasha replied and kicked Tariq.

'Don't do that,' I glared at Pasha. I was not frightened, which was strange.

He laughed out loud and called Tariq *kuni* – slang for sex slave.

The call to prayer played from a cellphone and the Afghans filed away to start a *jammat*.

'You can't pray with them. They are all Shias,' Tariq mumbled.

'Prayer is prayer,' I said.

'*Munafiq*,' he said, but then his eyelids drooped and he fell asleep.

They prayed with their hands to their sides and I followed the style. It made the militiamen feel at ease. They invited me to join them for food. Pasha smoked hashish and spoke in Urdu.

'He is a Karachiwala, not one of those stinky Taliban. They kidnapped him. He runs a business.' Pasha spoke on my behalf.

The other militiaman questioned me about my faith and family. They were Turi tribesmen, all Shia who had been

184

fighting Taliban for many years with or without the Pak army. But Pasha himself was not Turi, he was an Ismaili from Baghlan in Afghanistan. He had spent five years living in Karachi.

'You can get *charas*, *sharaab*, boy or girl, everything is available in Karachi for everyone. You don't have to be rich to enjoy life. I drove a taxi in Karachi. From airport to Defence and Kharadar,' he said. 'Do you drink?'

I shrugged my shoulders and he got up enthusiastically and returned with a can of vodka which had an emblem of a red rooster. He poured it into a plastic cup.

'You like the red cock?'

I told him that the red cock was delicious. There was a commotion outside.

'What's going on?' I asked.

An Afghan entered the room. He had a cleft lip that he covered with a thick moustache.

'That lady wants to see if you are okay,' he said, gesturing to me.

'What lady?' Pasha asked.

'The one from the Taliban village,' he answered. It had to be Bilqees.

'Let me talk to her. She is worried,' I said.

'Sit down. You Karachiwalas always run after women. Learn to be a man,' Pasha said.

The conscript went outside. More arguments in Dari followed and a burqa-clad figure peeked inside. Her face was unveiled but covered in dust.

'Is she your wife?' Pasha asked me.

'No, but we were almost married,' I said.

'At your age?' he laughed. 'Go and talk if you must.'

I walked to the door. My leg was stiff from sitting on the floor and I had red cock breath.

'You want something?' I asked softly.

'Yes,' she said. Her cheeks were red from exertion. 'Is Tariq okay?'

'Yes, he is sleeping in a corner.'

'You drink with that man? I thought you were a good Muslim,' she said with a frown.

Pasha yelled. 'Qais *bhai*, come here – there are more things to talk about.'

'I will see you later,' I said to her. 'I will be fine. Go back and rest.'

I spent the night sipping vodka and listening to Pasha.

'Once upon a time, I wanted to get married. But I have bad luck. Every time life starts to get on track, bad things happen. When I was young the Taliban murdered my parents and younger sisters, nine people in all. I was serving with the Afghan army when I heard the news. They burned the house down. Our things were looted – just because we were Ismailis. We grew up together and still they had no remorse.'

'I am sorry to hear that. When was that?'

'That was ten years ago. I killed those Taliban with my bare hands. I throttled two with no weapons. See?' He stretched his fingers out. They were big brutish hands with no hair.

'I escaped to Karachi and led a good life. I even met a nice Agha Khani girl. You might laugh today, but she loved me,' he said.

'What happened?' I lay down, keeping Tariq against the wall, away from Pasha.

'The Taliban found me. Karachi is full of their spies. There was an attempt on my life. I had to leave in a hurry. I joined the Milli Ordu, the national army. Last year, Captain Haider asked me to join his secret team, they call it a task force. It is a great honour. We get special orders from Washington on where to go and whom to capture to kill. Doesn't matter where it is, we can cross borders without even the NATO knowing about it. I am valuable to him as I know Urdu and have a Pakistani ID. He is a good man, even saved my life once.'

'How did he do that?' I asked, yawning.

'It was an ambush. I got stuck in a Humvee and he got me out, cutting the seatbelt. I asked him why and he said, "Rangers never leave a warrior behind".'

186

I was dozing off but kept asking questions, hoping he would fall asleep.

'What do you do for him?'

'The only thing I am good at. Kill.'

'So who did you come to kill at Ghazigar?'

He fell silent. I thought he had fallen asleep but he then continued.

'We came to confirm the drone strike and capture any information on the fighters. Kill any that survived. We have a kill list for some people who were at that place.'

'You have killed many Taliban?'

'I killed for *badla*, and my family's honour. But now it is different. I slice their throats as they sleep next to their wives.' He ran a finger over his own throat. 'Sometimes their babies are sleeping between them. I am out before the baby wakes up. But sometimes, bad things happen. Sometimes babies wake up. Sometimes they cry.'

He turned away on his side.

'I tell you Qais *bhai*, I am not a good man. You believe me?'

I believed him. I had met several sociopaths socially in the last few months. That is what a war zone is – a place for sociopaths to be social.

18
No Man's Land

'Get up, we are leaving,' Pasha said.

There was a flurry of activity. Men were on their feet, equipment was being packed and papers were being burned. I had no effects other than the stolen ID. I was the first one out and sat on the hard ground as the vodka swirled in my stomach.

'Hurry up, we have to vacate,' Pasha yelled.

'What's going on?' I asked but got shoved out of the way.

'The Pakistan army is moving in,' Pasha said. 'If they find this outpost they will shoot first and ask questions later.'

'What about us?'

'Wait here until transportation arrives,' said Pasha.

Jack and Wade talked over their communicators. They had their helmet, body armour and battle fatigues on. They were dressed for war.

Two jets screamed towards the eastern mountains. They flew low and the valleys echoed with their sonic booms. I saw the green circle of Pakistan Air Force. One fired a flare. A loud boom shook the ground.

'The *jang* has begun,' Pasha said.

'What war?' I screamed over the sound of shelling. The earth shook beneath our feet and made my heart thump.

'Why is everyone out in the open waiting to be bombed?' I asked.

'This is to show that there are civilians here,' Pasha said, lighting a cigarette.

That was what Mullah Nazeer had said – before Ghazigar was bombed.

For the next hour, we waited in the sun. I picked up tidbits as I overheard conversation from the radio, which was tuned to the BBC Pashto service in the background. American helicopters had attacked a Pakistani army post at Salala ridge. Hundreds of soldiers were dead. All roads were closed and a whole division of the Pakistan army was moving into No Man's Land. The Turi tribesman talked about the Americans crossing the Durand Line. This was the big war everyone was waiting for, to sort this mess out for once and for all.

'But Pakistan can't fight the US,' I said.

I said this a few times but nobody cared. The orphans sat in the dirt. They had spent most of their life waiting.

More war planes flew overhead. An anxious stir spread through my arms and into my fingers. I was having an anxiety attack. I recalled the Shock and Awe campaign on CNN, the green-lit footage, the sirens of ambulances, and the pillars of smoke in Baghdad. What would it be like if they bombed Karachi? How many people would die? Shereen and my mother were there. Everyone I knew was there.

I picked up a pebble and massaged it on my palm. My mother used to tell me stories of the 1971 war when Indian jets bombed Karachi. I was an infant then and she had stuffed cotton in my ears because the jets created sonic booms. My mother told me that my father had cried when the army had surrendered. He would have cried more if he had lived to see Pakistan face this kind of existentialist threat – a conventional war with the Americans.

A boy slapped the neck of his friend. His cap went rolling away. They jumped over each other and rolled around in the dirt until one of the soldiers kicked them.

'What is wrong with you?' Pasha enquired.

'I am worried for Pakistan,' I said.

'You are afraid of one bombing campaign. Afghans have had bombs falling over cities for forty years. All they did was move rubble from one place to another. Don't worry. This is another game by your snake government. They will kill random Shias and go back to their barracks,' Pasha said.

It was dusk by the time the 4x4s arrived. The men quickly changed the Pak plates to Afghan plates. The shelling had now stopped but our eardrums still trembled from the shelling.

'The Pakis ran out of ammunition,' said Jack.

'Don't worry, they will be back in Washington asking for more,' Wade said as the men climbed into the vehicle.

'Where are you going?' I asked.

'We are crossing into Afghanistan,' Jack said.

'Take us with you. I am from there. We don't want to be in Pakistan,' Bilqees said.

'It might be easier with the civilians,' Pasha said.

'Anyone who wants to come with us is welcome. The rest can stay in Pakistan,' Pasha said.

The group with Afghan IDs joined them. I stood there unsure. There are some borders that are never supposed to be crossed and the Pakistan-Afghanistan border was one of them.

'Qais *jaan*, come with us,' Bilqees said. 'You have Afghan ID.'

Jaan is used as a term of friendship in Afghanistan, but on our side of the Indus it is used between lovers. I was falling for her and even her voice made my heart beat faster.

The shelling started again.

'Hell, let's go. No decision is a bad decision,' Wade said.

We climbed onto the pickup trucks and drove down a dirt road without lights in the dark. Once we reached the canyon floor we took a path through the riverbed but found the road blocked by a big boulder.

I heard the hissing sound of a tyre losing air. There were nails on the gravel. The pickups' tyres burst open.

'This is a trap,' Pasha said as the vehicle rims ploughed through the gravel.

'Watch for snipers.' Jack checked coordinates on his GPS device.

A beam of light cut through the darkness. I heard the aerial whistle and then a mortar round exploded ahead. Hot scree flew around as flames lit the canyon.

'Ambush!'

'Back up. Now!'

The vehicle reversed over rocks as multiple blasts echoed in the canyon. An RPG took out the front vehicle and it blazed with yellow flames. The door opened and men scurried out of the hot metal box. One man was on fire and rolled on the ground, but was hit by bullets. Two more came out and ran in opposite directions. That distracted the shooters.

'Get out of the cars. We are sitting targets,' I heard a yell.

I shoved Bilqees out and ran to the side.

Jack rolled out of the pickup and propped himself up on one knee. He fired a short burst from his rifle and then moved across the line of fire on the balls of his feet.

'There are several insurgents up in the hills. They are using Dragunov rifles. They seem to have good aim, so don't take risks,' Jack said. He looked back and then ran across to get a better vantage point.

I saw Tariq crawling on the riverbed. I yelled to him to join us. The militiaman next to him got hit but Tariq survived the hail of bullets.

The vehicle that had gotten struck burned, lighting the valley with an intense yellow glow. The snipers continued taking shots and their tracer bullets arched flat from the walls of the canyon. This was a fire fight where the bullets zipped past silently

191

without the explosive discharge of a rifle fire. It was from the point of view of a target.

'Get to the side of the walls.' Pasha ran to the stuck 4x4, unloading an RPG from the pickup. He was only armed with a Colt automatic.

I fell behind the rocks and yelled to Pasha. He ran towards the sound of my voice. Bullets plopped in the sand by his feet as he came within reach of the overhang. Then I heard a gasp. Pasha looked at his chest to see blood. His expression changed to a grimace and he fell down.

'Call JTAC for air support. We are across the line,' Wade yelled.

He was behind an overturned vehicle. More rockets struck the remaining vehicles. The dry scrub caught fire. A fireball appeared ahead and I was thrown back as shrapnel struck my left shoulder. I crawled behind a boulder and squeezed into a crevice. The shrapnel round burned and I took a handful of cold sand and put it on the wound. I squeezed tight against the rock, away from the fighting. I heard firing, shouting, and cars grinding across the valley floor. I assumed some escaped but I could also hear screams as men burned or bled to death.

It took a while for the screaming to stop. A few minutes passed and I heard a vehicle coming from a side road onto the valley floor. Doors slammed and there were battle cries in Pashto followed by the hissing static of walkie-talkies. I peered out and saw black-clad fighters with bulky flak jackets turning over dead bodies and salvaging weapons in the lights cast by the vehicle. Two fighters dragged a body into the headlights' trajectory. It was stripped of the helmet and protective armour, but Wade's body was easily recognisable. His chin almost touched his chest. A man wearing an armband shot a video as another man fired point-blank into Wade's head. The body did not move, save for the shudder caused by the bullet's force, as life had already left it. The walkie-talkie hissed and the men left as quickly as they came.

Before the sound of their engines had died, more vehicles drove into the canyon from the west. These were more cautious and had searchlights lighting the path ahead. I heard commands given out in Dari on loudspeakers. They waited with their engines running as a helicopter gunship hovered overhead. The men surveyed the battleground and loaded up dead bodies. A few injured survivors were put on stretchers; I heard a woman crying and I wondered if Bilqees had survived. Once finished, the gunship flew away and the vehicles drove off, firing a volley of machine-gun fire.

It took another twenty minutes for the sounds of the thrashing metal, combustion engines and the savagery of war to extinguish itself and give in to nature. I remained still until the silence filled the void and I heard a long moan followed by a wheezing sound. It was horrifying and I knew it was the sound of life leaving a dying body. I did not have the strength to investigate and knew the person was beyond help. The sound continued for a very long time before it died out. I squeezed more deeply into the crevice until I was part of the cold rock. The bright starlight and burns on my shoulder kept me awake for a long time. I saw a shooting star and wished to see my daughter before I died. I fell asleep soon after.

*

I woke up in bright sunlight. Dew covered my eyes and my back was sweating. My first instinct was to find a drink. The smell of gunpowder still lingered in the air. The valley floor was cratered from mortars and the walls were blackened with gunpowder imprints. The burned vehicles still smouldered, as if left as part of a film set, and crows cackled ominously in the background.

I got up and carefully crossed the dry riverbed to the giant boulder. The haunting moaning from last night had come from that direction. I feared the worst as I saw multiple scavengers picking up pieces of remains that could have been plastic or organic. I shooed the crows away from the mass behind the boulder. It was Jack's dead body but the lower half had lost its human configuration and looked like a pulpy mess of trailing

193

intestines. I stared at the grotesque sight when I heard someone behind me. It was Tariq and he was holding his head between his hands.

'I am bleeding,' he whimpered and sat down on the valley floor.

'Is anyone else here?' I called out.

'I am here too.' I heard Bilqees's voice.

I waited for her to come down. Her face was uncovered and she looked flushed but still beautiful. I gave her a broad smile.

'Are you okay?' I asked.

'Yes, but I am very thirsty. Let's find water.'

We searched the burnt vehicles. I found a few water bottles in the back of one and we both drank while I stored away the rest. I gave Tariq some water then went back and looked for other odds and ends in the vehicle but did not find anything except some blankets. I went back to Jack's body and tried to untangle his backpack, which was still attached to him. I shooed the crows and loosened the straps from his body. The smell was noxious. I threw up but nothing came out except bile and the water I had just consumed.

Captain Jack's backpack was Umro Ayaar's *zambeel*. Apart from food supplies, it had gloves, electric lamps, ropes, tourniquets, handcuffs, a sewing kit, a hacksaw, emergency flares, and a medical box. The equipment was worth thousands of dollars in the thieves' market in Karachi. All I had in my possession was a steel mug and the wallet I had taken off the dead man. I thought of Riaz Khan's claim that one American soldier consumes more than a Waziri village.

I ripped open a pack of beef jerky.

'It's halal.' I showed Tariq the mark.

'Why would Americans eat halal?'

'Because it does not bother them if it is *haram* or *halal*. They import one kind.'

'We need to get out of here. Do you know the way?' asked Tariq.

I ignored his question and carried on rummaging through the backpack. The iPhone was locked and I could not get the passcode. In his top pocket I found a set of laminated cards and a flat wallet.

'That's a blood chit,' the boy said. 'There must be money with it.'

The chit had cards with high-minded script in Dari, Pashto, and Urdu with appeals to help Americans. A ziplock bag contained five-hundred dollar bills. I pocketed the money and opened the wallet. It contained credit cards, a driving licence from Maryland and a picture of three teenage boys posing with a bearded man holding a large fish. On the back was written *Pensacola Florida, Oct 1998*. Jack's date of birth was 5 October 1986.

'Are we ready to go?' Bilqees said. Her coarse brown hair shone in the sun and her eyes were bloodshot but she was a lovely sight.

'Yes, soon,' I replied. I wanted to impress her as a good man.

I removed his helmet and the body armour from his upper torso. His skin was smeared with dust and soot but his face was untouched. One eye was still open. I recalled the words from the blood chit, the reward for helping an American soldier and the consequences for killing one.

'We should bury the body.' I closed a cold blue eye.

'Why?' Tariq asked. 'He is American.'

'He was a good man,' I said. 'He deserves to be buried.'

'I hate Americans. They kill thousands of our brothers and leave them to rot and be eaten by jackals and you want to bury his body. Did they bury the bodies of Mullah Nazeer after the drone attack? You are soft in the head,' Tariq said.

His grumbling convinced me further to bury this soldier. I found a flat spot and uprooted and cleared the area using Jack's knife blade. Bilqees used the helmet to carry loose gravel and after a while we had a shallow grave.

It took all my strength to drag Jack's body over. It was a terrible half-assed job but I piled stones on top until it was covered. I placed his helmet on top.

I said words that I recalled from Hollywood movies. Holy Father this, Lord Jesus that. Earth to earth, ashes to ashes, dust to dust. It was mostly wrong but I mumbled on until I ran out of words.

The valley floor reverberated from a loud boom. The sky was filled with aerial explosions that looked like black flowers blooming in the clear bluesky.

'They are shelling again. Let's go before we get caught in the fight,' Tariq said and started walking towards the west.

A helicopter flew overhead followed by a four-engine propeller airplane with large cannons. Both were marked with US Army insignia.

I checked the GPS. It showed the nearest town as Jan Sareh Kalai. I wrote the coordinates on my forearm and picked up Jack's vodka flask and pistol.

'Leave the American things. They will bring trouble,' Bilqees said.

I considered this, took a swig of the vodka and then ejected the bullets from the magazine and placed the empty gun and flask on the unmarked grave.

'Better to trust in Allah.' She clasped my wrist and we walked across No Man's Land into Afghanistan.

19
Angels and Demons

I smelled the watermelons well before I saw the field. The round fruits were placed in the sand like forgotten trophies. I picked one, cut a triangular piece with Jack's knife and tasted the pink flesh. The juice filled my mouth and I cut a full slice, holding it out for Bilqees. She took off her burqa and sat on the sandy field. Even though it was early winter, the sun was fierce and we were thirsty. This appeared to be a safe resting place for us and I fed fruit to Tariq but he could not move his jaw. I squeezed juice into his mouth as drops ran down my arm. I untied his dirty bandages and examined his head.

'What's wrong with him?'

'He might have a concussion,' I said.

'What's that?'

I explained that it was internal bleeding in the head. She asked me if I was a doctor. I said no. She named other professions that she knew of – engineer, farmer and shopkeeper.

'I am a businessman,' I said to keep her from guessing further.

'Better if you were a pilot.'

'We have to find water and medicine for him or he will die.' I retied the dirty bandages.

'There has to be a village nearby. I can ask for help,' Bilqees said.

'I will come with you. Wait.'

'I know this land. It's better if I go alone. I will say I have a sick son and a man with a soft head,' she smiled.

'Why do you keep saying that? What does it mean?'

'A fool with a weak mind can't speak,' she walked away. 'So don't talk to anyone.'

I ate more watermelon while I waited for her. A trail of chubby black ants crawled up my legs and I spat out black seeds for the column. It was a childhood activity from idyllic summers. A shrine attendant whom we called Laal kaka because he dyed his facial hair with henna, told us tales of how my grandfather had solicited the help of djinns during the Partition riots. Rumour had it that the scalps of the enemies were still kept wrapped in the shrine's basement. My cousin and I had once colluded to open a leather-bound trunk we had found there. We had barely lifted the lid when Laal kaka found us out. 'Don't ever touch the dead. You will release the djinns!' he had yelled.

We had been so scared we never mentioned this to anyone. But the memory and the putrid smell of the trunk had left behind a strong impression. It was the scent of death, which I had smelled earlier.

I fell asleep as vultures perched up on the rocks, and woke up to find Bilqees's oval face looking down. I had slept without dreaming.

'I found a settlement. We can take shelter with them,' she said.

'How far is it?' I helped Tariq to his feet.

'Not too far, we can walk. Let me do the talking. I know the Kuchi *zaban*,' she said.

'Are you a Kuchi yourself?'

'Yes.'

'Tell me about your life.'

'I don't want to talk about it. It is not good.'

I persisted and she gave me a short and unemotional account of her life. She identified as a Ghilzai Pashtun from Lashkar

Gah but she grew up in a refugee camp until her uncle adopted her. He had a shop in Herat. Once the Taliban took over, his business was shut down and he was forced to marry off Bilqees to pay his debts. She ended up a widow when her husband died.

'How old were you?' I asked.

'Ten. I stopped going to school, but I can count. Want to hear?'

She counted in Dari and I figured out that she would be at least a dozen years younger than me.

'Do you watch movies at the cinema?' she asked as we came across a ridge that overlooked tracts of tilled farmland.

I nodded and chewed on a twig. I felt for a cigarette but had none.

'What movie did you watch last?'

'*Avatar*,' I said. I had seen it at the Atrium cinema in Karachi. Shereen had loved it.

'What is it about?'

I explained the story and the plot, blue aliens who live in a jungle under threat by greedy corporations. She struggled with the concept and frowned. I stopped and asked her about the last movie she had watched.

'*Khuda Gawah* in Herat. The pictures were big inside the cinema. It made the actors appear like giants. Have you seen *Veer Zara*?' She bit her lip.

'Uh-huh,' I said, wondering how it would be, to bite her lip.

'I saw it but on VCD. It is my wish to see it in the cinema.'

I chuckled out loud. She frowned.

'Did you not like it?'

'It is like any other Bollywood movie. They show Pakistan as imagined by Ibn-e-Safi where everyone wears a sherwani.'

'It is a beautiful movie,' she sighed. 'How long she waited for her man. That kind of love is no more.' Bilqees stopped as we came to a bridge.

A dog barked somewhere and I heard the repeated thuds of a hammer. A face peeked from the rooftop of a farmhouse nearby, a child shouted, the hammering stopped. Goats and children roamed around with cowbells and colourful clothing. It was peaceful except for the farm dog. He was a black brute with a large mastiff-like head and a broad chest.

Bilqees walked to the dog and placed a steady hand on his head. The dog sniffed and then stepped to the side. She crossed the rickety bridge. I took a step forward and the cur growled. I stayed behind, holding Tariq by the shoulder.

We faced a good half an hour of ferocious growling before a boy in a bright blue dress called out to us. The boy gave a command to the dog and he moved aside. We crossed the bridge and went past the outer wall to a large clearing with several thatched huts, a mosque and a few old buses parked beside a forlorn road. Two tribesmen stood with Bilqees; one of them had a dyed red beard. She pointed back and I raised my hand in a universal symbol of a salaam.

'*Walekum salaam*,' I heard from them.

I shook their hands and mouthed a salaam. Bilqees explained Tariq's condition as they loaded sacks onto a Jeep CJ-7 with a Mercedes emblem. The red-bearded tribesman shook his head when she asked for a ride to the next town.

'My car is full – I came to pick up relatives and drive to town. The wretched police have destroyed the opium because I did not have money to bribe them. My watermelons are not ripe and it's already late in winter. We have many mouths to feed, and no money. My child is dying of a strange illness: she loses weight daily.' The man lamented for a while. Bilqees listened patiently and asked if there was any other transportation available.

'It's a few hours' walk to the main road. You can find a bus to take you to Khost. You can stay the night here with your man and boy.'

The boy in the blue dress took us into a hut enclosed with *khas* bushes and covered with tarp. We took off our sandals and sat down. Two women came inside and sat down next to Bilqees. More women joined and we were served green tea and biscuits. The boy placed a pink plastic tub filled with water and a plastic bag filled with medicine in front of me. I took off Tariq's bandages and cleaned his wound with hydrogen peroxide and gave him anti-inflammation medicine. A meal of leftover naan bread and beans was served to us in the meantime. I re-tied Tariq's bandages and put him under a blanket.

At sunset, there was a call to prayer and Bilqees came over to me.

'Go and pray with the men,' she whispered.

'Why?'

'I told them you are softheaded but not a *kaffir*.'

'Did you say I am your man?' I reached for her hand.

'Yes. Now go and pray,' she said as a smile formed on her face.

Outside, men washed themselves in the passing stream. I cowered behind a bush and clutched the pleats of the shalwar to make my toilet. Afterwards I washed my hands in the freezing stream and saw the inked numerals from the GPS coordinates I had written on my forearm – the exact position where we had buried Jack's body. I traced the numerals and memorised them for later. I had been incredibly lucky to not end up like Riaz – headless in a Taliban body bag or like Jack in an unmarked grave in No Man's Land. Someone must be praying for me.

After prayers, I sat with the men and acted the part of a softheaded man. There are enough traumas in Afghanistan to explain my behavior as normal and they left me alone. After the *isha* prayers, the paraffin lamps were put out and the boy provided bedding. I lay down on the one next to Tariq. There was an opening in the roof and I saw the starlight. In our village, we used to lie on *charpai* under mosquito nettings and wait for another day of fun and games. I fixated on the gentle rustle of the breeze on the vetiver bush, the canine howls, and Tariq's gentle breathing. I felt calm and energised at the same time – a feeling I used to get before a squash match. It was what my coach Naseer used to teach as 'compressed stillness'.

The calm did not last long and I felt the need to piss. I walked out but the fear of the black cur kept me on edge. When I heard a low growl, I quickened my pace towards the road and took a piss standing up beside one of the old buses. They had been stripped of tyres and engines. All that remained was a creaking shell silhouetted in the starlight like a raised rectangular box. As I tied the cummerbund, I heard a rustle. Fearing the dog, I climbed into the bus.

'What are you doing here?' Bilqees whispered.

'I needed to go to the bathroom,' I said, delighted to find her by this happy accident.

'Go by the stream,' she said.

'I am done.' I walked down the aisle to the end where the seats had been removed and rugs and blankets were piled on the floor.

'Someone lives here?'

'It's for farm workers who pick opium,' Bilqees said. 'I sleep here tonight. Go now.'

'I am not going anywhere. I will stay here with my woman.' I sat down across from her with my legs folded underneath. The Plexiglass sheets on the windows and the rooftop exit kept the bus warm but allowed the starlight to filter in.

'I think you are afraid.'

'The black dog does not like me,' I said.

'You are afraid of the *jangi spai*? You have to show him that you are bigger,' she laughed. It was the first time I had heard her laugh. It was deep and full.

'What are *you* afraid of?'

She thought for a moment and frowned as if the memory was an unpleasant one.

'Djinns, witches, ghosts,' she said.

This time I laughed and edged closer to her.

'Are you not afraid of the supernatural?' she asked.

'I am only afraid of the natural things – like guns, bombs and drones.'

'Have you never encountered a demon?' was her next question. Outside, the stars and the constellations moved around the bus.

'I would love to see a demon,' I answered.

'Why do you say such horrible things? You are crazy.'

202

'If there are demons, then there must be angels who will protect us from them.' As I said this, I pointed to the figure of a winged creature drawn on the metal sheet of the back wall.

'Is that an angel?'

It looked like Icarus but I nodded.

'*Kheli hub.*' She leaned forward and her face fell under the light but her eyes remained in shadow. I raised her chin with my thumb and index finger until I could see her eyes. They glistened in the starlight with a look that has inspired romantic poets all over the globe.

'If we are together, we have nothing to fear from natural and supernatural.' I cupped her face and kissed her forehead.

She sighed. I kissed her again, this time on her lips. She turned her face away.

'Should I stop?' I asked.

She shook her head and closed her eyes.

I traced her lips with my finger until her mouth opened. I bit her lower lip. She pushed me away and looked at the angel.

'It is not an angel. Looks like a Zarathus god. I have seen it in my uncle's shop,' Bilqees said.

'I think it is *Yunani*. Your uncle was an educated man?'

'He taught himself. He owned an antique shop in Herat. You could find Aladdin's lamp in his shop if you tried.'

'Where is he now?' I moved my hand from her armpit to her left breast.

'The Taliban killed him.'

'Why?' I put my hands on her chest but she turned away.

'They found him playing a harmonium. They told him to stop, but he was slow to respond so they hit him on the head with a rifle. He bled to death in his shop. After that I was married.'

'And your husband?' My hands were now on her shoulders.

'He used to work at the shop. He wanted to be a *Qari* – one who recites the Quran – but once the war began he got distracted. My uncle told him to go to Iran but he refused. He died in an American ambush.'

'They ambushed him?'

'No, it was he who did an ambush. They called the sky machines, and the earth shook. They bombed valley, village, pastures, and rocks. Even the cows were blown up.'

'Was he Taliban?'

'Maybe, he never told me.'

I told her she reminded me of a Pakistani actress.

'Which one? Do I know her?'

'Doesn't matter.' I kissed her again. Her leg touched my hand and my hand travelled up her thigh, but she pushed it down. I put my arm around her waist. She had curves, folds, and all the things that make a woman. We kissed frequently and I explored whatever she allowed. I felt like I was back in college except back then we were always short on time but here, under the halo of an angel, the stars moved around the bus and time froze.

I woke up as she was leaving. I heard dogs barking outside.

'I go now.' She walked out of the bus.

I savoured visions of last night, my hands on her roundness, the weight of her breast, the curve of a cheek, a wisp of hair and that lower lip. After half an hour I walked outside. The sun lit the cold desert with a pink glow and tumbleweed ruffled among bushes. I could smell fresh manure and ripe fruit. The black devil dog stood valiantly on the bridge as I walked to the thatched hut. It was a good day to wear a *shalwar*.

*

We spent the next few days in that village. The villagers had no financial wealth but they shared what they could with complete strangers who had walked into their lives from the desert. During the day, I took care of Tariq, and at night Bilqees took care of me in our space bus. I even made peace with the Kuchi shepherd dog although I did not pet his monstrous head. In three days Tariq recovered enough to walk by himself and Bilqees said that we must leave.

'Do we have to?' I hugged her. I had made little progress in lovemaking but had come a long way in love.

'Yes, we are a burden to these poor women. They have few men here.'

'Let's give them this.' I took a $100 note of Jack's money and gave it to her.

'That's 50,000 Afghani. I will get change,' Bilqees said and went to see the women in the village.

The next day was cloudy. After an hour's walk we came to the main road and joined other passengers. The bus had filled up by the time Bilqees had paid the fare and found seats in the front. Tariq had kept pace but he got squeezed in the back of the bus along with traders with their plastic bundles filled with odds and ends. One man even travelled with his own small stool.

It was a twisted and battered highway that ran through a wasteland of grey rocks and craggy mountains with tips covered in dirty snow. The road was littered with burnt-out oil tankers and broken vehicles. There were frequent check posts with American Humvees and green pickup trucks, sandbags and the obligatory *pathak*. Every time we stopped we went through a process. First the bus conductor collected all papers in advance. He then handed them to an Afghan soldier who checked the IDs. Then the passengers filed out and were frisked by other soldiers. Finally the vehicles were checked by armour-wearing NATO soldiers with K-9 units. I was nervous about the ID as the dead Jan Muhammad Arish was younger, but in the turban and beard I could pass for him as long as I didn't open my mouth.

After a gruelling ride, we arrived at the Khost lorry stand. I got out of the bus first and waited for Tariq to emerge. After all the other passengers had disembarked, I climbed into the bus and carried him out. He was in a dazed stupor and I carried him to a teashop and found him a seat. A boy appeared and I ordered tea and water.

'Tariq, wake up, can you see me?' I said to him. He moaned and kept his eyes closed.

'We have to take him to the hospital soon,' I told Bilqees.

'Only in Ghazni,' she said.

'He can't take a bus ride like this again.' Doubt formed in my mind about her intentions. Why was she so fixated on Ghazni? Whom did she know there?

'We have enough money to take a *siracha*. It will be faster,' she said.

'Can you get water, snacks and cigarettes?'

'Softheaded men don't smoke,' she said, but returned shortly with a water bottle, a bag of mulberries, and a pack of Pine cigarettes.

'I found a ride,' she said.

I lit a cigarette and we walked over to a white Corolla with a large sticker that said *Super Saloon*. There was one other passenger, a young man who wore jeans and a heavy bomber jacket. The driver wanted to add more passengers but Bilqees promised him an extra tip and we took off with the three of us in the back seat.

'Cover up, woman,' said the driver as we passed through the last city security checkpoint.

'I am not your woman,' Bilqees said.

'The Taliban monitor this road with binoculars. This provides opportunities for their snipers. Uncovered women attract attention. After Gardez it is safer,' said the driver.

Bilqees went under her burqa and we drove slowly on a road covered with ice. The battered lane snaked its way through high passes behind, and we followed overloaded Bedford trucks. It was cold and rainy outside and the driver struggled to find visibility in the drizzle and fog. I had been threatened with death and decapitation, but the fear of falling down thousands of feet into the crevices was terrifying.

After a torturous climb, we descended towards the dry valley. The traffic had slowed to a crawl. The rain had caused an accident and a truck lay on its side with its spilled contents. The driver waved us around as we skirted the edge of the road. The truck's back panel was painted with a depiction of Burak, the angelic horse that the Prophet rode on his spiritual Mairaj. The equine

206

face looked serenely towards the sky. The drizzle turned into a cloudburst.

'This road is the death highway. There are frequent IED bombings as well as ice storms. It's never safe,' said the driver. His short beard was laced with green spittle.

'The Russians made this road in the seventies and then bombed it in the eighties. Then the Taliban made it and the Americans bombed it. Now the Americans make things and the Taliban bomb them,' said the passenger.

'Yes, but it is worse now,' the driver agreed.

'The Taliban gain strength as they leave,' said the passenger.

'You want them to stay?' asked this driver as we gathered speed.

'I want NATO to stay. I have daughters and migraines. I want schools and hospitals.'

Outside Gardez we found an ambushed tanker blazing on the road near a police checkpoint. Delayed again, we stopped until the police cleared the area.

'This is a fresh ambush, we missed it by minutes,' said the driver.

'The angel saved us,' Bilqees said. 'If that truck had not overturned, we would have hit the IED.'

The road to Ghazni got better after that and we sped past decaying military vehicles and an abandoned warehouse with stencilled Cyrillic letters. A long iron girder from an upturned crane pointed towards the traffic like the middle finger of a dead giant. Far ahead I saw huddled figures standing in the middle of the highway, looking up at the sky. The driver did not slow down.

'Watch out for the children,' I yelled in Urdu.

At the last moment, the kids moved away as the driver threw out fistfuls of coins, and the bodies rushed into the vortex of the swirling dust.

The passenger in the jeans looked at me curiously. I opened my mouth and made a face.

'He is sick. Put on music. Or are the Taliban eavesdropping in the car?' Bilqees said.

'No, they can't hear us here,' the driver said. He took off the grill from one of the vents and took out a hidden cassette from inside the air duct.

'This is my favorite *attan*. Naghma is like our mother and she sings songs that make us dance and remind us of good times,' the driver said.

It was a lively song and Naghma sang with passion and bravado. Bilqees hummed under her breath and I took her hand in mine for the rest of the journey.

20

Ghazni *Kheli Khub*

Ghazni was neither beautiful nor prosperous. It was a dirty city of destroyed rubble mixed with early snow. But it was a city nevertheless with electric power, hospitals, and billboards of hijab-clad women selling mobile phone plans.

The problem was Tariq. His head was swollen and he was unconscious. No anti-inflammatory drugs could fix him any more and he needed a hospital and professional medical care. Once we dropped off the other passenger in front of a fenced building that promised skills in HTML and Java language, we raced to the hospital.

'Private or provincial?' the driver asked.

'Provincial,' Bilqees replied.

We drove along the river road, past glass buildings protected behind iron gates, concrete barricades and barbed wire. There was plenty of police as well as ISAF forces manning check posts. My hopes rose as I saw restaurants and civil society. I was nearly free, with enough money to get to Kabul and then the Pakistani embassy. I would demand to see the ambassador, in my best English and with the proper authority of the landed gentry of

209

Punjab. How could they deny me entry into my own country? I could be on a flight to Karachi and home in no time.

'What are you thinking about?' Bilqees asked.

'Nothing,' I said. She had seen a rare happiness on my face.

'You seem happy.'

'I am a city person.'

'I told you that you would like Ghazni,' she said and squeezed my hand.

The hospital was a bright blue freshly painted building with a sign outside declaring it a provincial hospital and *shifa khana*. Turbaned men and covered women were camped outside and the corridors were filled with patients seeking the attention of medics.

'Find a doctor,' I said.

Bilqees ran after attendants who rushed from one room to another while I found a spot on the floor to rest. The hospital had bright corridors but smelled of dirty bandages and iodine. It was noisy with cries from men with shrapnel wounds, children who were double amputees and burned women. The trauma victims were wheeled to the emergency ward as their relatives ran beside the moving stretchers. I felt an unsettling fear. This was a place of death. I closed my eyes as I held Tariq's head in my lap and waited.

Bilqees convinced a medic to look at Tariq. He took him to a changing station, checked his vitals, and wrapped bandages around his head like a mummy. He then wheeled him to the emergency ward.

'He should be fine now. Let's go and find a room,' Bilqees said. But I refused to move.

After an hour, the medic came out with a folder in his hand. I asked him about Tariq's condition in English. He held out an X-ray of a human skull.

'He has shrapnel stuck in his head. We have to do surgery, but we don't have a surgeon here. Maybe tonight we will attend to him. You can go, we will take care of your son,' he said.

I grabbed his hand with both of mine. 'Tomorrow, I will see you tomorrow,' I said.

'Let's go now, it will get dark soon,' Bilqees urged.

Outside, the sun was setting and muezzin called the faithful to prayers as a cold wind swept across the high plateau. Bilqees hailed a rickshaw and we drove into old Ghazni. It was made of short hills, mud houses and parched landscape populated by slow-moving stick figures wrapped in colourful clothing. We got dropped off on the edge of the river and walked through a bazaar until we found a money-changer. I gave Bilqees two hundred dollars and pocketed the last bill. She changed the money and took me to Bakhtiar Hotel.

'My uncle knew the owner of this hotel,' she said and led me up the stairs past dirty snow and trash. Inside, she named a few men but the attendant did not recognise them and she paid for a private room on the second floor. I climbed the dingy stairs to the room. It was furnished sparingly with a bed, two chairs, and a low table. There was a mirror on the wall, a broken wardrobe, and an open window that overlooked the river. I struggled to close the window as Bilqees left to rent an electric heater. I asked about the bathroom.

'It is at the end of the corridor. I'll go and buy some things. Stay here,' she said.

'Yes, madam,' I said in English.

The toilet was communal, with western-style toilets. I kept a cigarette lit and the burning tobacco disguised the other smells. Outside I washed myself in the sink, returned to the room and slipped inside the smelly blankets. I slept through the night and woke up late to find Bilqees sitting on the chair sewing her burqa. She had bathed, and I noticed that she had put on dark lipstick.

'Did you sleep?' I asked, yawning. I had not had sleep this good for months.

'I don't need sleep. Eat something. This is all I had time for before curfew starts.'

She opened a plastic shopping bag and took out oranges, dried mulberries, a packet of biscuits and a bottle of Cristal branded water. She had also bought me thick cotton socks.

211

I ate the biscuits and the oranges. She ate nothing.

'Aren't you hungry?' I asked.

'You eat, I will later,' she said.

I lit a cigarette and moved the heater next to the bed. I felt like lying down again as it was still cold, but Bilqees sat by my side.

'Something on your mind?' I asked, drinking water from the bottle.

'You don't trust me, Qais *jaan*?'

'I do,' I said as I put on the cotton socks.

'You are with me because you don't speak Dari fluently. You would not trust me in Pakistan.'

'I gave you the money, didn't I?' I took another swig from the water bottle.

She reached under her burqa and took out the Afghani currency.

'I am not talking of money. You can have it.'

I looked at the currency notes, took a thousand and pushed the rest to her.

'You keep it, I only need a little bit,' I said, drinking some more water.

'Would you marry me?' she asked without any attempts at being coy.

The water spurted out from my mouth as I exclaimed in surprise.

'I am old,' I said.

'You are not that old.' She ran her fingers along my elbow. 'I am not a bad woman myself. I was pretty once.'

'You are still pretty. But you don't know me. I have other responsibilities also, as a father to a daughter,' I said.

'I am nobody's responsibility. I have worked with and without husbands. I raised my sister's boys until they ran away with the Taliban.'

'Why did they run away?' I hoped to get her off the topic of marriage.

'To make them *ghazis*.'

'Or *shaheeds*,' I said. 'They turn boys like Tariq into suicide bombers. Taliban idiots.'

Bilqees shrugged her shoulders. 'All Afghans fight. It's our condition,' she said.

'But these mullahs are cruel and stupid.'

'You think men like Pasha are better than the Taliban? He probably raped boys. You liked him because he knew your city.'

I remained silent. Outside I heard a loudspeaker start a religious sermon. The mic was off, the sound was warped and it reminded me of a sci-fi movie in which an Englishman is kidnapped by aliens who look like upstanding slugs dressed in black suits.

'I used to think all men were the same until I met you,' she said. 'Tell me about Karachi. I heard that people in Pakistani are without faith and women show their stomachs in public and they have more flavours of *sharab* - wine - than styles of pilau.'

'Same in Kabul,' I said. 'Even more in Dubai and Delhi.'

'India is not Muslim, but Karachi is *fahaash*.' She picked up the Afghani currency and put it inside a hidden pocket.

'It is my city. I can only live there.' I tried to remember the name of the movie. Scenes appeared in my mind but not the title.

'Tell me about it,' she said. 'Is it beautiful?'

'Not really. It's big, dirty, and polluted. But there are nice areas and the people are beautiful, especially the girls. You can talk to them for hours, they laugh, dance, sing and in the summer, they wear lawn dresses that are almost see-through and you can see the shape of a woman, from ankles to neck.'

'What about men?'

'Men dress in western suits with silk ties, polished shoes and smooth socks.'

'Did you dress like that as well?'

'Yes. A long time ago, I used to get fitted for a suit every new year.'

'What else do you miss?'

'I miss the ocean and the horizon. I miss my daughter.' I stopped. Every time I mentioned Shereen, her face tightened.

Or maybe I just imagined it. I touched her shoulders and kissed her on the cheeks.

'Maybe you'll take me to Karachi one day?' she said.

A loud explosion shook the room. The boom, like so many before in the last few months, hurt my heart. From the window, I saw a ball of flame burning the building across the river. There were shouts and gunfire from the rooftops nearby.

'What is happening?' I asked, running to the door.

'Bomb blast, but it is far away.'

I heard horns tooting, ambulance sirens, and loudspeakers in the mosque. The noise of a helicopter filled the room. I looked through the window and saw black soot coming from a building. The noise multiplied as another helicopter joined the one already circling.

'Come and sit,' Bilqees said. 'Death is always around; life can end anytime.'

I heard yells outside. There were feet stomping and running above us on the rooftop.

'Hold me,' she said, hugging me closely. Her body trembled like a leaf.

'I thought you were only afraid of the supernatural,' I said.

'I am not shaking from fear.' She let out a small laugh.

There were shouts outside the hotel. I looked at the door. It was locked. I looked back at Bilqees's face – her eyes were closed and her neck arched up.

She made me feel brave. I took a deep breath and kissed her neck. She sighed and her hands caressed me.

We helped each other out of our shalwars with passionate urgency. I ran my hands down her body and her legs wrapped around my waist. Into my lovemaking, I put all of my learning and my yearnings.

'*Kheli khub*. That was wonderful.' Her lips pouted to form the word *khub* as overwhelming pleasure filled my heart, mind and loins.

Close by, a gun fired. I hoped the gunfire was not directed at the helicopter for it would surely target the hotel with a missile.

214

We would burn down to a crisp, or worse, the police would break down the door and parade us outside while those American dogs snarled and snapped at my genitals. Fear distracted me from the job at hand, but I remained committed and mouthed love talk in pidgin Dari. But it was one of those rare moments when I could have recited 'twinkle twinkle little star' and nobody would have given a damn.

The sex was over before the second helicopter flew away. The garbled speech continued from the loudspeakers and I remembered the name of the movie, *The Hitchhiker's Guide to the Galaxy*. The Englishman had gotten the girl and returned home.

'Now marry me,' Bilqees said. She had covered her body but her eyes sparkled.

'I don't know how,' I replied.

'Be a man and find two witnesses and a mullah. That's all.'

'It's not that easy. I don't have papers in my name.'

'Qais *jaan*, I am not asking for the moon,' she said and looked away.

I thought about this, and realised it was not as hard as I was making it out to be. She could be a good wife. I could take her to Karachi and show her *Veer Zara*.

*

Later that day we took a bus to the hospital. Inside, there was more commotion than before as it was freezing cold and everyone had squeezed into the building. I could not find the medic or Tariq in the mayhem. An old man bundled up in woollen clothing swept the front entrance to no avail. He was not part of the hospital staff and talked out loud to himself as he struggled to keep the water from coming into the corridors.

'Kaka, no point in cleaning the doorway, it is futile,' said an attendant.

'I am not going to let a little rain get the better of me,' said the old man.

I finally found the medic and asked him about Tariq. He told me to wait and came back in half an hour and then took Bilqees and me to the doors of the emergency ward.

'We have to drill a hole in his head, but I have not been able to put him on the surgeon's table. He is busy with other emergencies,' he said.

I felt that this was an opening. It would be impossible to get an operation without a bribe. 'How can we get him on the table?' I asked.

'That's not my job but the operation manager's. Unfortunately, he is corrupt.' The medic strode off through the door of the emergency ward.

'How much? We are poor people ourselves,' I said.

'It's not for me, you understand. It's for the manager who does the paperwork. But the boy needs an operation soon.' The medic shrugged his shoulders and once again, walked away.

'Do you have the money I gave you?' I turned to Bilqees.

'You are going to give it away. Don't be a fool,' she said.

'Give me what you have. Please, Bilqees *jaan*.'

'You don't understand these things. He is trying to get money out of you because you talk in English.' Bilqees grabbed my hand but I jerked it away.

'Wait!' I called out to the medic. I took out the plastic sheaf that contained my ID and the $100 bill. I gave him the bill.

'Is this real?' he asked, holding the note in his palm.

Bilqees spoke quickly. They had an argument as she accused him of open bribery.

'Is she your wife?'

I nodded and he walked away.

The hundred dollars bought us the surgery. In a couple of hours, Tariq was wheeled into the operating room with four other stretchers. By this point, Bilqees had disappeared. It was a welcome relief from her incessant grumbling.

It was evening when the surgeon came out. He wore blue scrubs and had a thick beard that hid a kind face. He looked as if he had not slept in days.

'We have removed the shrapnel from the head. We had to open the skull and fix it.'

'Is he okay?' I asked.

'He is alive, but is hemiplegic.' he pronounced his p like an f.

'What does it mean?'

'He is paralysed on one side.'

'For how long?'

'Forever,' said the doctor, then went off to speak with other families.

I slid against the wall until I was on the floor. The corridors were filled with words – paralysed, shrapnel, bullet, mine, mandible gone, brain out …

*

I walked back through the Ghazni slums. It was freezing cold and my open-toe sandals did not help. Snot-nosed children in colourful sweaters watched as I skipped over trash and sewage. They reminded me of the slum where I used to distribute *laddus* as a child, on the Prophet's birthday. It was a compassionate act but mainstream theologians had put a stop to the Prophet's birthday celebration as a heretical activity.

I stopped by a video store with posters of Bollywood movies. A Pashtun movie played on screen but the song was by a Pakistani band. The shop sold things like phone cards, cigarettes, batteries and had a computer connected with Skype.

I stood there staring until the owner got suspicious.

'What do you want?'

'How much?' I said, pointing to the phone.

'What city?' he asked.

'Karachi,' I said.

He told me to write down the phone number. I picked up the pen but stopped. Was my family under surveillance by the ISI or CIA? And Sonia? She would have spent the ransom money on a trip to Dubai and bought handbags. The only person whom I could manage was Zahid. I wrote his number down and the man

217

dialled it through the computer. The phone rang and he gave me the headphones with the mic.

'Hello,' I said as Zahid picked up the phone.

There was silence. I waited. My heartbeat galloped all the way to Karachi and back.

'Qais. Have you forgotten?' I said in English. I did not want to speak Urdu.

'Shah-ji, is it really you? Where are you? I will come and meet you,' he said.

'I am in *dushman mulk*,' I said.

'India?' he asked with surprise.

There was silence. I needed to be clearer. Pakistan had many enemies.

'*Sarhad ke par*. Near Kabul. How is Shereen and my mother?'

'They are well, living with your Uncle Jamshed. He is a true gentleman. Shereen passed her exams and is waiting for admissions.'

'Does she think I am dead?'

'No, we never lost hope. It's been over three months with no contact or demand for ransom,' he said. He was having a hard time speaking in his excitement.

'Zahid, once I get to Kabul, I will need help.'

'You have my word. Worry not, I will manage at my end.'

The Afghan pointed at his watch. My time was up.

'Okay, I've got to go.'

'Wait, Shah-ji. Don't go,' Zahid was saying as I hung up.

I paid him for the call and bought two packets of Sunsilk shampoo. In the hamam, I scrubbed out the grime, the dirt, and the worries, and went to the mosque. When I returned, Bilqees was not in the hotel room. There was nothing I could do for Tariq, but I promised myself that I would not fail my daughter.

21
Nihilism

*I am holding a red plastic phone in my hand. When I answer it, a
female voice sings Faiz Ahmed Faiz's poetry.*

'Who is this?' I ask.

*'You don't remember me, Qais? I am waiting and you are marrying
another woman?'*

'Jameela?'

'Is she more beautiful? Can she fulfil all your desires like I did?'

*'Who is this? I buried you at the Kala Pul graveyard in 2008.
What sorcery is this?'*

'I wait for you in heaven, Qais, forever ...'

*

I woke up in a cold sweat with the dirty blanket in my mouth.
I jumped out of bed and ran downstairs. In the lounge I found
two burly men in woollen overcoats watching TV. I sat down
with them, not wanting to be alone. The TV played an Arnold
Schwarzenegger sci-fi movie dubbed in Farsi. I had seen the
movie before at Nishat cinema in the eighties. In the movie,

Arnold's wife turns out to be not his real wife, but simply a memory planted in his head.

I took a bus back to the hospital. Tariq was in the communal ward on a stretcher bed. His head was bandaged up and his eyes were closed. When I placed my hand on his forehead, he opened his eyes.

He remained silent as I stroked his hair.

'Tariq, *beta*, you rest now,' I said.

He raised an arm and took it to his head and scratched at the bandages. 'Can I remove this? Where am I?' His eyes darted back and forth.

'Don't remove it. You might bleed. You are in a hospital in Ghazni.'

He looked around and tried to get up, but panicked.

'I feel like my body is under a big weight. Remove it from me, can you?' Tariq tried to get up. His body did not respond and twisted and turned in a grotesque manner. An attendant came by and increased his morphine dose.

I returned to the hotel on my last dime and found Bilqees waiting there.

'You should not go out alone,' she said. 'What if the police stop you?'

I ignored her and sat down.

'I am fine and I am out of money.'

'I have some. What do you need?'

'I need enough to get me to Kabul.'

Bilqees stood up and sorted things out. I smoked. Outside, two bulldozers were moving the rubble from the bomb explosion that had flattened the building across the river.

'I can take you, but first you must do something with me.'

'What can I do for you?' I walked over to her and hugged her from behind.

'I need you to take *faal* with me.'

'How would that help?'

In Pakistan, *faal* was foretold on the footpaths outside shrines. The parrot would pick a random envelope and the astrologer would read the future. The *tuta faal* had almost disappeared, as the religious goons had denied it as *shirk*.

'Do this for me, Qais *jaan*. If fate is not good, then I will leave,' she said.

'I don't want you to leave.' I held her hand.

We crossed the bridge again, and made our way through dirty alleys and derelict gardens into a shrine complex. In the middle was a green dome and outside was the usual Islamic paraphernalia – a red, gold and green flag inscribed with Quranic scripts. The tomb had a sarcophagus covered with cotton and velvet. I sat next to an old man who swayed gently.

'From Qandahar?' he guessed without looking at us.

'Nah, Sistan Baluchi,' I said in Dari.

'Come to see the shrine of Sheikh Saani?' asked the old man. He was tall and thin and wore a green turban. This was the first time I had seen a green turban in Afghanistan.

I nodded.

'You're a long way from home.' He extended his hand, then asked, 'What are you doing here?' His left eye had a severe cataract.

'*Gardish*,' I said making a reference to aimless travelling.

'This is no place for *gardish*. Go home.' He laughed. His breath smelled old.

Bilqees sat down. She then asked him if he would do *faal*. He nodded and went to a cubbyhole from which he took out a bundle of books wrapped in soft cloth.

'You have children?' he asked, as he mumbled verses and unwrapped the bundle.

'Yes, a daughter,' I replied.

'Not with me,' Bilqees said. 'From his dead wife.'

I winced at her bluntness.

The old man found a tattered book with a torn cover. He closed his eyes and sat still.

'We do *faal* as guided by Sheikh Hafiz,' he said.

He opened the book and read out '*Garchan yaaran faregh-and az yad-e man az man ishan-ra hazaran yad bad*. Do you understand it?'

'My *yaar* is free, I still have thousands of memories,' I said.

'Open the book by chance and read,' he said and handed it to me.

'You go first,' Bilqees said.

I said *bismillah* and flipped the book open.

'Read where your finger lands not from the top,' instructed the old man.

'Ze-eshq-e natmam-e ma jamal-e-yaar, be-ab-o rang-o khal-o khatt cheh hajat ruy-e ziba-ra. The beauty of my *yaar* does not need my imperfect love. For they have a beautiful face, colour, glow, a perfect mole and peach fuzz.'

'Sheikh Hafiz desired a young lad,' I whispered to Bilqees.

'My turn now,' Bilqees said.

I handed her the book. She ran a finger down the fore edge of the book. She stopped in the middle, opened that page, and pointed her finger to a couplet.

'Read. I don't know how,' Bilqees said.

The old man took the book, mindful of where her finger was placed.

'Jahan faani-o baaqi feda-ye sahahed-o saqi, Keh Soltani-yeh alam-ra tofayl-e eshq mibinam. The world of the transient and the permanent can be sacrificed to a friend or cup-bearer, because I see legal and lordly matters as mere intruders in the way of love.'

The old man gave her a look that made her blush. She stood up and walked away.

The man smiled and wrapped the books. I asked him how much I owed him. He told me to donate money for the shrine upkeep.

'Come. There are four more sheikhs buried here, all Sheikh Saani's closest disciples, and the one at the foot of the tomb being Iskander, a king who left his kingdom to study. That is the kind of love he had,' the man said.

I walked with him for half an hour. I don't remember what he talked about. He spoke mostly in Dari, but with a soft accent. But whatever he said made Bilqees happy.

We walked back past the broken citadel, amid the mounds of debris, stones and plastic trash. There were Hazara girls walking along in bright costume. A young girl, hardly six, was dragging a propane tank as her brother pushed a wheelbarrow next to it. Her posture showed the enormity of the weight. She fell down, cried, and then continued walking.

We found a vendor selling samosas. I bought a plate. The sun sank over the hills and the birds chirped in the trees. We sat together as a couple among other couples.

Across from us was a sandy field. In a corner, a pair of shoes marked the goalpost. The other goal was a wall. The goalkeeper was an eleven-year-old with a toothy grin and a stump for his left leg, which explained his position in the team.

The one-legged goalkeeper dove for the ball and saved a goal. He rolled around, sat up, then threw the ball; the boys went running up the hill towards the other end. He hopped on his one good leg, re-tracing the goal line with his stump. The smile never left his face as his eyes followed the ball. I thought of Tariq in that ward.

'My last husband could not give me a boy. Now I feel a seed of a boy growing inside. Your boy.' She placed my hand on her stomach. We stayed like that for a while.

Then she said: 'I will take you to Kabul but don't leave me behind when you go to Karachi.'

'*Inshaallah*,' I said.

'Promise me that you will take me along.'

I made a promise. I intended to keep it.

*

Before leaving Ghazni, I made one last stop at the hospital. I gave my email to the medic and wrote my real name down as Tariq's next of kin. I said goodbye to Tariq but he was in a morphine-induced state. I kissed his forehead and read *Ayat-ul-Kursi*.

The lorry stand was on heightened alert. There had been a series of bombings, and swarms of blue-uniformed Afghan soldiers moved around with walkie-talkies. Brown Humvees and green pickups were parked by the road, with tripod-mounted guns. A bone-chilling wind blew the tri-coloured Afghan flags on their poles. Nearby, a group of children collected plastic bottles and brass bullet shells to be sold to recyclers. A solitary figure dragged a blue suitcase along on the other side of the road.

'This is the bus we catch,' Bilqees said. She had been nervous all morning and had begged me to postpone the trip by one day. Unfortunately, we had overstayed at our hotel and had to vacate.

'I told you – I will not abandon you, so why are you so nervous?' I asked.

The boy with the suitcase waited for the buses to roll past. His head was bandaged. My mind was still with Tariq. The wind picked up and the boy's shalwar ballooned around his legs. He looked back a few times at the two men in big coats. Then he crossed the road towards the checkpoint.

'Let's go. The bus will leave soon,' Bilqees said.

Two Afghan soldiers raised their hands. Their guns were pointed to the ground. Next to them were two American soldiers. They were in full armour, wearing helmets and sunglasses, holding M-16s in their hands. Their dogs yanked at their chains, barking at the boy, who stumbled onward. One of the Afghans lifted his rifle.

'Stop now!' a soldier yelled.

I covered my ears and screamed. A white flash was followed by a blast that echoed in my ears. Everyone moved back from the explosion and stared at the burning pickups. Security vehicles and ambulance's sirens screeched. We sat on the ground as the rising flames and smoke seared our skin and filled our lungs. The Humvee burned on the ground in front of the crowd. The bullets sank into the sand, their mission incomplete. Afghan policemen cleared the area for a helicopter to land.

Then they released the dogs. They snapped, growled, and scared the children. I held Bilqees's hands. A piece of blue cloth floated amid the black soot in the dazzling white light.

'All I want to do is get to my village,' one old man sobbed, holding his head in his hands, too ashamed to let others see his tears.

The soldiers commanded the women to separate from the men. A woman wheezed, affected by breathing in the dust; her husband stood up to help her, and was beaten by the guards as he yelled 'asthma'. There were more shouts. Bilqees squeezed my hand.

'Qais *jaan*, what was the name of the actress I reminded you of?' she asked.

'I am not going to let them take you away from me.' I held her hand.

A soldier pressed the muzzle of his rifle on my chest and gestured to Bilqees.

'Wait, that is my *khanum*,' I said, but she was pushed away with the other women.

My voice was lost in the crowd. Two low-flying jets roared overhead. Some cheered while others cried.

'Where are you taking the women?' I asked.

'Sit down.' A soldier gave an order, and I was struck on the shoulder. I watched helplessly as Bilqees joined a flock of multi-coloured burqas being guided into an alley. I kept my eyes on her until her burqa blended with the floating fabrics. The sight made me recall an old English movie where an ostrich swallows a diamond and the hero chases it over the hill, only to find thousands of ostriches on the other side.

The men were pushed towards a shack and our papers were checked. A few soldiers sat on camp-style chairs talking on their phones. One of the soldiers had the hairstyle of the film *Titanic*'s lead actor. He moved along the line, checking papers, while the man next to him, a fleshy fellow with broad Turkic features and a thick moustache, stared at the line and smoked. Even in the cold weather, he had rolled up his sleeves and a shotgun lay across his lap.

When my turn came, I handed him the Afghan ID. The Turkic put a stubby finger on the photo.

'You?' he barked.

I nodded.

'Punjabi?' he said with a tight smile.

I remained silent.

He stood up and peered at my face. I looked back unblinking. He then punched my stomach. It was a short, precise punch, but it had his entire weight behind it. My insides rose up my chest.

'Liar.' He yanked my collar up to check the label.

'He is a Punjabi Taliban. He is one of the terrorists!' He punched me again.

I stepped back out of fear. He clasped my body in his hairy arms and squeezed. I couldn't breathe and I instinctively placed my elbows between his shoulder and neck. He was stocky but I prodded until I found a soft spot and drove in my elbows. He finally let me go and I fell down.

I looked up and saw the *Titanic* star on his feet. He had lifted the shotgun and was looking at us with a vacant, bored expression. I knew he was going to shoot. He did.

*

I woke up in a small cot. My face burned with pain. I lifted my hand to touch it, and found a bandage covering my left eye.

'I can't see. I can't see,' I babbled.

'You have no bullet wound,' I heard a careless voice say.

I was left alone until I starved. I yelled but to no avail. My eye throbbed and I feared crying as the water could seep through the bandage. I stared in the dark, and imagined starlight and food.

The next day, two bored Afghan soldiers escorted me to a police van. They were tough but not brutal. A picture of the mujahideen Ahmed Shah Masood hung from the rear-view mirror.

'Where are you taking me?' I asked but got no response.

We were stopped by an American K-9 patrol for a thorough checking. The guards talked in Dari to each other.

226

'American dogs don't like shalwars,' said one, spitting to the side.

'They treat dogs better than they treat us,' said the younger one, who had a clean-shaven face.

'They are eager to recognise them as masters,' the other one said. He talked with a lisp and his eyes flickered constantly.

'What happened to the females that were with us?' I asked one.

'They are in prison, but will be released,' said the guard. 'The Americans want Punjabi terrorists.'

We drove into a bungalow with high walls and a perimeter fence. There were more uniformed soldiers and flags, which indicated an army base and rational men. I could always convince rational men.

I was shown into a clean waiting room. After an hour, I was escorted to a lab technician and told to look into a machine for an iris scan. Once finished, he asked me to show my fingers.

'You have all your fingers,' said the operator. His uniform was two sizes too big for him and he had on a facemask and plastic gloves.

'Men in your profession have lost a limb or two by the time they get to your age,' he said, placing my fingers on a reader. 'Start with the index finger.'

After I finished, I waited. There were four men with me, all heavy-browed and bearded. Two of them were soldiers. I heard the other two men waiting with me speaking in Punjabi and caught their eye, then raised my eyebrow in a silent salutation. They looked at each other and then in my direction and winked. I thought of winking back, but how can you wink with one eye?

'Latrine, please,' said one of the Punjabi men, holding his pinkie finger up in the air.

The soldier gestured for him to sit back down. The second Punjabi leapt up and grabbed the guard by his throat. They crashed into the wall. The Punjabi's hands were on the guard's throat. The second Punjabi man ran through the door, pushing the other guard out of the way. The guard fell down but made the decision to chase the runner, leaving the two men wrestling on the floor. I heard swearing, shouting and gunfire from an automatic weapon.

More soldiers rushed into the room. They hit the Punjabi man's head with a rifle butt. Another hit him under the neck. I heard thuds and cracks. The man folded like a ragdoll, and collapsed on the floor with his tongue out.

I remained seated. I had been through too much to be a hero. A third dead Punjabi would mean nothing to the Afghans.

In the next hour, the dead man was dragged away and the blood on the floor was washed with antiseptic. The room was empty, except for the two guards who had accompanied me. But their manners had changed, and they were energetic.

'Dhal-eating motherfuckers, they come here to kill Afghans. I killed both,' the younger one said. One of the attackers had clawed his throat before being beaten to death and I could see the livid marks.

I heard an order outside and both men went on the alert as an army officer entered the room. He was wearing a smart cap and spoke in a loud voice.

'What's your name?'

'Syed Qais,' I said.

'You are identified as Nadeem Muhammad Dar, a Pakistani on the TerroristWatchList4. You are now under arrest,' he barked, then walked out of the room. I was then taken back to the first room for another round of iris scans.

'How am I identified?' I said.

The assistant looked at me with a vacant expression and then turned his screen. On it were capital letters that said: DENY ACCESS, DO NOT HIRE, SUBJECT POSES A THREAT.

In the silence I heard a laser printer working. I had always wanted one for my office but could never afford a printer this good.

'Sign this.' He handed me the printed page. It had text in English and Dari.

'What is this?'

'A confession from you as a suicide bomber.'

'I will not sign it,' I said.

He shrugged his shoulders, stood up and motioned to the guards. One had a wooden truncheon in his hand. He hit me on my right bicep. The sheer pain jarred my senses. Before I could recover, I was hit on the left shoulder and thigh in quick succession, and the truncheon was shoved in my solar plexus.

I lost contact with the world for a brief moment. When I returned, the survival instinct made the decision.

'What happens if I sign it?' I croaked.

'We transfer you to the Americans in Bagram. Otherwise you can remain here as our guest.'

I signed the confession of a suicide bomber.

22

Ghosting in Bagram

I am completely naked. My instinct is to cover myself. I have no recall except what I see – a bright corridor with locked doors on both sides. I run to the end of the corridor and find black padded cloth hanging from bronze eyelets. I can't unhook it, so I pull it. A mechanical noise alerts me and I see a ceiling camera zooming in on my face. I wrap the cloth around my body and pace up and down the corridor ...

I can trace my story of how I travelled from Karachi up to the confession I signed as a suicide bomber. How I ended up here remains a mystery. I have tried hard, but cannot find the missing pieces.

I am transferred to a place called DFIP. I am standing in a yard, clothed but with no shoes. I feel the cold gravel and sand under my feet. I walk into a steel chamber with no seats. The door closes and I see the silhouettes of other men.

We are on the road for hours, and slide on top of each other. The windowless chamber makes breathing difficult and crying impossible. We pee in our clothes.

More soldiers in fatigues and polished boots appear ... and a fence beyond which lie snow-covered mountains. Somewhere, a large propeller cargo aircraft taxies on a runway. I am escorted to a large, low building.

'Take off your clothes,' says an amplified American voice. This is repeated in other languages. I take off my clothes and walk to a tiled room. A high-pressure water hose hits my body and there are no corners to hide. The water stops, and a soap bar appears in my hand.

'Two minutes,' says the voice.

I am paralysed. More shouting follows. I soap up furiously and scrub vigorously. I can't remember the last time I took a bath. After two minutes, the hose starts again and the dirt and crud runs out with the water.

'Walk through,' the voice commands.

In the next room, a nondescript American soldier with fair hair and white gloves takes an iris scan, as two other guards stand armed and ready. The soldier holds a plastic shoehorn and commands me to bend over. I try to remember why he looks familiar. He gestures again. I bend over and he performs a cavity search to make sure I am not concealing a weapon.

'Area 3 cleared, moving inmate to cell,' he says into his walkie-talkie. Now I realise why he looks familiar. He resembles the character of Hutch from the television show *Starsky and Hutch*.

And here I am sitting naked in the corridor of an American jail.

I try the doors as the servo motors on the camera are focusing. A bolt is released and a door opens. I walk into a well-lit cell with another ceiling-mounted camera. The door closes behind me. I find a pair of pyjamas and a shirt. I put them on as well as socks and a woollen sweater. In a corner is a metallic sink with knobs for hot and cold water with an attached commode. The floor is covered with black foam with interlocking, jigsaw puzzle-style ends. The other corner has a cot and a Chinese blanket and a prayer rug from Bangladesh. It also has a copy of the Quran published in Pakistan. I notice that the steel toilet has a sign that says it's made in America.

231

Then the lights go out. There are no windows. I try the door but it is locked. I close my eyes but can't sleep. After a couple of hours, the lights are back on. They are exceptionally bright and my good eye fills up with water. I hear footsteps. They stop outside my door. The bottom part of the door slides up and a tray is pushed inside. It has a milk carton, a water bottle, a banana, rice, and a curry dish cooked in a fashion particular to army messes. The hot food makes me drowsy. I fall asleep.

It is dark when I wake up again. The food tray has been cleared by magical elves. The next meal is spaghetti and meatballs with apple sauce. That too puts me to sleep. Lights switch on and off with a frequency that make days and nights shorter than Allah intended. The food is doped but there is nothing to do except sleep and dream.

The stillness of the cell is conducive to dreams. Reality stretches thin and dreams become dense. I look forward to a dream world where I win hearts and medals. There are happy moments with ex-lovers and dead friends; childhood days and forgotten moments are relived and then there are new variations on old memories. But in the waking hours, I cannot describe tangible details of the dreams, except the one about the train.

*

Late afternoon is a good time to start journeys, I think. I finish a beer with an old friend. The surrounding is plush, like a Dubai mall; the older men are at ease, while younger men pose and women are frozen in the hour-glass of youth. There seem to be no children around, and everyone appears to be rich and self-satisfied.

In the restroom I glance in the mirror and exchange a glance with a man who is struggling to tie a Windsor knot. I join old friends. We are in the early hours of a reunion, and we share accomplishments – all equally poignant, all equally awesome. Someone mentions that the train is about to leave; there is a general shuffle and the restaurant gets divided up into passengers and well-wishers.

I don't know which group I belong to, but some friends are boarding and Cash is always ready to travel. There are tearful eyes, the kind you get when your parents know that they are sending away a boy who will come back as a man. I see elderly women sniffling and I get a bear hug from a friend – he holds me for a long time. I almost want to stay.

The train is lined with red velvet and has grand chandeliers. I make my way through the crowd – there is no hurry – I grab drinks and grilled meat, pukka sahab food. My life is reenacted in various compartments: my childhood, my coursemates, friends, and lovers. No one is fighting; everyone is flirtatious. Someone tells me, 'Your father is out on the upper deck, with the seniors.' There are no women of my family here, no siblings, so I am surprised that my father is on the train and I wonder what he is doing here. I am waylaid though, by would-be lovers – their pull is strong, as is their beauty. I nuzzle, kiss, whisper and cuddle. I notice that everyone is on their feet; there are no seats on this train, no beds, no place to rest.

I encounter more friends; they remind me about an ex who looks ravishing tonight. I pass by an uncle hanging out with his drinking buddies. He asks me to join them. 'What's the hurry?' he says. I keep moving and find a beautiful young boy smoking a joint. I take a good hit – and another; it feels like my mind is billowing in smoke. I grasp the rail and climb to the upper deck – and find myself on the train's rooftop, which is set as a terrace. I see green mountains in the distance, and great gorges and a benevolent blue sky. The train passes between orchards, and passengers pluck apples that hang from nearby branches. It is sunny here, and older men sit on chairs reading newspapers and having conversations as a group of aunties drink tea out of Thermoses.

I see my father. He is dressed in a tweed jacket; he has a red fez and a pocket-handkerchief. His Olympic gold medal is around his neck. I go for a hug – he has never seen me as a mature man – but he pushes me off the train …

I free-fall past portholes; the faces peering out become sadder, wide-eyed, pale with red splotches, and hairless. The train zooms towards a shadowy space., I lose focus. Hear my father's voice, saying: 'You don't belong here.'

*

My father never wore a fez or a gold medal around his neck. But he valued the medal and wanted his son to be a champion, just like him. While he was alive, I did my best to be one. When he passed away, my life plans fell apart. I took the dream as a sign. I knew I had to train myself so that I wouldn't become a ghost in my own mind.

I looked at my cell. The squash courts in which I had practised were slightly larger. Coach Naseer had told us that the precursor to the game of squash was a game called rackets, which was invented in an English prison. A prison is a good place to do squash training, even without the equipment. I looked at my right hand and imagined a racket, a Spalding carbon graphite, and gripped the handle. My other hand palmed the plum-sized black leather ball. I crouched and hit the ball, a controlled and easy swing. The camera's servo motors zoomed. The ball bounced and I played a backhand shot and then a drop shot. Back to the T and to the corner. Volley into the nick, run cross-court and go for the kill shot. I did this until the lights turned off.

Eventually, I made human contact with my jailers. The fair-haired guard shackled my hands and tied me onto a wheelchair. I was wheeled across a long, covered glass walkway to a large room. Here I sat in my wheelchair and went through another batch of iris scans, finger printing and was given a number called an Internment Serial Number. I was instructed of my rights as a detainee at the facility called DFIP and the charge I was held under: 'Conspiring to kill coalition and Afghan forces'.

'I am not the man you think I am,' I said in English.

'Talk in your language, Punjabi,' said the Afghan who was a translator.

'I can speak English better than you.'

'You are a Punjabi terrorist. A beast made to carry burden for your mullah masters.'

'Are you comfortable with English?' asked the fair guard. I replied yes and put the Afghan, named Majeedi, out of his job.

'Yes, sir. I was kidnapped by the Taliban and imprisoned. I ended up here by chance. I am from Karachi. I only want to go home and see my daughter. I am innocent.' I choked up.

'You will be given a chance to contest your charges,' said the American. His uniform had the name *Lennox* on the front. His face glistened with the exertion of enunciating words in English for the benefit of my ear.

'How do I prove it?' I asked.

'You will get access to the Red Cross and will be given a personal representative who will act on your behalf.'

He introduced me to a tall man with a red beard called Lieutenant Colonel Cox, who would be my representative. He wore plain clothes but I could see that he was a military man and probably closer to my age than all the young people I had met in this jail.

'Are you a lawyer, Colonel?' I asked.

'Not technically. But I am here to help you and represent you. So tell me the truth.'

He described the roles of the others in the room, with military and legal terms that made sense only to them. There were analysts, recorders, and judge advocates who would lead the prosecution. Colonel Cox led the first round of questioning as two more men and a woman entered the room. The men sat in the back but the woman sat next to Cox. Her hair was covered by a long scarf with the dull pattern of a faded American flag. She wore khaki-coloured clothes with a bright blue shirt. She was the one identified as the recorder.

'Let's start from the beginning. State your name,' said Colonel Cox as he placed his notepad, pens, voice recorder and an iPad on the table.

'Syed Qais Ali Qureshi.'

'Nationality?'

'Pakistani.'

'Profession?'

'Insurance surveyor – passed my examination with Lloyds in 1995. You can check with them. I also have a website under *continentalsurveyers.pk.co.*'

'What brought you to Afghanistan?'

'I was kidnapped,' I said.

There were more terse questions around my imprisonment at Ghazipur. I told them all I could. It was evident that they had more information than I had on all these subjects.

'Who did this Asad group work with? Lashkar Jhangvi, Jamat Dawa, Harkat-ul-Mujahideen, TTP Swat?' asked the woman. I was impressed by her pronunciation.

'I wrote letters in their code. They were hand-delivered. I only knew Mullah Nazeer who died in the drone attack.'

'Tell us more about Hukum Khan.'

'I have told you everything. I am not even sure that that was his name.'

'All I care about are the trivial bits,' said the woman.

Cox looked at the voice recorder and selected a track. My voice played back like a gurgling stream, probably from a session that I did recall.

'His rifle was a 303. I had used one in my army training.'

'What did he look like?' someone asked.

'Medium height, grey beard, piercing eyes, gold tooth - a warrior.,'

The tape stopped playing.

'You remember who you are talking about?' the woman asked.

'Which division were you with in the Pakistan Army?' Colonel Cox resumed his questions.

'I did NCC as a college cadet. I was never a soldier. I am a civilian.'

'You need to tell the truth if you ever want to get out,' Cox said. 'You have to understand that as your PR, I will be on your side when we go in front of the DRB.'

'I have not lied to you. I tell you what happened again and again, but my mind plays tricks,' I said.

'Were you smuggling bomb triggers from Pakistan? Or grenades?' asked the woman.

'I was kidnapped by the Taliban and ended up on this side of the border by accident.'

'With this woman Bilqees and this boy Tariq? Where are they now?' Cox asked.

'I got separated from Bilqees. She was my woman. Tariq was in the provincial hospital when I left. You can check on him.'

'Where is Bilqees?'

'She was taken into custody after the explosion at the bus stop. I don't know where she is. I have been worried about her.'

'Was she your wife?'

'No, but I wanted to marry her.'

They consulted each other.

'Did you know anyone in Ghazni?' Cox asked.

'No, but Bilqees knew some people.'

'Was she your contact and your liaison?'

'No, she is a poor widow. Nothing to do with the Taliban.'

'So you have no interest in jihad and killing Americans?'

'Absolutely not. I deal with insurance claims, my work is banned by the extremists.'

They stopped asking questions and went through their notes again.

'You were rescued by an American?' Cox continued.

'Yes, after the drone attack. He was operating inside Pakistan. They called him Captain Haider, but he said his name was Jack. He was killed in an attack. I buried his body.'

'Did he mention his last name?'

'I don't remember.' I stood up. Someone pulled me back down and I toppled over. No one helped me as I struggled to sit back on the chair. I noticed that the woman's nails were bitten.

'We need you to tell the truth, otherwise you will remain locked up here. There are Pakistani Taliban who have been here for over ten years now,' Cox said.

'What about this Jack?' the woman asked. Her scarf had come loose and I could see that her blonde hair was cut in a bob style.

'Why did you bury him?' Cox asked slowly.

'I wanted Bilqees to see me as a good Muslim man and not one of the Taliban brutes,' I said. 'You can find his body. He was a US ranger and they said they never leave a man behind.'

'You know where the body is?'

I nodded and Cox handed me his notepad. I wrote the GPS coordinates slowly.

'How do you remember these?'

'I used association tricks. I matched numbers to events in my life. Twelve was my father's birth date, I was born in '69, my sister got married in '94, so on and so forth,' I said.

'Where did you learn that? During your spy training?'

'No, in school. I read *Reader's Digest*,' I replied. I had this feeling that every good deed I had done in life was being turned around to prove a point.

'We will see if these coordinates lead anywhere,' Cox said. 'Now let's talk about Ghazni.'

More terse questions came from Cox and the woman. She never told me her name, but I gave her the name Amelia. The Americans acted as a team and stayed on script – repeating the questions with precision but expecting a different answer each time. It was as if they were grinding sandpaper on to my memory. By the time they were through asking about one life experience, you never wanted to think about it again. It was like the Day of Judgement.

But even Allah is not as pedantic as the Americans.

*

A few days later, I was transferred to the general prison.

'You will have access to the yard, library and vocational training and a doctor. You can have your eye looked at as well,' Cox told me. 'Always remain in view of the security camera and you will be fine. Afghans don't like Punjabis.'

I was locked in a cell block with other men. The DFIP facility was filled with low-level jihadis from all over the world. Punjabis,

Arabs, Yemenis, Kashmiris, Uzbeks, and even Dagstanis. They were a sorry lot, full of misery and depression, and spent their time reading the Quran or sitting together in corners having discussions. I remained aloof, and borrowed Robert Ludlum thrillers and Jackie Collins romances from the library. The prisoners left me alone, except for the ones with mental problems. An Afghan kicked me in the head once and the Arabs tried to get me involved in a debate about politics, but I avoided them.

The weather got warmer in the spring and we spent more time in the yard. Beyond the fence lay the mountains of Afghanistan, and beyond that, Pakistan. The Arabs played football and the Afghans played basketball. I spent my time ghosting a game of squash against walls. One Afghan with a pleasant face and watery eyes would watch me play and one day he asked me what I was doing.

'Playing squash with Jehangir Khan. Do you know of him?' I replied.

'But there is no one here.' He took out a cigarette from his top pocket.

'I am training. We call it ghosting.'

'He was a great champion. Do you smoke?'

'How do you get these?' I asked, licking my lips.

'My wife, she buys them for me.'

His name was Islam Khan, and we made casual and careful conversation. He believed his internment to be temporary. His DRB review was next month and he was confident he would get out. 'My wife would never abandon me. She is a strong woman and I know she will continue fighting my case. Also, times are better. The Americans have also changed their policies under Obama – he is half Muslim and understands that Afghanis have rights.'

I wondered if Bilqees would try to find me and pay me a visit. We were not legally married but we did have something. Or did we? Maybe she had completely forgotten about me and moved on to some new opportunity. Her emotions were always so controlled, I could never tell if she saw me as a free ticket to a better life or if she really loved me. With her I knew I would always be in No Man's Land.

Weeks passed, summer came and went. I passed time and tried all avenues to talk my way out of this conundrum. I told my story to anyone who would listen. I even met a Red Cross representative – a Swiss man named Marcus. He listened to me attentively and promised me contact with my family via video conferencing.

'A phone call would be fine. I don't want them to see me like this,' I said. 'I can also write letters - maybe you can deliver them.'

He promised me he would but I was not allowed any phone calls. It was another promise that did not materialise. A part of me believed that this was best for the family. Shereen had moved on and given up on her father. Sonia had spent the ransom money and Bilqees had found another Afghan man.

*

'Your DRB is in two weeks. It will determine your eligibility for release,' Colonel Cox said.

It was late summer when I saw him again. 'I have seventy-five detainees to represent and there is only one me,' he told me when I complained about my review. 'The board will not have much time to conduct your review. We have five DRBs every day. Your information must be clear and concise. I assume you have no witnesses you can bring to the DRB?'

'Sir, you are aware that I know no one here. I can't even speak their language,' I said.

'Don't worry, we have a few days.'

He informed me of the procedure and worked diligently to develop a synopsis of my case, which he referred to as the 'baseball card'. Two days before the DRB review, I met a crew of Americans, all of whom asked me the same questions. Cox conducted a rehearsal on my behalf and read out my baseball card. It sounded like I had a reasonable case.

'Don't talk much. Remain quiet and respectful and we will do just fine,' he coached me.

The fact that he said 'we' made me smile. Maybe it was the American way of doing business, but it gave me hope. I agreed to everything. We shook hands.

The day of the review, I was wheeled to a big room. There were many important Americans as well as observers from the Red Cross and Human Rights Watch. A massive camera on a tripod recorded all proceedings. My synopsis was read out to the president of the board. The prosecutors, who were dressed in military uniforms, read out the charges. The questioning went back and forth. I remained respectfully quiet as I focused on understanding the legal jargon they were speaking. Cox made a fair case from my side.

'Are you one hundred per cent sure that this man is not working for a foreign power and that being an insurance agent is not just a cover-up for his activities?' asked the president of the DRB. He had silver hair and a clean-shaven face, and wore black-framed glasses.

'I can't be sure of that,' Cox replied.

'Sir, I have nothing to do with the Taliban. The Taliban hate us.' I spoke up.

'Be quiet, you will get your statement,' Cox said.

We switched to a confidential hearing without spectators and cameras. This time the prosecutors presented a case with evidence that I was a suicide bomber with plans to target American civilians and other westerners. I pleaded my case again and the president dismissed the hearing and the review was adjourned.

As I was wheeled out, I asked Cox about the decision.

'It could take months for a decision, but don't worry. The hearing went well.' Cox smiled. 'This is the time for you to take vocational classes. You should spend the time honing your skills in a trade. You can be a tailor, farmer or machinist.'

'Sir, I am not a peasant. I am an insurance surveyor, certified by Lloyds of London,' I said. It was as if they had not listened to

241

anything I had said. They still considered me to be a madrasa-trained terrorist captured by Americans.

The next day I looked for Islam in the yard but he was not there. I assumed he had been released. I read pulp-fiction, prayed, and wrote letters to Shereen. I was told that I might be allowed to post them eventually.

It was getting cold again when I met Amelia. This time I was taken to a sunlit room with posters showing American forces helping civilians. We exchanged greetings and she went through her notes. Lennox stood behind her but he had unshackled my hands this time. She opened her bag and took out a Snickers bar. She unwrapped it halfway and then pushed it across the table.

I peeled the wrapper and took a bite. The peanut chocolate melted in my mouth. I asked her if she had cigarettes.

'No cigarettes for Qais,' she mimicked my accent. She then switched on the recorder and announced the date and time.

'How are you? Did you go back to America?' I asked politely.

'Did I tell you we found the body of Captain Haider?' she said, ignoring my question.

'Good. I tried to do a decent job of the burial but had no tools.'

'They tell me you read a lot from the library.'

'I read thrillers and spy fiction.' I immediately regretted mentioning the world spy.

'I know what you read,' she said. I noticed that she had lip-gloss on her lips and blonde fuzz on her upper lip. 'But you don't read the Quran.'

'I read the Quran to follow the way of the Prophet,' I said.

She said something back to me in Arabic.

'You know Arabic?' I said, surprised.

'Yes. Why, did you not learn it?'

'I know Punjabi, Urdu, and English. That is enough.'

'But you believe in jihad?'

'No.' I stopped talking. Over-explaining was the worst thing I could do for my cause.

'Why not? It is the duty of every brother.'

'Not this brother.'

'What about the Prophet?' the woman said. 'Would you kill someone in the name of the Prophet? Like the man who drew a cartoon that showed your Prophet as a sex maniac.'

'Anyone who defiles the Prophet cheapens himself. They are as you say in America, "white trash",' I said.

'Go ahead, finish your thought about your prophet,' she said. The rare insult that I had harboured had no effect on her. I hated her composure but it is easy to be calm when you are not the prisoner.

'Our stories of the Prophet are different. He got married at twenty-five to a woman who was fifteen years older. He remained married to her for twenty-five years and took no other wives. He spent the best part of his life as a loving father and a husband. That is our truth.'

'What about your wife? Was she older?'

'No, she was my age.'

'Did you kill her?'

'Why would you say such a thing?'

'All widowers feel like murderers.'

'You know that I am innocent. You have done all your research, checked my fingerprints, website and passport details, but still you keep me prisoner. What year is it now?'

'It's December 2012.'

'Maybe the world will end and nothing will matter,' I said.

She remained silent. I looked back at her. She wore a red blouse under her plain brown jacket and smelled of lavender flowers.

'What I like about you, Qais, is that you are intelligent and well read.'

'I am a rational man. I have tried to reconcile to my situation.'

'How does it make you feel about us?'

I shrugged. I did not want to answer her question as one question or the other always led me down a path where I would get cornered into admitting something I never did.

'Do you hate the Taliban more than you hate us?' she continued.

'I don't hate Americans. You have treated me more fairly than they did.'

'They beat you and killed your friend. Did they rape you as well?'

I shook my head.

'Perhaps you prefer not to tell me about such things.'

I shrugged.

'Would you kill a Taliban?' she asked, switching tones. I knew I was being prepped up.

'I already have.' I told her about Badar. I wanted to impress her. I wanted her to know that I was not always this vulnerable and that I was a strong man.

'Will you work with us against them?' she asked.

'But what value can I bring?'

'You can let us know when your friend Hukum Khan contacts you.'

'He was my captor, not a friend. He murdered my friend.'

'He has links with Ilyas Kashmiri's organisation but vanished after Ilyas died in a drone attack. Does that make you sad?'

'I don't know Ilyas. I keep track of cricket players, not terrorists. Anyway, why do you think Hukum Khan will contact me?'

'Because he knows the extent to which you can be pushed.' She switched off the recorder. 'Would you like to know what I wrote on your baseball card?'

I nodded.

'Goes by Syed Qais, real identity established and matched. Forty-two years old, widowed and an insurance adjuster by profession. Quick-witted, independent-minded and educated but sarcastic in manners and a frequent liar. If kept in general prison population, he could face reprisals for being a Pakistani. Recommend reaching out to the judicial council for release.' She leaned back and clasped her arms behind her neck. 'All this – if you agree to be our man in Karachi.'

She kept her posture. I had never seen a woman in that pose. I thought of Riaz and how much shame he carried for being called a *mukhbir*.

244

'I agree. Thank you, Miss ... I don't even know your name,' I said.

'My name doesn't matter. But my recommendation does. It will take time, but it will set you on the path to freedom.'

She remained seated as Lennox put his hands on the wheelchair to wheel me back.

'Remember, you are now in our system. We have your fingerprints, DNA and retina scans. Every time you travel, we will know; any time you use your credit card, we will know. We will monitor your phone, email and your movements. If you make contact with a jihadi outfit, you will be extracted from Karachi before you can say Guantanamo.'

'I will never say that word to you, Amelia,' I promised her.

23
What Doesn't Kill You

I was booked on a PIA flight PK-252 to Islamabad. Two Afghan soldiers accompanied me to the ticketing counter and then handed me over to airport security. After passing through a state-of-the-art X-ray machine, I sat alone in the boarding lounge. The airport was busy; flights were coming in and out, both for civilians and private contractors. Men wore fashionable suits, girls were dressed in skinny jeans with a chadur on top. I had no luggage and carried only a brand new Pakistani passport. After being a person of interest for so long, it was good to be nobody.

After Amelia'a recommendations I was put on a fast track for release. I was provided access to Justice Project Pakistan (JPP) lawyers. I talked with a Pakistani woman named Aafia who was interested in my wellbeing. Within a few weeks I was released from DFIP and moved to a safe-house in Kabul. Outside I heard klaxon horns, ambulance sirens, rickshaw squeals and the infrequent whine of a high performance, high-revving Japanese motorcycle engine. After a few weeks, I was taken to the Pakistan embassy where a young man took my bio-data, fingerprints, and a passport photo. A week later I was presented with a machine-readable Pakistani passport.

*

The bad English and Urdu accent of the PIA flight attendant was the first reminder of being home. I was back in the land of the pure – where we assumed we spoke better English than the British and prayed longer *namaz* than the Arabs.

It was a short flight and we spent more time circling in the air than we did getting to our destination. I was met at the tarmac by ASF police officers and Aafia from JPP. She was dressed in blue cotton-lawn, and her hair was pulled back in a tight ponytail. We hugged; she smelled of perfumes and hairspray. I play acted a few tears to show my gratitude. It did not take much effort.

She was quite businesslike with the airport officials and swept us through the airport. I was overwhelmed by the chaos as I came out of the terminal. There were flights landing from Abu Dhabi, Dubai, Karachi, and other places. The crowd was populated by guys in tight jeans, women in blouses, capri pants, and burqas, and older men in white *harams* in preparation for *umra*.

I was rushed past the hotel counters to a restaurant up the stairs. A mustachioed Punjabi gentleman put a flower garland around my neck.

'From Mir Jehangir. He could not make it but will see you tomorrow,' said the man.

The JPP held a press conference. Miss Aafia rattled off a statement in English, about how hard the JPP was working to unite jailed Pakistanis with their families. Cameramen jockeyed to get the right shot. One aggressive journalist wearing a green dupatta stuck her microphone in my face.

'Sir, were you kidnapped by the Taliban? How did they treat you? Did the Americans torture you? Are you a CIA agent now?'

Aafia spoke on my behalf. I felt a headache coming on and my eye throbbed with pain.

'Shah-ji!' I heard Zahid making his way past the photographers.

'I am glad to see you,' he said.

'Me too, brother, me too' I patted his back. I had not done that for a long time.

In half an hour, the pantomime was over and I walked out with Zahid to the parking lot.

'Is there any luggage?' the driver asked.

'No luggage,' I said. 'When do I fly to Karachi?'

'Tomorrow evening. Gives you time to rest for a day,' Zahid said.

'What about Shereen?'

'She is fine. I have not told her everything. To the last day, we were not sure what state you would be in after your ordeal. But mashallah, you look fine. All you need is a shave and you will be your handsome self again.'

'Where are we going now?' I enquired. It was good to be among friends, but I had dull aches everywhere, including my heart.

'Hotel One. It's nice, you will like it.'

We drove past the tall skyscrapers bounded by the Margalla Hills. I soaked up the advertising and the hustle and bustle of Pakistan. It was election time and political parties were making promises to create a new Pakistan – free from American influence and western debt.

'I thought there was a flight to Karachi every evening,' I said. My eye throbbed from the stop-and-go traffic.

'There is someone who wanted to meet you in Islamabad,' Zahid said. 'We will get you fixed up in Karachi.'

'What about Major Bhatti?'

'He doesn't have the same pull he had last year. There is a new ISI chief. He was based in Karachi for years as the Corporal Commander. I know him well.'

'And that means what?'

'It's all fixed. If he contacts you, play it cool. He can't touch you.' Zahid took off his police sunglasses and put them on my face. 'I have failed you once. I will never do it again.'

Hotel One was a four-star hotel in the posh F/6 sector. I had a room on the ground floor, and I immediately took a long, hot shower. I examined myself in the harsh light of the bathroom mirror. My face had aged and I had lost weight, but apart from my left eye, I was back in one piece.

In my room I found a blue sweater, a white shirt, a pair of khaki pants and Hush Puppies shoes. The size 34 pants were big around my waist and I had no belt to hold them up.

There was a knock on the door. I opened it to find a long-bearded attendant with a tea setting and a plate of samosas and pastries. The teapot was covered with a tea cosy.

'I ordered tea and snacks. I am starving.' Sonia emerged from the corridor. She wore a black-and-white striped sleeveless shirt that showed off her toned arms.

'Sonia.' I took off my sunglasses.

'What happened to your eye?' she asked.

'I had an accident,' I said. 'Actually, a few.'

'Oh Cash.' She found my hands and slipped her fingers through mine. Her fingers were smooth and I felt ashamed of my bitten fingernails. The attendant cleared his throat. Sonia opened her purse.

'Do you have money?' she asked me as she handed him a tip.

'No. Is this black tea?' I asked the attendant who was setting the tea on a table.

'Brooke Bond, sir.' He poured the tea into porcelain cups. The smell made me feel nauseated.

'Could I get green tea?' I asked.

'Since when did you start drinking green tea?' Sonia added a spoon of Everyday creamer into her cup.

'Did you think eighteen months would not change anything?' I said with a laugh.

249

'Has it been that long?' she said. 'Did you meet somebody special?'

'I was kidnapped by the Taliban, not by Bollywood producers,' I said sarcastically.

'As far as you are concerned, women seem to fall out of closets in the most unexpected ways.' Sonia finished her tea. 'Who is this Aafia?'

'Justice Project Pakistan. She helped arrange for my release.'

'Good for you. Cigarette?'

I nodded and Sonia opened a new pack of Gold Leaf.

The first pull of the Gold Leaf thawed the ice that had formed in my mind. The series of cruel events that had been part of my life these last two years fell into place. All the trauma of the kidnapping, the killings, the bombing, the imprisonment and the final memory of the young woman I had left behind settled like a jigsaw puzzle. And the person responsible for all my misery was sitting right in front of me.

'You heard about Riaz Khan?' I asked.

She nodded but refused to meet my eyes.

'Did his family get anything from his life insurance?'

'No. We did what we could, but it wasn't much. What about you?'

'You tell me what happened here first.'

Sonia talked a lot. She did that when she was nervous. It wasn't very helpful. The important thing was that my family had never cashed my life insurance. I had never been given up for dead and Mir Jehangir, my cousin, had created a fuss in the media and the foreign ministry. Sonia showed a picture of a handsomer version of myself with the tagline: *Son of hockey gold medalist missing in Waziristan*.

'So we kept trying to contact the Taliban through Major Bhatti. He was a gentleman.' Sonia picked the last samosa. She also ate more when she was nervous.

'Did you sleep with the gentleman?' I asked.

Sonia put the half-eaten samosa down and punched my shoulder. It was a good punch, but it barely raised my heart-rate.

250

'You are a nasty son of a bitch. You should have been left to rot with the Taliban.'

'Well, you slept with Vicky.' I did not want to fight with her, but I could not stop myself. How gorgeous she looked and how depleted I had become.

'Yes, I did. So what? It's not like you would have married a Catholic.'

Sonia left the room as the bearded attendant re-entered with a metal teapot. I poured a cup of green tea. He lingered around for a tip but I had no money and had driven off my friend.

I was finishing my cup when Sonia returned with a duffel bag.

'Here you go, asshole. Your blood money.' She threw the bag on the floor.

I was quiet. She left. I picked up the bag and pushed it under the bed and closed my eyes.

I woke up to a knock. I opened the door to find Zahid.

'Are you okay, Shah-ji?' Zahid asked. 'You have been asleep for hours.'

I nodded and smiled. I thought I had barely closed my eyes.

'You should call home now.'

'Yes,' I said. 'Can I use your phone?'

'Here is a phone and money. Get sleep tonight. We go to Karachi tomorrow.'

'Where are you going?'

'To run some errands.'

He left and I looked at the Nokia phone. After some deliberation, I dialled Shereen's number. She picked it up after two rings.

'*Abu*. Is that you?' She sounded like her mother – and perhaps this is why I had avoided calling her.

'*Abu*, I know it's you. Zahid uncle told me to expect a call from this phone. Are you okay? When are you coming home?'

'Tomorrow. I missed you, *beta*.' I stopped to have a moment. Tears flowed freely. I had never cried in front of my daughter.

'*Abu*, you need to come home. I will take care of you. Just like mama did.'

251

I did not want my daughter to grow up that quickly. I wanted her to enjoy her childhood. She was going to be seventeen this year. I had to spend every remaining moment of my life with her.

'I will be home soon.' I wanted to sound commanding but the old Cash was lost in this new Pakistan that I was discovering.

'Hello, Qais, is he there? Shereen, did you talk to him?' my mother yelled into the phone. She laughed and cried at the same time. I told her to relax. But she remained *Ammi*.

I ended up talking on the phone for the next hour. My sister called, I talked to her, then her husband, Uncle Jamshed, other aunts, uncles, even Rabia. I had forgotten how much people loved me, and how much my family cared. They had seen me err, suffer and destroy myself – but they still cared. All that caring made me tired and I switched off the phone and watched PTV channel, which replayed nostalgic shows from my childhood. I fell asleep listening to Tina Sani singing an old ghazal: *'Nah maza hai dushmani mein, nah hai lutf dosti mein. Koi ghair ghair hota, koi yaar yaar hota.'*

The next morning, I did all things civilised. I used the toilet, showered, shaved, and went for a walk. Men with long beards walked together in groups. They looked like Taliban with their shalwars hitched up, long beards dyed black and high turbans. At the very least they were Taliban informers. I watched them, as did the security guards in camouflage uniforms. They were probably CIA informers. I remembered Amelia's warning. *You are now in our system and everything you do will be recorded forever.* Some kind of fear was going to be a part of my life forever, whether it was the Taliban, the ISI, or the Americans. So be it, I conceded. This was Pakistan, after all. It didn't matter about the new or old; it was still beautiful, broke and broken.

At a restaurant called Karachi Klassics, I ordered mutton biryani and drank Fanta. An Afghan boy with a white skullcap carried a reed basket for a fat housewife. She chatted on her cellphone in a mix of English and Punjabi. If Bilqees had our son he too could end up like this – as an errand boy for a housewife or a suicide bomber for a mullah, I thought. Bilqees knew nothing about me except that I was an insurance man in Karachi. Maybe that would be enough. Maybe she would find me one day. How would I feel about it? I got the food to go.

At Hotel One, I saw a black Toyota Corolla with a government plate. A government Suzuki jeep stood at the corner. The striking figure of Baz was there, and a few other plain-clothed men with oiled hair and dyed beards.

'Captain Baz, how are you? Everything working?' I greeted, pointing at his torso.

He ignored me and led me into the sunny breakfast room. I could smell fried parathas and fried eggs. The TV showed an anchorman talking about a scandal with the current government. At a table sat Major Bhatti and Sonia drinking tea.

'Good morning, Mr Qais,' Major Bhatti said. He did not get up or extend his hand. He still played his power games.

'Major Sultan Bhatti, *kya baat hai.*' I responded and kept my hands to the side.

Baz sat down as well. Rahbar the SSG commando sat at another table by himself. There was no one else, or maybe they had cleared off the area to help with the abduction.

I pulled a chair across from Sonia. She was dressed in white and had piled her hair in a chignon. She looked porcelain perfect.

'Tea?' she said.

'No, *yaar.*' I gave her a smile and I asked for green tea from the nervous waiter.

'You made it back. Escaped as a hero from the bloody Taliban,' Major Bhatti said.

'The Taliban are not as bad as we make them out to be. They were hospitable, made me their brother and married me off to their women,' I said.

Sonia stopped buttering her toast.

'Good to see you still have your sense of humour.' Major Bhatti took out his iPad from the leather case. It was a new tactic

253

for passive-aggressive people – to slow down a conversation by staring at touchscreens and pretending to read.

'And you, sir, you still have your sense of duty?'

'My duty goes on. The world is in a precarious state. We must be vigilant. The threat is everywhere. Even your home city, Karachi, is infiltrated by the Taliban. You can ask your friend Zahid about that,' Major Bhatti said as he swiped through news items on his iPad. 'But I am glad you are back to sort out your problems.'

'I don't give a damn about the blood money,' I said as the waiter returned with green tea. I poured it into a cup and added lemon. Nobody said a word.

'We do,' Baz said. 'The *diya* stands, irrespective of what has happened to you.'

'As does the Jandola drone attack. The Americans would be interested to know who sold the weaponry that was stored in the godown,' I replied.

'What does that have to do with anything?' Baz asked.

'That night when we had the firefight outside the Duck Hunter's Lodge, did you ever wonder why nobody died? Not only did the mobile phones stop working, the wireless did not work either. The army never came to rescue us. It was a big set-up by the good Major. All he did was shoot blanks at his Taliban friends,' I said.

'Qais, I was there, you have lost your mind,' Sonia said.

'Shut up, Sonia. I am not finished. The honourable Major here sold off Riaz as an American spy and I was the gravy on top – the rich Punjabi industrialist to Hukum Khan. You know what they did to Riaz? They beheaded him in front of my eyes,' I took off my sunglasses. My left eye was throbbing with pain.

'You have been brainwashed. You believe a terrorist like Hukum Khan over officials of the army?' Baz said. 'That is a dangerous precedent for a man coming out of Afghanistan. I can take you to a safe-house and you will vanish. All I have to do is say the word.'

'Say it,' I said. 'Arrest me now and get it over with. I have been jailed by everyone else, why should the Pakistan army be left behind?' I stood up in a hurry.

Baz glared, but I did not shy away. I had his balls in a proverbial vice grip. It was good to be home.

Major Bhatti said pleasantly, 'Come, now. There's no need to be uncivilised here. Who is going to believe your story? Colonel Aftab, your good soldier, has emigrated to America. Your insurance company does not care and neither does Miss Sonia. You remember the saying, what doesn't kill you makes you stronger?'

'Or stranger,' I said and laughed out loud. 'You can play any game you want but you are not getting any money.'

'We will see about that.' Major Bhatti stood up to leave. 'In the meantime, don't do anything foolish. You are a loss adjuster. Adjust your loss and bugger off.'

He left, followed by Baz and Rahbar. The army always gets the last word in Pakistan.

I finished the green tea and walked up the stairs to the room. Inside, Sonia hugged me fiercely.

'You were awesome,' she said. 'That's the Cash I love. He did not even ask about the money. Where is it?'

I reached under the bed and pulled out the duffel bag.

'You didn't open it?' She made sure the door was locked.

I shook my head.

'That is not like you at all, Cash.' Sonia unzipped the bag and pulled out plastic bags till she found a bundle wrapped in a newspaper. She took out the currency bills.

'Sixty thousand dollars and the rest in Pak and Afghan rupees. This is how your captives wanted the ransom. I had it ready. Did you doubt me, Cash?'

I looked at the notes, the pale green dollars, the turquoise blue Afghanis, and the purple Pakistani notes. The only person I doubted was myself.

I picked the largest denomination Afghan note. It was a souvenir for Shereen.

'Did you get paid for the survey?' I asked.

'Yes. Anthony is satisfied and I got a bonus. This is all yours. Do what you want with it.' She sat on the edge of the bed. 'What are your plans?'

'I don't know. Maybe give it to Riaz's widow.'

'You have changed. That's a lot of money to be given away to charity,' she shifted her weight, crushing the blue Afghan notes. I grabbed the notes from under her. She giggled and rolled into my arms and clasped her hands behind my neck.

'Do you ever wonder what it would have been like if we had got married?' she asked.

'There are two tragedies in life. The first is if you don't marry your soulmate,' I said.

'And the second?' she asked curiously, looking at me with the eyes of a gazelle skipping over shifting sands.

'Is if you do,' I said.

I hugged her. Her body was slender and the skin was smooth. I closed my eyes and breathed her in.

'Are you wearing that Jasmin Noir again?' I asked, opening my eyes.

'Yes.'

'*Kheli khub*,' I said, but choked on the words.

'What was that?'

'Nothing.' I pulled away.

'Are you okay?' The disappointment in Sonia's voice was thinly disguised.

'Not really. I have been through a lot. I am a bit emotional.'

'Even courageous men need time to recover. Promise to meet me in Karachi, *yaar*, once you recover.'

'I promise, *yaar*.'

I hugged her again and she kissed me on the cheek. We stood in an embrace. She left as the muezzin called to prayer.

I gathered the money and wrapped it up in the *Jang* newspaper from the day before. The headlines screamed of political failures of the government, threats from the Indians, and revisited a scandal that involved a one-time Pakistan ambassador to the

US who shared his last name with the most wanted Taliban leader.

The great migraine continues.

I opened the Karachi Klassics biryani container, but I felt no hunger.

I lit a cigarette and chuckled.

Sonia still made me lose my appetite.

Acknowledgements

This fictional story has been inspired by my travels, imagination, and watershed events that have defined the geo-politics of the region. Many individuals have contributed to the story – sometimes without realizing it.

I would like to thank my agent Kanishka Gupta for his perseverance and Rosemarie Hudson for her support in overseeing the UK edition. I would also extend my gratitude to Ijaz Syed for his early feedback and to my wife Saadia for keeping it real.

Because this is a novel, names, places, and timelines are not always authentic. The story and the characters are my own invention and thus my responsibility. No one else can be blamed for any shortcomings.

S. S. Mausoof